PENGUIN BOOKS
Cold Kill

# Cold Kill

P. J. TRACY

PENGUIN BOOKS

PENGUIN BOOKS

UK | USA | Canada | Ireland | Australia

India | New Zealand | South Africa

Penguin Books is part of the Penguin Random House group of companies
whose addresses can be found at global.penguinrandomhouse.com

First published as *The Sixth Idea* in the United States of America by G. P. Putnam's Sons 2016
First published as *Cold Kill* in Great Britain by Michael Joseph 2016

Published in Penguin Books 2016

001

Set in 12.5/14.75pt Garamond MT Std

Typeset in India by Thomson Digital Pvt Ltd, Noida, Delhi

Printed in Great Britain by Clays Ltd, St Ives plc

A CIP catalogue record for this book is available from the British Library

ISBN: 978–1–405–93532–6

www.greenpenguin.co.uk

# Prologue

Confine a dozen scientists and engineers to a seemingly endless desert of hard-packed sand with no recreational diversions and, inevitably, they will design and build a golf course.

'This is not just any golf course, Donald,' Arthur kept insisting. 'This is Augusta, a near-perfect replica of the first nine holes, minus the grass and the water hazards, of course.'

'Both of which are somewhat critical components to any dandy golf course, wouldn't you say?'

'Stylistic details, Donald, a matter of preference. Tennis is played with equal enthusiasm on lawn and on clay. Think of this as golf's version of a clay court. I think it's ingenious, really.'

'We could really use some caddies and a clubhouse.'

'I'll give you that.'

Arthur always dressed in the plaid knickers and cap of his hero, Bobby Jones, which looked especially ridiculous in the deserted New Mexico hinterlands. But that was the charming thing about Arthur – in his knickers and cap he *was* at Augusta, on the Masters course Bobby Jones had built, and he made you believe you were right there with him.

Donald Buchanan and Arthur Friedman played the makeshift course almost every morning while the rest of the men slept. Most of the scientists preferred to work through the chill of the desert night and sleep through the most brutal heat of the day, but Donald and Arthur were paced to a different clock.

'I have an idea,' Donald said as he lined up his drive.

'Jesus Christ, the last time you said that, you and Teller damn near blew up half the world.'

'That is a ridiculous exaggeration.'

'It could still happen. Nice drive,' Arthur said as he watched a golf ball sail up into the dry air against a backdrop of blue sky and mountains. 'So what's this idea of yours?'

'A bomb that doesn't kill anybody.'

'That defeats the purpose of a bomb, doesn't it?'

'Not necessarily. If you could invent something that would destroy infrastructure – power grids, delivery systems for weapons, communication, transportation – the enemy would be crippled with no cost of human life. The world would never again see the horrors of Hiroshima and Nagasaki.'

'Without infrastructure, there are no resources, no order, no money, and nothing to buy with money even if you had cash in hand. Anarchy would fill the vacuum and people would die anyhow. Friends and neighbors would end up killing each other over a crust of bread or a vial of penicillin.'

'Perhaps. But the death toll would be minimal in comparison to a multimegaton atomic bomb.'

'So you're seeking a more moral weapon.'

'I'm seeking a less morally repugnant one. Infrastructure can be rebuilt but humans cannot.'

'And how do you propose to invent such a device?'

'I don't know yet. But the electromagnetic pulses the bombs generate intrigue me.'

'You need a nuclear detonation to create an EMP substantial enough to be an effective weapon, which is exactly what you're trying to avoid.'

'Yes. But there has to be a way to generate EMP without a nuclear detonation. And if we could harness something like that, perhaps miniaturize it and selectively direct it . . . It's something to think about, anyhow.'

'Indeed. But for the time being I'd think about what you're going to do with that nice drive you just made, because it landed in a sand trap.'

They both laughed, because the whole damned golf course was a sand trap.

By the time she was nine, Alice had moved five times. She had been too little to remember the first two moves, but the last three were sharp in her memory.

It was always the same. Father would come home one night and tell them all that in two weeks, they were going to live in a wonderful new place with a bigger house, a nicer town, and better schools. Alice and her brother and sister, older by five and six years, all would start crying because they knew they would never see their best friends again, and then Father would send them from the table before they finished their dinners because crying was not allowed.

Father was very strict about a lot of things, like not crying, but he was never mean, like Melinda's dad, who had slapped Melinda's face once when Alice had been *right there*, watching. If Father sent you from the table he always brought snacks up to your room later, and by the time you woke up in the morning he was smiling and gentle again.

'Come into the living room, Alice. We'll have a little talk, just me and you.' He sat in the big brown recliner Mother hated because it didn't go with the white floral sofa, and patted the footrest for Alice to sit on.

She hitched up the legs of her pedal pushers just above the knees, because that's what Father did when he sat down in pants, and for some reason it always made him smile to see her doing it. She sat obediently, almost reverently, before her father, big eyes eating him up, little mouth open in breathlessness. Father-daughter talks were rare in this house and almost exclusively disciplinarian, like when her older sister was caught smoking or using mascara. But Alice never did anything wrong, so she wasn't afraid; just excited.

He handed her a well-thumbed paperback novel, the kind her mother removed from the bookcase and hid in a closed cabinet of the buffet whenever guests were expected. 'These are trash,' she'd told Alice's father, 'and totally inappropriate for a child.' Alice remembered that day because her mother had raised her voice, and she'd never done that before.

Ever since, only big fat books with no pictures on the cover were permitted in the bookcase. Alice read every one her father gave her, even though she had to look up an awful lot of words in the battered Webster's dictionary, but the best days were when Father went to the cupboard of the trash books and selected one for her to read. They all had pictures of bad women on the cover. You could tell they were bad because they wore bright red lipstick and blouses that bared their shoulders and showed the tops of really big bazoomies. There was just such a picture on the cover of this book, but instead of a man pulling on the woman's arms, she was running from a really big fire.

'Don't show your mother this book.'

'I won't.'

'Don't show anyone this book ever. Not your mother, not your sister or brother, not your friends. Hide it in a very safe place. Even after you grow up, you must keep it hidden. It's our little secret. And remember the part about the generator – I marked it for you. Read it again and again until you have it memorized. Is that clear?'

'Yes sir. But what's a generator?'

'It's a machine that makes electricity. You can use it to run things in case the power goes out.'

'Oh. Okay. I'll memorize that part.'

'All right. Run along now.'

Two days later, she and Mother drove Father to the airport. He had to travel a lot for his job, and he always had a briefcase handcuffed to his wrist.

Alice loved going to the airport. Everything echoed in the big spaces with their tiled floor. She always wore her patent leather shoes, even though the buckles pinched her feet, because they made hard clicking sounds, just like the high heels the stewardesses wore. Her brother and sister stayed home, but Mother always took Alice with her. She was the baby, and the last time Mother had left her home with her siblings, they'd locked Alice in the hall closet for the whole time she was gone.

Father always squatted down in front of her and held her by the shoulders when he was about to leave. This time it felt like he might actually hug her, but it didn't happen.

'Are you reading the new book?'

Alice nodded. 'I'm halfway through . . . but it's a little scary.' She peeked around her father to make sure Mother wasn't listening. 'It's just a story, right? Nothing like that could ever really happen, could it?'

'No, of course not.' He looked away for a moment and touched his stomach the way he did when he had a tummy ache. 'But read it all anyway.'

'I will. I already memorized the part about the generator.'

Father beamed at her. 'That's my good, smart girl.' And then he kissed Mother and walked out the door to where the plane was rumbling, propellers turning. Alice watched him trot up the metal staircase and disappear.

After Father got on the plane, Mother always took her to the counter where the stools twirled and the food was delicious – grilled cheese sandwiches that tasted way different from the ones they made at home. 'That's American cheese. We use Velveeta,' her mother explained. 'I think Velveeta tastes better, don't you?'

Alice nodded dutifully, although she didn't think that at all.

There was a big window opposite the counter so you could watch the planes take off and land. When they heard the rumble of the engines on Father's plane get louder and louder, they both looked up.

'Can I go wave at the window?'

'*May* I go wave at the window, and yes you may.'

Alice leaped off her stool and trotted to the window, her head tipping back as she watched the plane rise higher in the sky.

There was a terrible, loud noise that shook the window under Alice's hands, and she saw a big yellow and orange and black flower of fire bloom against the sky where Father's plane had been.

Five men were sitting around a large table in a darkened room. None of the men knew the names of the others. They referred to one another only by numbers. Some of them were fidgeting, all of them were pointedly avoiding eye contact with any of their compatriots, except for the man at the head of the table. He was watching everyone, noting their demeanor, reading their expressions, assessing their level of discomfort at being part of this group. This day, more than any other since they were selected, would test the limits of their courage and loyalty.

The mission had already been approved by them all, but planning was a far cry from execution. You never knew who was going to break until they were tested.

He placed one hand on the black rotary telephone in front of him, fingers loosely curled and perfectly relaxed. A few men started at the strident ring when it finally came. 'Zero,' he said into the mouthpiece. It was the only name he would have as long as he managed this project, which would be until he was unable to perform his duties. At that point, he would be replaced by another.

He listened for a moment, replaced the heavy receiver gently back into its cradle, then folded his hands in front of him. 'The mission is complete. The plane is down. There were no survivors.'

# One

*Present Day*

Sixty years later, the large table and the darkened room still existed in a mansion in upstate New York, but the five men who had originally held court there had been replaced three times over. Some had died of natural causes over the years, others not so natural – if you outlived your usefulness on this panel, you outlived your usefulness on earth. They still referred to one another by numbers only, just as their predecessors had, but everything else had changed dramatically over the decades.

For instance, the current five were now sitting in an observation deck in a much larger, adjacent ballroom that had been renovated into an apotheosis of technology – banks of monstrous supercomputers whirred and hummed, lovingly tended by a small, carefully selected cadre of America's brightest minds. At the moment, they were chattering quietly in nervous excitement, their eyes fixed on the digital countdown clock hanging above an enormous flat screen that showed aerial photos of various cities around the world.

The third-generation Zero had only been a part of this elite group for fifteen years, and yet he had seen the astronomical rise of something miraculous, something that had been a mere pipe dream of a man named Donald Buchanan. According to the countdown clock on the wall, two minutes would tell them all if that pipe dream would cross over from the realm of science fiction to reality.

'T minus ten seconds to Operation Silver Dune Alpha Test,' a voice from the computing floor called out, and the room went silent and still – no one moved, no one spoke, no one breathed.

It took a few moments, and then every person in the room burst into applause as a section of the screen went dark.

'Detroit is now off-line,' a voice dutifully reported, as if the men in the observation deck couldn't see that for themselves. 'Permission to restore?'

'Granted,' Zero replied.

# Two

Chuck Spencer settled into his first-class window seat, pulled down his tray table, and started unloading his briefcase. These were the last of his father's effects to be sorted through, and the three-and-a-half-hour flight from L.A. to Minneapolis would give him just enough time before he met Wally tonight.

When the miscellaneous pile of papers and old photographs started to tower and slip, he put the rest of the contents on the empty seat next to him. It wouldn't be empty for long with the plane fully booked, but the papers might discourage his unknown seatmate from bending his ear. Clearly he was a busy man who shouldn't be disturbed. See all my papers?

Grousing his way uncomfortably through his early sixties, Chuck was annoyed by a lot of things now that never annoyed him before. And this plane was one of them. A 757? An A320? Whatever. This one's entrance was in the front of first class, so you got to watch every passenger file by as they boarded, never knowing which one would take the seat next to you. Would it be the tremendously fat man wearing far too much – what was that? English Leather? Did they still make that? Or maybe the elderly woman who had a tissue tucked into the sleeve of her cardigan, which meant she was probably carrying bird flu or some other potential pandemic. He breathed a silent sigh of relief when she passed by, rewarding her with a friendly smile for having the decency to fly coach.

One of the last stragglers to board was a pretty woman definitely young enough to be his daughter and perhaps young enough to be his granddaughter. She had a sweet face and an obvious case of nerves. Her eyes were darting this way and that, probably making note of the emergency exits and any potential terrorists she might have to subdue mid-flight.

She slowed, then stopped to stand next to the empty seat Chuck had cluttered with his paperwork, and gave him a timid smile.

Chuck smiled back and started gathering up his papers. In the ever-capricious lottery of air travel, this lady was the jackpot as far as seatmates went. She was thin and would take up no room at all, she was attractive and seemed quite shy, she didn't smell like English Leather, and she wasn't coughing or sneezing or carrying tissues up her sleeve. 'Sorry about the mess.'

'No worries.' She sat down abruptly once he'd cleared the seat. 'I'm Lydia Ascher,' she mumbled at her lap, frantically trying to fasten her seat belt.

'Chuck Spencer.'

She was obviously terrified of flying, and that could go one of two ways. Nervous fliers either went dead silent during takeoff and pulled up on their armrests as if they could hold the plane up with the sheer force of their will, or they chattered like magpies and looked you straight in the eye and pretended they weren't on a plane at all. The latter was the worst-case scenario for anybody who valued solitude of any kind, even on a crowded plane, as Chuck did.

He stole a crafty, peripheral glance at his seat-mate, trying to assess her demeanor so he could form an isolation strategy if need be.

Since she was just sitting there rigidly, staring at the seatback in front of her, Chuck figured her to be one of the silent types who suffered their terror alone, and thank God she wasn't investigating the puke bag. He relaxed a little, then turned his attention back to his papers.

A few minutes later, he realized he was completely distracted by a creeping guilt. This poor thing sitting next to him was clearly fighting off demons, and he was just sitting there doing jigs in his mind because she was mute. And really, what could be so bad about having a conversation with a pretty young woman if she chose to engage in one, especially if it helped calm her nerves?

Chuck finally decided to breach the silence, for better or for worse. 'Don't worry, it'll be a smooth flight. No weather between here and Minneapolis,' he reassured her.

She turned her head slowly to look at him, as if she were afraid any sudden movement might tip the plane on its side. 'It's that obvious, huh?'

'Only to anybody who pays attention, but your secret is safe with me, because nobody pays attention to anything but their phones anymore.'

She let out a great sigh and leaned back in her seat. 'Isn't that the truth.'

Chuck let the comment hang, and she didn't pursue it, which was fantastic. When a flight attendant announced that the doors were being closed for takeoff, he leaned back and closed his eyes. Just as the plane began taxiing and he was starting to nod off, he felt a light hand on his arm.

'Thank you, by the way.'

Chuck straightened from his dozy slump. 'Uh . . .'

'Oh my gosh, I'm sorry, I woke you up.'

'No, no,' Chuck insisted in classic sleep denial. He'd never understand what compelled most humans to deny they'd been wakened. Phone call at four in the morning? No problem. Hell no, I wasn't sleeping, what can I do for you?

'Yes, I did, and I'll shut up. I just wanted to thank you for trying to make me feel better.'

'I'm sorry it didn't help,' Chuck finally said earnestly, looking down at her white-knuckled grip on the armrests.

She gave him a sheepish look. 'I'm pretty hopeless.'

'Is there anything that distracts you?'

'A stiff Bloody Mary would distract me.'

He was surprised to find himself chuckling, even more surprised to be enjoying this little conversation with a complete stranger, another of his later-in-life peeves. 'We can take care of that once we're airborne. What can I do for you between now and then?'

She let out a shaky sigh. 'Well, you could tell me your life story.'

'Trust me, reading the in-flight magazine is a lot more interesting than my life story.'

Lydia let out a breathy giggle, part anxiety, and maybe, Chuck thought, there was a little mirth mixed in, too. 'I don't believe that for a minute.'

'Then you haven't seen this month's edition. You can now buy a seven-foot gargoyle statue for your lawn for two hundred dollars.'

She looked at him in disbelief. 'Really?'

'Really. Are you interested?'

'I'm only interested in what kind of person would *want* a seven-foot gargoyle statue in their garden.'

Chuck was pleased to see that Lydia seemed to be relaxing. It made him feel good; paternal, even, in spite of the fact that he had no children of his own. And then the pilot came on the PA and announced, 'Flight attendants, prepare for takeoff,' and the poor girl gave him a look of pure, crystalline terror.

'I hate this part the most,' she whispered, her voice all apologies. 'My grandfather died in a plane crash. On takeoff,' she blurted out.

Chuck's thoughts slammed to a halt and he suddenly felt a little panicky himself. He'd never actually met anyone who knew someone who died in a plane crash. No wonder she was terrified. And how did you respond to that? He could lecture her on the physics of flying, how it worked, why it was so safe, but that would probably just make things worse. She was in the red zone already. 'It's going to be okay,' he said lamely.

Lydia just nodded, her wide eyes fixed straight ahead.

'Lydia? Why don't you tell me *your* life story.'

Chuck had no idea what had made him say such a dangerous thing, but apparently it had been the right thing. She seemed to calm a little as she began speaking to the seatback in front of her, and by liftoff she was making eye contact with him, and he knew both her parents were deceased and she lived on a small lake an hour from Minneapolis.

By the time the aircraft had banked over the Pacific and turned toward the country's midsection, he found out that she was a successful artist who was returning home from some important gallery visits in L.A., and her posture seemed much looser, almost normal.

Somewhere over Nevada, Chuck realized he was genuinely enjoying himself despite the fact that the conversation was one-sided. They ordered Bloody Marys and the serpentine route of their conversation somehow ended up on the topic of her mother's childhood, and that was the moment the lopsided conversation grew another leg. As she was listing every city that her departed mother had lived in as a child, ten cities in ten years, to be precise, Chuck's jaw went slack, because he had lived in every one of them.

Good God. His own childhood was a mirror of this girl's mother's. He probably went to grade school with her. What kind of odds were we talking here? 'This is really weird. I lived in all those towns at about the same time your mother did,' he said.

When she didn't reply, he turned to look at her. She was staring at the clutter of paperwork on his tray table, her eyes wide and her mouth open. He quickly looked down at the tray table, hoping there wasn't a nude centerfold in the pile. He didn't see anything offensive at first glance. Maybe she was just having a fear-of-flying seizure or something.

Finally she reached over and pulled a photograph from the middle of the pile. 'Where did you get this?'

'It belonged to my father.' He pointed to one of the men in the photo. 'That's him, and the rest are some guys he worked with about fifty years ago. Why?'

She shook her head in disbelief and pointed to the man standing next to Chuck's father. 'Because that one is my grandfather.'

'What?'

'That man right there. He was my grandfather. The one who died in the plane crash.'

Chuck gave her a skeptical look. 'Whoever it is might look like your grandfather, but I guarantee it isn't. There were only eight men in the world who even knew about this project, including the President. See? That's President Eisenhower at the end of the line.'

'I know. I have this very same photograph at home. These were the men who supervised the manufacture of the hydrogen bomb.'

Chuck just stared straight ahead for a moment, sorting through all the calculators in his brain, estimating the odds of being seated next to one of the very few people in this world who would know who the men in that photo were. 'I never knew any of this until my dad died six months ago and I started going through his things.'

'Your dad never told you?'

'I hadn't seen him in years. When I started cleaning out his house, I found this mess' – he gestured at the stack on his tray table – 'and a whole lot of other records. Up until that moment I never knew what my dad did for a living. I always thought he was an engineer.'

Lydia raised her brows. 'The project's been declassified for a couple decades now.'

'Like I said, we didn't see each other. We didn't talk. It was kind of a weird childhood.'

'So was my mom's. Let me guess. Your dad traveled all the time with a briefcase handcuffed to his wrist. You moved every year or so, and men in suits came and talked to all your little friends, asking if you ever told them what your father did, right? And all you knew was that he was an engineer and worked for American Iron Foundry.'

Chuck closed his eyes. 'Jesus. That's exactly what it was like. This is unreal. Wally's never going to believe this.'

'Who's Wally?'

'A new friend. When I did a little research on the Web and found out what Dad had really been doing all those years, I started a website dedicated to finding other descendants of those eight men, or maybe even some of the original men still living. Just for fun, you know, like going on Ancestry-dot-com. Kind of a strange mystery I wanted to follow. Wally and several others found my website and signed into my chat room. He lives in Minneapolis. That's what I'm doing on this flight. We're getting together tonight. And suddenly, I find myself sitting next to another descendant. It's kind of freaking me out.'

Lydia smiled. 'It is pretty unreal.' She reached into her purse and pulled out a business card. 'Give me a call and let me know how your meeting with Wally went. If you're going to be in town for a while, maybe we can all get together.'

'I have a better idea. Why don't you come along tonight? Hell, the three of us have more in common than a lot of siblings.'

Lydia was tempted, but clearly not as obsessed with the past as Wally and Chuck, maybe because she was a generation further down the line. 'The thing is, I've been away from home for ten days, and I am truly whipped. Tomorrow? I could come into the city and meet you both for lunch, say around noon?'

'Terrific.' He scribbled on a cocktail napkin. 'That's my cell and my hotel. Give me a call when you're close and I'll meet you in the lobby.'

# Three

There was something terribly wrong about growing up in a family of secrets. Chuck had never understood why his parents never talked to each other or to him; why strange men in suits questioned his friends; or why they had to move every year or so. It seemed that every time he started to make new friends in a new town, they packed up and left. Maybe it was his fault.

Children drew the straightest lines between cause and effect, so Chuck concluded that by making friends, he doomed the family to another move. He started to withdraw after that twisted epiphany, hoping that would enable them to stay in one place for a while. It never worked, but it was, apparently, a perfect recipe for a solitary existence, because he'd been a failure at relationships all his life, and very nearly friendless.

Ironically, the death of his father had led him to Wally, a man with an almost identical childhood, sharing a history so similar to Chuck's, they might have been siblings. Even though he had yet to meet the man face-to-face, they'd made a strong connection in the past few weeks through their Internet exchanges and phone calls. And then today, along came Lydia, another connection. Chuck felt like he was acquiring a family one person at a time. He'd been a little disappointed that she hadn't wanted to meet with him and Wally tonight, but he understood what it was like to come off ten days on the road – he'd done plenty of business traveling before he'd retired. At least she'd agreed to a cup of coffee at the airport before they went their separate ways.

He'd never been to Minneapolis before today, but it seemed almost magical as he drove through downtown to his hotel. Christmas lights sparkled gaily from the streetlamps and garland seemed to be looped everywhere, trumpeting the festive season. Shining store windows proudly displayed their holiday swag, and cheerful people bundled up in their winter clothing strolled the streets as if they didn't have a care in the world. There was even a pristine dusting of fresh snow to complete the Christmas card feel, and more snow was sifting lightly down from the darkening sky.

But after his day so far, Chuck felt a deeper magic drawing him to this city like an unseen magnet. First he'd found Wally here, then the unbelievably serendipitous meeting with Lydia. It was like the cogs of fortune had finally caught, telling him there was a more important reason for him to be here than just the simple pursuit of an old mystery. It sounded stupid and New Agey, even in his own private thoughts, but with his spirits so high, he didn't care.

He found the Chatham Hotel, parked his rental in the ramp, and checked in. The place was a little too modern and hip for his personal taste, but the service was impeccable and the room and amenities were on par with the hefty nightly rate. In a bigger city he would have paid twice as much and gotten much less.

Once he'd settled into his generously sized suite, he pulled a Heineken and a fifteen-dollar bag of cashews out of the minibar, unloaded his laptop and external backup drive, then dialed Wally's number from his cell. He couldn't wait to tell him about Lydia, but he'd save that until they were together.

'Wally!'

'Hey, Chuck, are you in town?'

'Just got to the hotel. And you're not going to believe what happened to me today. Are we still on for six?'

'You bet. Think you can get here all right?'

'I've got your address programmed into the GPS already.'

'Great. And I've got some things to tell you, too. I've been going through some of my father's old files I never bothered to look at before, and . . .' Wally paused for a moment. 'Chuck, hang on, would you? There's somebody at the door.'

'Sure, Wally.' Chuck put his cell on speaker and walked over to the big window that looked out onto the street below. Minneapolis was even prettier four stories up.

There were some muffled voices coming out of his phone as Wally greeted his visitor, but then he heard a much louder noise, almost like a crash, then shattering. 'Wally?'

'Who are you? What do you want?!' he heard Wally shouting, then a protracted, 'Noooo!' before the connection went dead.

Paralyzed, Chuck stared at his phone in horror for a moment, then called 911 while he scrambled for his briefcase and car keys.

# Four

Chuck's shaking hands felt slimy on the wheel of his rental as he tried to focus on the directions the GPS was squawking at him. The female voice was supposed to be soothing, he supposed, but right now it seemed shrill and grating. He felt acid churning around the expensive cashews in his stomach. Jesus. Who would attack a nice man like Wally in his own house?

*Stupid question*, he chided himself. It seemed like there was more senseless savagery in the world now than there had ever been. Then again, there hadn't been a twenty-four-hour news cycle when Christians were getting fed to lions and gladiators were chopping off people's heads in the Coliseum or when the Roman Catholic Church was burning witches. Maybe humanity was just as brutal and depraved as it had always been, you just heard about it now, every time you turned on the TV.

The GPS harpy commanded him to turn right on Gleason in fifteen feet; still, he almost missed it because the snow had started to fall harder and the headlights of passing cars turned into fuzzy, disorienting halos in his aging eyes.

He pushed his speed as far as he dared on the residential street that led to Wally's cul-de-sac, but after fishtailing on the slick pavement and nearly sideswiping a parked minivan, he slowed down.

When he was less than a quarter of a mile from Wally's, he heard the sickening bellow of sirens and saw a raft of flashing lights ahead. But maybe that was a good sign. The police had responded fast, he prayed fast enough, and Wally would be okay. Shaken by his home invader, most certainly, but okay.

But his tenuous optimism morphed into a leaden sense of doom when he saw billowing plumes of ugly black smoke and orange flames rising above the bare trees and into the dusk. Emergency vehicles of all kinds were jumbled every which way in the middle of the street, and there were uniforms everywhere, frantically barking out orders and admonishments to the gathering crowd of wide-eyed, frightened onlookers.

There were barricades across the street a good two blocks from Wally's address, and officers were stopping every car, turning them back.

'I'm sorry, sir. We're evacuating the area. No through traffic. There's been a natural gas explosion.'

'My friend lives at 1240 Gleason. Can I get there another way?'

The cop gave him a pained look. 'I'm sorry. That's the address where the explosion occurred.'

Chuck shook his head. 'No, it can't be. You must have the wrong address, or maybe I do, because I was on the phone with Wally when he was attacked.'

'Wally?'

'Yes, dammit, Wally Luntz, 1240 Gleason. On the phone I heard someone come into the house, then there was a struggle, but there was no explosion, just Wally screaming for help.'

The officer winced. 'I'm sorry, sir. I'm afraid your friend died in the explosion.'

For a moment, Chuck thought he might throw up, and he pressed his sweaty brow against the cold steering wheel. 'Are you sure?'

'Yes sir.'

'Oh my God.'

The officer squatted next to Chuck's open window, giving him a few moments to compose himself. 'I know this is a shock for you, sir, but you said you heard Mr. Luntz being attacked, is that right?'

All Chuck could manage was a nod.

'I think you should talk to a detective. Can you manage that?'

Chuck nodded again, or maybe he was still nodding.

# Five

As Christmas crept up on the calendar and reliably cold weather settled in for the long haul, Minneapolis homicide detectives Leo Magozzi and Gino Rolseth were enjoying day six of their seven-day vacation. Only they weren't enjoying it at all.

A few weeks back, it had seemed like a great idea to take some time off after chasing around armed terrorists in the north woods and spending the emotional equivalent of twenty years in FBI debriefings so repetitive and boring the idea of pulling out your own fingernails had suddenly seemed like a terrific alternative.

But in retrospect, vacation in the middle of dreary December in Minnesota had been even worse, and they were bored out of their minds. The need for distraction of any kind had become absolutely essential, which was why, on a frosty winter evening, Magozzi and Gino were in the western suburbs, currently freezing their balls off while simultaneously getting the crap kicked out of them in a bush-league, two-on-two broomball game by a couple of Neanderthal firemen buddies out of Station Seven. It was cold, painful, and humiliating.

'Come on, Detectives!' Freddie Wilson taunted them, expertly sweeping the stupid ball back and forth on the ice with his tricked-out tournament broom, daring them to move on him. 'You're only ten points behind! Make an effort!'

Gino gave him a ferocious sneer and shouted back, 'You look hungry, Freddie! Wish we had time to eat chili on the job!'

'Oh yeah? Looks like you've had plenty of time to eat on the job, Rolseth!'

There was a chorus of 'oohs' from the handful of spectators along the boards of the outdoor hockey rink, the crowd evenly divided between law enforcement and Fire. These interdepartmental matchups were more like the WWF – the more smack talk, the better.

Magozzi watched Gino's demeanor change from competitive to bloodthirsty just as Freddie bent into shooting position and made a searing shot toward their goal. Gino launched himself across the crease, making a half-twist swan dive onto the ice as the ball sailed over his head to home for the score. One more goal for Fire, one seriously messed-up shoulder for MPD.

The firemen on the sidelines raised their hands and cheered. The cops booed and started chanting, 'MPD! MPD!' along with colorful words of encouragement to Gino and Magozzi.

Gino rolled over onto his back, clutching his throbbing shoulder, wondering if it would have to be amputated. At least it wasn't his shooting arm. He stared up at the dingy snow clouds above, which turned into Leo's cold-reddened face.

'Are you okay, Gino?'

'No. I need morphine.'

'Time out, take five!' Magozzi heard the referee shouting, with no regard to the dying man writhing around on his patch of ice. What an asshole. Freddie and his fellow firefighter Jim Ames, über studs of the illustrious, hard-core broomball world, slid over to stand above Gino.

Freddie offered his hand and lifted him up off the ice as if he weighed less than a two-day-old kitten. When the guy wasn't fighting fires or eating chili in the station house, he was throwing around iron.

'Nice move, Rolseth.'

'Fuck you, Freddie, I know where you live.'

'No, I mean it,' he chuckled. 'You were just a millisecond too slow, otherwise it would have been a bomb save. Better luck next time.'

'Yeah, right.'

Magozzi gave Freddie a friendly bump on his inhumanly large arm. 'Nice guns. But don't forget, Gino and I get to carry real ones. All the time.'

Freddie and Jim both laughed. 'Yeah, well, we've got big hoses we get to use all the time, so I guess it's even.' He looked back at Gino, who was tentatively testing his injured limb. 'Happy to see that.'

'What?' Gino snapped.

'You're moving your arm. If you'd dislocated your shoulder, you'd be screaming right now –'

Suddenly, all the firemen's phones beeped loudly in unison, creating an electronic orchestra around the boards and on the ice. Jim Ames pulled out his cell phone from a zippered jacket pocket. 'We gotta go, Freddie. Gas explosion in South Minneapolis.'

'Aw, too bad you guys can't finish the game,' Gino said smugly. 'Leo and I were just heating up.'

Freddie snorted. 'Yeah, you're melting the ice now,' he said smoothly as he and Ames jogged away.

'Be safe, guys,' Gino called after them, meaning it. Then he turned to Magozzi. 'Can I shoot him in the back?' he asked, also meaning it.

Gino shrugged off his parka in the warming house and slapped a cold gel pack on his shoulder.

'Sorry about the shoulder,' Magozzi offered, rummaging in his duffel, pulling out a bottle of ibuprofen and tossing it over. 'Take four.'

Gino gladly washed down the pills with the warm dregs of his Gatorade. 'What an asinine sport.'

Magozzi gave him a long-suffering look. 'I hate to remind you, but . . .'

'Yeah, yeah, yeah, I know, it was my idea. Next time I recommend any recreational activity I ever enjoyed before I hit twenty-five, you have my blessings to pistol-whip me.'

'Deal. Is the offer retroactive?'

'No. You were an accessory to the crime because you were stupid enough to let me talk you into it.' He sagged onto a wooden bench and started stripping off his snow pants, wincing in pain whenever he moved his shoulder the wrong way. 'God, this hurts. The only thing that's going to save this day is the lasagna Angela has in the oven. Hey, you wanna come over for dinner?'

'Are you kidding, I always want to come over for dinner, but Grace and I have plans tonight. Thanks for the invite, though.'

# Six

Mid-December, and Magozzi was sitting outside in a light jacket, looking at Grace MacBride's naked magnolia tree. Minnesotans were notoriously foolhardy when it came to maximizing their time outdoors, and although Grace wasn't a native, she'd learned to adapt to the weather. This fall she'd put up a partially enclosed patio area at the back of the house, with insulated windows and a radiant heating system beneath the stone floor. The open front of the patio was flanked with big propane heaters that kept the space surprisingly toasty.

A gentle snow continued to filter down from the sky where a half-moon was rising. It was the first snow of the season, and although the temperatures had been low enough to freeze a broomball rink, there hadn't been any bone chillers yet. When was the last time that happened in Minnesota?

Grace had put Christmas lights on the magnolia. Not that she thought of them as Christmas lights, of course; just decorative twinkle lights that had forgotten their original intent.

Magozzi was born and raised a Catholic, and he'd always been a little disturbed by the pervasive array of downtown trees adorned with twinkle lights all year round. The decorative fad had tried to creep into the Minnesota landscape, and although restaurants and clubs jumped on the bandwagon, the state as a whole had been unable to fully embrace this particular trend. In the Midwest mind-set, Magozzi thought, Christmas lights meant something special, something rare you waited for all year. If you had them all the time, they lost their magic.

Just like fireworks. Used to be you waited all year for the Fourth of July. Now they blasted them off at concerts, store openings, and amusement parks almost every night so you could watch them from the Ferris wheel. No one noticed anymore. They'd become too common to be special, and Magozzi missed that.

'I'm getting really old.' Magozzi talked at the magnolia tree rather than at his male companion one Adirondack chair over. Males didn't look at each other when they talked in this part of the country, and that unspoken rule crossed species lines. Tonight Magozzi's companion was Charlie, Grace's dog, who woofed politely at Magozzi's words, but didn't look at him either. He knew the rules.

He heard the back door close, then Grace's footsteps, then smelled something delicious wafting out of the kitchen and into the night air. These were the familiar sounds and smells he associated with most of their time together over the past two years – the back door closing, Grace's boots on the three wooden steps down to the yard, Charlie's chewed-off tail thumping against the back of his very own Adirondack chair as his mistress approached. And, of course, the aroma of spectacular food always simmering on Grace's stove. They were warm, happy memories, but for some reason they seemed to be receding into what had been, instead of punctuating what was. Even here, in the place that had always felt like home because Grace was in it, things were a little off-kilter.

For instance, occasionally, like tonight, Grace wore some sort of silky, billowing slacks that moved like water around her legs and drove Magozzi nuts. But tomorrow she might appear in her old signature outfit of black jeans and T-shirts and tall, stiff riding boots. Sometimes she carried her Sig in the shoulder harness, sometimes it was in the new belt holster. It was confusing and disturbing, as if she were trying to shed her old personality with articles of clothing and couldn't quite pull it off.

Magozzi didn't like change. What if she wasn't trying to shed parts of her old personality, but parts of her past? He was part of that past, and he wasn't sure he would belong in whatever present she was making for herself.

'You're awfully quiet,' she said, handing him a glass of wine. They tried a new one every Tuesday during their weekly dinner, and tonight's was some French stuff that had more syllables than most spelling bees.

'Charlie and I were bonding. Men don't talk or look at each other during the process.'

Grace settled into the chair to his left and took a tasting sip of her wine. 'Tell me what you think of this one.'

Magozzi raised his brows. 'Last week you told me I had the palate of a carrion eater. Tonight you're asking my opinion on wine?'

'I was being polite.' She tossed her head a little, and the moonlight got all tangled up in her hair. She'd let that short, scary, pixie cut grow out over the fall and early winter, and she wore it loose tonight, brushing her shoulders like a tease.

He took a small sip of the wine, then a larger one, wondering how those stupid tasters ever spit out something this good. 'This stuff is killer. I could drink it with oatmeal.'

'I have something better in mind.'

'I can smell it.'

She sipped her wine and stared out at the falling snow. There were often comfortable silences between them, but tonight the silence seemed itchy and weird, at least to Magozzi. It was the emotional equivalent of an arthritis sufferer getting stiff joints before a rain.

'What is Monkeewrench working on?' he finally asked, cringing because it sounded like a lame, first-date line.

She looked at him, and her blue eyes sparked with interest. Maybe it hadn't been such a lame question after all. 'Actually, while Annie and Roadrunner are trotting all over the globe cherry-picking new clients, Harley and I started a new corporate security project.'

Magozzi's brows lifted. 'No more educational software?'

'We'll always do educational software, but this was a fresh challenge. We're enjoying it. And Annie and Roadrunner are enjoying being on the road. I think we all needed a change.'

As far as Magozzi was concerned, Grace MacBride had changed quite enough in the past year, thank you very much. She'd cut her hair, she'd run away to sail the Caribbean with another man, and even if it hadn't been a romantic relationship, she'd gone to someone else to get what she needed, leaving Magozzi behind. And he was beginning to wonder if he would ever get over it.

And then she did something so out of character he almost jumped out of his chair: she reached over and put her hand on his.

Grace never touched him beyond the darkness of the bedroom, where touch was an inherent and unavoidable part of the process and therefore meaningless. It seemed ass-backwards to him, that touching in bed was almost incidental while touching out in the open, in the light of day, somehow seemed more profound. Not that it mattered. Being touched by Grace, no matter what the illumination, was pretty much all he cared about. But it was strange.

'You're touching me and we aren't having sex at the moment. This is weird, Grace.'

She shrugged and almost smiled. Her shoulders went up to her ears and down again just like normal people, but Grace didn't do that. Shrugs indicated uncertainty and she never experienced that. 'Hormones, Magozzi. It happens.'

'Why didn't it ever happen before?'

'I was stronger then. What do you think of the patio?'

'I love the patio. I feel like I'm having an après ski glass of wine at a Swiss chalet. I can almost see the Alps right there, by your security fence.'

She rolled her eyes, but there was a faint smile on her lips. 'Nice of you to say so, but this isn't exactly a Swiss chalet.'

And that was true. Grace's house was a tiny structure with a tiny yard in an average city neighborhood. She could afford a real Swiss chalet if she wanted one, but she'd chosen this piece of real estate specifically for its size, because it had been easier to turn into an unbreachable fortress where she could shut herself in and shut everybody else out. 'Do you ever think of moving, getting a different place?'

She shrugged. 'I'm comfortable here.'

'Charlie wants a bigger yard, I can tell.'

'Charlie's agoraphobic.'

'You used to be agoraphobic, too. Animals take cues from their owners, change with them, you know.'

'And this from a man who's never owned an animal?'

'I might be watching too much cable TV. Do you know how many animal psychology shows are on now?'

Grace didn't giggle exactly – that would have been outrageous – but she was clearly amused.

42

'What about you? Do you ever think of getting a different place?'

'I'm comfortable there,' he echoed her earlier comment, and suddenly whatever strange tension had been tightening the air around them eased.

'Come on, let's go eat.' She took his hand and led him into the house.

# Seven

Chuck had only sketchy memories of driving back to the hotel after leaving the fire at Wally's house. One minute he was at the fire, talking to a Detective Hudson, the next he was walking through the lobby of the Chatham to the lounge. He told himself he wanted a beer, needed a beer, but the truth was, what he wanted and needed was human contact. You could live a solitary existence for most of your life, but when you really came up against it, sitting alone in a hotel room was a miserable prospect. It would be nice to prefer the company and solace of particular people, but if you didn't have that, a bartender was the next best thing.

'Good evening, sir. What can I get for you?'

'Beer, please. Whatever you recommend.'

The bartender expertly tapped a perfect pour into a frosted glass and watched Chuck lift it to his mouth with a hand that still hadn't stopped shaking. 'Are you all right, sir?'

'I'm not sure. I lost a friend tonight.'

'I'm sorry to hear that. Maybe you can patch things up.'

'I don't think so. He's dead.'

'Oh my God, I'm so sorry.'

Chuck stared down through the perfect foam head of his beer and felt sick. 'His name was Wally.'

The bartender noted Chuck's pasty face and his hunched posture and poured two fingers of amber liquid into two crystal lowballs. 'This might go easier on your stomach than beer right now. To your friend Wally, sir.' He touched his glass to Chuck's.

'You're very kind.' Chuck downed his drink and set his glass on the bar, thinking that bartenders were actually quite brilliant. The scotch went down smoothly and settled like silk in his troubled stomach, much more soothing than beer.

When he tried to pay, the bartender refused, saying, 'On the house, sir, with my sympathies.'

Chuck pressed his lips together and swallowed, wondering when people had become so nice, wondering if he'd missed that all these years.

After his second scotch with the sympathetic bartender, Chuck started to think he might actually be able to go to sleep – the unexpected infusion of alcohol in a body unused to it had calmed him a bit. And for a time, at least, he'd stopped dwelling on what had certainly been the worst day of his life. Even so, the circumstances surrounding Wally's unexpected death still tormented him. He was no detective, but you'd have to be an idiot not to see just how wrong the whole thing was, how unlikely it was that your house would blow up from a gas leak just after you were attacked in a home invasion. Nobody had that kind of bad luck.

He finally pushed up out of his stool with a weary sigh, thanked the bartender again for his kindness, and discreetly tucked a twenty-dollar bill beneath his empty glass. It seemed like a ridiculously small price to pay for a sympathetic ear and a little companionship when he'd needed it most.

The hallways on the fourth floor were deserted and silent, until Chuck approached the last turn before the hall that led to his room and heard the whispers. They were urgent, hissing like angry snakes ready to strike, and they stopped him dead in the adjoining hallway.

'What if he's not back from the fire?'

Chuck felt his body freeze as his heart leaped forward. Who was that? How did they know about the fire?

'Then we wait,' another voice hissed. 'Get me in his room, dammit, then go down to the lobby and cover that.'

Chuck heard the metallic clunk of a room door opening, muted whispers, and then brisk footfalls coming toward him. He looked around instinctively, frantically, for cover, because this was wrong, wrong, wrong, just like Wally's attack and his house explosion had been wrong. He saw a vending machine alcove just a few feet away, scrambled toward it, and crouched beside the ice maker, making himself as small as possible. On any other day, he wouldn't have had such an outlandishly paranoid reaction, but today wasn't like any other day. There were times when you knew you had to listen to that crazy inner voice that screamed duck and cover, and this was one of them, even if he would be embarrassed about it later, because surely there was some rational explanation.

He got down on his hands and knees and peeked around the corner as the footsteps drew closer. He saw a male figure flash by, but not fast enough to keep him from seeing the gun in his hand. Jesus God, who were these men? Burglars?

*They were waiting for you. With guns. Get the hell out of here.*

But where was he going to go? One man was in his room, the other was waiting for him in the lobby.

And then he saw the fire stairwell.

He was breathing hard after running down the first flight of stairs. Good Lord. Ten steps? Twenty? One stinking floor from the fourth floor down to the third, and already his breath was gone and his heart was pounding. Jesus, he'd never make it.

He stopped and bent over, clutching the stitch in his side which had no business being there after such a short distance. *Breathe. Deep breaths, all the way to the bottom of your lungs, then exhale slowly. Yeah, right. Men with guns are after you, so gee, Chuck, just take a minute and imagine yourself in a hammock on a beach somewhere.*

But oddly, taking that brief, ridiculous pause did one thing. He remembered that day he'd sat in front of the TV, weeping unashamedly as he watched the World Trade Center towers pancake into the ground with an odd grace, like gallant warships going down like ladies. Old people, burned people, wounded people trudging down as many as eighty flights of stairs, and he couldn't make one?

Remembering them made him feel small and ashamed, and quieted his fearful heart and panicked breathing. And then, clarity, and thought, the hallmarks of a charmed and relatively uneventful life.

*You have choices.*

There was one man in his room, one man guarding the lobby. Where should he go? A couple of floors down? All the way to ground level? Where was it safe?

The very acknowledgment of a choice panicked him all over again. What if he chose wrong?

It took less than five seconds to make a choice. The people in those crowded, crumbling stairwells never asked those questions. They went down, down to ground level without hesitation, because they didn't belong halfway up in the sky, they belonged on solid ground, where humanity was milling around, waiting to help them.

Strange, how calmly he descended the last three floors, and only for a moment did he hesitate at the ground floor. Now the choices were only two. Right, through the hotel, or outside.

He looked at the glowing red exit sign over the outside door and thought of it as a message just for him.

Those men were inside the hotel. He would go outside.

# Eight

Magozzi watched the bright lights of Hennepin Avenue strobe a rainbow of colors on the dashboard while Gino weaved through traffic on the way to the Chatham. It was a newer boutique hotel in the heart of the small downtown Minneapolis theater district, and from what he'd heard, it had posh rooms, a great restaurant, and a modern art collection a small museum would envy. People weren't supposed to get murdered in the Chatham universe.

'Well, shit, look at that,' Gino muttered, leaning on his horn and veering around a news satellite van. 'The vultures are just waiting to pick the carcass clean. How do they sleep at night?' He made a sharp left and almost skidded onto the sidewalk, which would have killed several more people, because there were throngs of rubberneckers braving the arctic cold and snow to watch the aftermath of some poor soul's murder.

'Jesus, Gino, slow down. Our victim isn't going anywhere.'

Gino let out a grump, then nudged the car up to the curb. 'We're not going to get any closer than this.'

Police presence outside the hotel was conspicuous, and the crime-scene tape blocking the alley looked bizarre next to the sleek hotel façade, and would certainly do nothing for public relations. Well-heeled guests stopped and gawked, then rushed inside, probably marching straight up to the front desk to demand refunds.

The uniforms had their hands full, so Gino did the genteel thing and hollered, 'First responder?'

A young officer looked up from the barricade he was putting up in the street, then waved an arm and jogged over. His face was as pink as a summer cherry, totally clashing with the modest, reddish sideburns that peeked out from under the down-turned earflaps of his department-issue winter hat.

'Evening, Detectives. I'm the first responder.'

Magozzi looked at his nameplate. 'Officer . . . Szczypanski?'

'Good try, sir.'

'Thanks. You want to walk us through?'

'Absolutely. Let's get behind the tape first. The media is crawling all over, and who knows what kind of microphones they're using now.'

They ducked under the crime-scene tape and stood at the mouth of an alley. Harsh safety lights mounted to the backs of the surrounding buildings played off the fresh dusting of snow, casting shadows in pure black and white. Magozzi felt like he was stepping into an old noir flick.

Szczypanski pointed to a Dumpster by the hotel's loading dock. 'I found him right there. Well, actually I didn't find him initially. See, nine-one-one took a call about forty minutes ago. The caller was male, real panicky, saying that somebody was trying to kill him outside the Chatham Hotel, then the connection got cut off. I was closest to the area on this beat, only a couple blocks away, so I hightailed it over here on foot, searched the vicinity, and . . . well, I found him, right there, next to the Dumpster.'

'So you're saying the *victim* called this in?'

'It seems like it.'

'We need a trace on the number that called nine-one-one,' Magozzi said to Gino, but apparently Szczypanski was a go-getter.

'As soon as I found the victim, I called that in.'

'Good job. Any witnesses?'

Szczypanski shook his head. 'Nothing so far, but the sergeant just started the canvass.'

There were blood spatters on the fresh snow. Gino and Magozzi approached the Dumpster

52

slowly, taking in the details of the alley before they viewed the victim, who was sadly crumpled on his side next to the Dumpster, as if he were just another parcel of trash that had yet to be tossed inside.

Gino shone a Maglite on the victim's bloody, gray hair. 'He was shot in the head. Looks like twice.'

Magozzi made a circuit of the immediate vicinity like a dog circling his bed. He crouched down next to the body and checked the pockets of the man's overcoat, shirt, and pants. 'No personal effects, no phone. He was cleaned out.'

'Mugging?' Gino suggested. 'This guy is well-dressed, probably a hotel guest, and the Chatham sells rooms for what, five hundred a night? If I were a mugger, this is where I'd hang out. There's always somebody who's going to decide to take a shortcut through the alley on the way back to the hotel after a three-martini dinner.'

Magozzi felt the cold taking root in his extremities. He would have stomped his feet to warm them up, but he figured all his toes would break. He wrote 'new winter boots' on the mental shopping list he forgot almost immediately. 'I'm buying the hotel-guest angle, but I don't like the mugging angle. The MO doesn't fit. Neither does his nine-one-one call. Muggers don't give you a shot at personal phone calls. They jump out of the shadows and bring you down before they strip you clean. So this guy knew someone was after him and he ran. They caught him here, but he had time to punch in the three magic numbers and call for help.'

Gino was sweeping the alley and the area around the Dumpster with his light. 'There aren't a lot of prints in the alley, just by that metal fire door. I think this started inside.'

'Detectives?'

They both turned and saw Szczypanski trotting toward them. 'I got a name to go with the phone number that called nine-one-one. Charles Spencer, Woodland Hills, California. Verizon's his carrier.'

# Nine

The Chatham's lobby décor was modern, serene, and understated – dignified hipster meets Tibetan monk – but the heavy police presence outside the sparkling glass doors was ruining the carefully curated Zen atmosphere. Even the potted orchids looked stressed out.

A lot of guests were milling around, watchful eyes fixed on the door as they burbled to one another in hushed voices, endlessly speculating on the source of the evening's excitement. They were the information scavengers waiting patiently for a juicy detail or two to satisfy their salacious souls. It was off-putting, but Magozzi couldn't blame them, really; when your expensive hotel was overrun with cops and you had no idea why, your curiosity got piqued. It was human nature.

Gino nodded toward the concierge desk where a thin, fretful-looking man with a hotel nameplate on his finely tailored suit was standing alone, wringing his hands. 'Let's go talk to this guy, see if he can find us a manager.'

As it turned out the distraught man at the concierge desk was the manager. His name was Jacob Amundson, and he emanated the helpless despair of a good Roman citizen watching his city burn to the ground.

'Please, tell me how I can help you, Detectives. This seems very . . . serious.'

'It is,' Gino reassured him. 'Can we speak someplace private?'

'Yes, yes, of course.' He paused and his eyes diverted to the front of the hotel. 'Ah . . . before we speak, is there information I should pass along to my staff or clients?'

'Nope,' Gino said amiably. 'Not unless you want to tell them there's a dead man in your back alley.'

Jacob's face turned the color of the snow falling outside. 'Follow me, Detectives.' He whisked them into a small office just off the lobby and pulled out chairs. 'Please, have a seat.'

'Thank you,' Magozzi said, flipping to a new page in his notebook.

'What happened?' the manager asked, no doubt scouring his mind for the crisis management protocol he never thought he'd need.

'We'd just like to ask you a few questions.'

He cleared his throat. 'Of course.'

'We need to know if a Charles Spencer was a guest at your hotel.'

'Let me check for you.' He sank down into a padded chair at his desk that looked far more comfortable than the blond wood torture devices he'd offered to them.

He tapped on his keyboard for a few minutes, then turned in his chair. 'Right here, Detectives. Charles Spencer, from Woodland Hills, California, room four-twenty. I remember him now. In fact, I was at the front desk when he checked in late this afternoon, and he was excited about the snow. He's staying for three days . . . unless he's . . .'

'Deceased,' Magozzi said, watching the color drain out of Jacob's face for the second time in five minutes. He showed him the driver's license photo of Spencer they'd pulled off the computer in the car, and the man nodded slowly.

'Yes. That's him.'

'Was there anybody else staying with him?'

'The reservation was for single occupancy. He only took one key card. God. This is just dreadful.'

'Yes, it is. Mr. Amundson, we're going to need everything you've got on file for Mr. Spencer – calls in or out, any arrangements he might have made through the concierge, whether or not he had a rental, like that.'

He tapped at his keyboard and it was less than ten seconds before a well-hidden and muted printer began discreetly producing pages. He tucked them into a black folder with the hotel logo embossed on the front and passed it across his desk. 'All of Mr. Spencer's activities since his check-in are recorded in his room records, including the information on his rental car. If a maid visited his room, if he purchased items from the minibar, if he requested an extra towel or asked for a restaurant recommendation, you'll find it there.'

Gino raised his brow. 'Wait until Motel 6 hears about this setup.'

'Our officers are going to be interviewing staff and guests at our discretion, just so you know,' Magozzi said, feeling sorry for the guy as his perfectly arranged world of premium customer service came crashing down around him. 'We'll also need your security footage. Every single camera, inside and out, the sooner the better.'

The manager nodded in submission. 'I'll call my security chief right now. Is there anything else?'

'A key card for Mr. Spencer's room.'

'Nice place,' Gino said as he and Magozzi entered Charles Spencer's suite and started exploring. The space was clean – a little too clean in Magozzi's opinion, with the exception of a partially drunk beer and a bag of cashews sitting on a corner table.

He opened the lid of a small Tumi carry-on that was sitting on the luggage tripod at the foot of the bed. Neatly folded clothes, a leather shaving kit, a copy of *Scientific American*, and nothing else. 'There's no stuff here, Gino. When people check into hotel rooms, they usually do a little unpacking, leave a few personal items scattered around. There's no laptop, no iPod, no papers, no keys to his rental car.'

Gino shrugged. 'So maybe he's a light traveler. Or maybe his stuff's in his car, or he had it all on him and it got lifted in the alley along with his cell phone.'

'Maybe. Still, it bugs me.' Magozzi walked over to the windows that looked out onto Hennepin Avenue, where traffic was snarled in knots around the police barricades, just adjacent to the alley.

'Detectives?' Jacob Amundson's accommodating voice whispered from the open door. 'I don't mean to disturb you, but I've just spoken with my security chief regarding today's footage.'

'Thank you.'

'Well . . . unfortunately, thanks are not in order. There's a problem.'

'What kind of a problem?'

'Our IT team seems to think that there was some kind of breach in our server. Security currently can't access any footage from today, but I can assure you that we are doing everything to resolve the matter as quickly as possible. I'm terribly sorry. Nothing like this has ever happened before.'

# Ten

Lydia Ascher was sitting at her dining room table, enjoying the anticipatory butterflies in her stomach she always got when embarking on a new challenge with the confidence that there would be a successful outcome. This joyful anticipation was predicated on her fairly consistent track record of succeeding, at least modestly so, at all the unfamiliar tasks she tried, and she couldn't imagine why this particular endeavor would be any different. Thoughtfulness, careful preparation, and perseverance took you a long way in this life, and outside of rocket science itself, nothing was rocket science.

With all her equipment in place, she rubbed her hands together with a smile and addressed her current subject. 'It's bath time, Rex, so let's do this thing. Six easy steps. Says so right here in the book.'

Rex was unresponsive. So like a king.

'Okay, I'll talk us through it. Step one: Unload the pistol. That would be you, and we've got that covered.'

And then she froze suddenly. Did she *for sure* have that covered? She'd unloaded ten clips at the range tonight, proving herself a horrible shot who showed potential to improve with practice, and upon finishing she'd pulled back the slide half a dozen times just to make sure Rex was empty. But what if he wasn't? Was it possible for bullets to hide, and if so, would that hidden bullet blow up in her face while she was disassembling for cleaning? Or worse yet, fire right into the two-thousand-dollar plate glass window the barrel was pointing at right now?

Maybe she wasn't cut out for gun ownership after all. It hadn't been her idea, anyhow, it had been a gift from Uncle Ambrose, who was a lifelong city dweller with a pathological fear of the countryside. To him, her lake house an hour outside Minneapolis was Dante's seven circles of hell all rolled into one, and Ed Gein was behind every tree, waiting to turn her skull into a cereal bowl.

Lydia pulled the slide back again, miffed by her sudden uncertainty. Yes, empty. Of course the damn thing was empty. No need to be OCD, even if a mistake could blow up her face, her window, or maybe her house. 'Okay, step two: Manually retract the slide until the slide disassembly notch is aligned with the slide stop tab.' Once she'd achieved that, she read step three: 'Remove the slide stop from the frame.'

Easier said than done. Fifteen minutes later, she realized that shooting a gun was a lot easier than cleaning one. Big fat *F* for failure. And maybe that's just what you got and deserved when you were ridiculous enough to name your weapon, although it made sense to her. A gun was a scary thing, and anthropomorphizing it with a pet name made her pint-sized instrument of death seem less intimidating.

She wondered if men named their guns. Probably not, although guitar players named their guitars sometimes – she knew that because she'd been stupid enough to date one once. She'd also heard that some men named their penises, which had always seemed a little bent to her, but was a woman naming her gun the feminine equivalent of a guy naming his junk?

But back to the task at hand. She now had a partially disassembled, dirty gun, and if taking it apart was so difficult, what about putting it back together? What if she did it wrong and it wouldn't fire? What if tonight was the night the psycho serial killer showed up, her cobbled-together gun wouldn't fire, and she'd die a horrible death? And if she couldn't clean her gun, she couldn't practice with it, so she wouldn't be able to hit the psycho serial killer anyhow, and she'd still die, with a useless gun in her hand. She realized she was in the midst of a terrible conundrum.

She looked down at Rex. She wouldn't be in this pickle if she hadn't been possessed by a wild hair this afternoon, all amped to hit the range for the first time ever. Hell, the gun had lain untouched in her dresser drawer for six months, and she'd never even had the slightest desire to shoot it. Then suddenly, out of the blue, the minute she'd gotten home from the airport, the range had seemed like not only a good idea, but an absolute necessity. What was that about?

But in her deepest heart of hearts, she knew exactly what it was about. The man at the airport café.

For a woman who'd absorbed her mother's terror of flying through osmosis, it had been a fantastic trip home. In a hugely creepy-fun-amazing coincidence, she'd been seated next to Chuck Spencer, a man whose father had worked with her grandfather on the nascent hydrogen bomb, back when it had been top secret, back when only a handful of men in the world had known about it. What were the odds, with the thousands of flights a day? Astronomical.

Chuck had calmed her travel jitters and put her at ease right away, and he seemed like a great guy. Nice, salt of the earth, and a real gentleman for suffering her endless, nervous babbling without telling her to shut up.

But once she and Chuck had inadvertently discovered that their predecessors had rubbed elbows in the age-old quest for bigger and better ways to blow the earth to smithereens, he'd become abruptly fascinating.

They'd grabbed a quick cup of coffee together once the flight had landed, sharing more weird stories about their unconventionally employed family members, and that's when she'd felt it. The prickle. She'd turned her head then, and saw a man at a distant table whose eyes didn't look right.

Her first prickle had been at the age of five, and throughout her life it happened from time to time, and she'd come to think of it as a nuisance, and definitely something to be ignored as mild craziness or paranoia.

Until the age of twenty-nine. Having cocktails with friends at an upscale lounge in downtown Minneapolis. Looking across the bar and seeing a handsome man staring at her. Just staring, with eyes too bright, too shiny, too focused. But not drug eyes. Drug eyes were aimless and had no intensity. These eyes were like looking at stars in the nighttime sky – from Earth, stars just twinkled, but if you had ever paid attention in astronomy class, you knew the twinkle was caused by raging storms of gas in the stars' atmospheres. People were no different.

She never told her friends about the man at the bar or her curse of the prickles. Not even when she found out later that the man in the bar had raped and killed a young woman on that very same night.

Lydia never ignored the prickles after that. She also started drawing faces. Two years later, her haunting portraits became the talk of the art world. And four years after that, she still cried for that murdered young woman, and prayed that her rising art star was in some way a tribute.

She returned her focus to Rex, anxious to merge off memory lane. Interesting that noticing the bad man in the airport hadn't inspired her to pick up a pencil, as it normally would have, it had inspired her to pick up a gun.

*Listen. Always listen.*

'Oh, I'm listening,' she muttered to herself, picking up the phone and punching in Otis's number.

Otis was her geriatric handyman, whom she was certain didn't have a name for his penis or his guns, although the veracity of that particular speculation wasn't one she wanted to dwell on for more than the millisecond it had taken for it to pop in on her thoughts like an unwelcome guest.

'Otis.'

'Hey, Lydie, welcome back. How was your trip?'

'Great. Warm. I brought you back a shot glass.'

'Aren't you a peach! I only got two states left and my collection is complete.'

'What are you missing?'

'Rhode Island and Nebraska.'

'Sorry, but you're on your own with those. Hey, Otis, do you have to clean your gun after you shoot it?'

'You sure should.'

She thought of all the old movies, where pioneers and cowboys were shooting their guns all day and night, and you never saw them cleaning their weapons. 'Really?'

'Don't tell me you finally dusted off that little mite your uncle gave you.'

Lydia sighed. 'Yeah. And I'm having some trouble. Is it too late for you to come over?'

# Eleven

Lydia loved Otis. He was an unabashed chauvinist, as old-school as they got, and he could fix anything, build anything. In spite of his age, he was still strong and straight, and his mind was sharp. She paid him, of course, but he refused to take the current market rates for skilled labor, so to make up for the paucity of pay, she baked him pies. And she made great pies – a legacy from her mother, Alice. It was a perfect barter, a true symbiosis, and they were both happy with the bargain. Besides, it was a little window into the way things had been way back when. Men did stuff for women they couldn't or wouldn't do for themselves and women did stuff for men they couldn't or wouldn't do for themselves. Everybody had a job, a place in the larger scheme of things, and there was perfect balance.

She watched as Otis briskly took the gun apart, cleaned it, and got it back together within the space of a few minutes. 'Wow. You're good.'

'I did it fast, so you could see how easy it is. Just takes some practice, and I've had plenty. Now let's see if you can do it. We'll take it real slow.'

It took an hour, but she eventually got the hang of it, felt comfortable doing it on her own. Lydia Ascher, soon-to-be-gunslinger beyond compare, could take apart her weapon, clean it, and put it back together again. Astounding. Psycho serial killer was in big trouble now.

They celebrated the milestone event with strong coffee and the lemon meringue pie she'd baked as a thank-you to Otis for keeping an eye on her place when she'd been in L.A. When they ran out of rural life small talk – the snow that was coming, the cold snap, the gardens they would plant when spring eventually arrived – she told him about her wild meeting with Chuck Spencer and their shared family history.

Otis loved every minute of it. 'Well, my goodness, young lady, you've got yourself quite a pedigree.'

'Well, maybe an ignominious one.'

'I don't know what that means, but there's gotta be the hands of fate tangled up in there somewhere.'

She smiled and shrugged. 'Not really. It's just the six degrees of separation. Which is getting smaller by the minute.'

'I suppose so. But I do wish you an enjoyable lunch tomorrow. I'm glad you're taking the time to revisit family history with this Chuck fella. Those times are long gone now, and it'd be a damn shame if everything was forgotten. My Pop served in the big war. Never got much out of him until the end, and even then it was sparse, but I still keep everything he told me close, as a memory.'

As she was wrapping up the rest of the pie for Otis to take home, he came into the kitchen and touched her shoulder. She looked up and smiled, but her smile faltered a little when she saw his eyes. Norwegian bachelor farmer eyes, she called them. Blue as blue could ever get, even at his age, when eyes usually faded to a lesser color. They were warm eyes, jolly eyes, but they were troubled now.

'I'll be keeping an eye out. Just so you know.'

'An eye out for what?'

Otis just shrugged and looked down at the foil packet of pie. 'Trouble.'

Lydia felt prickles again, and God, did she hate that feeling. 'What makes you say that?'

'I got horses. They get skittish all kinds of times, when a storm's brewing, when there's coyotes afoot, if a little wind picks up, if a butterfly pops up from the grass. But you're not a horse, and you're not the skittish type.'

'Uh . . . no. I'm not.'

'Not usually. But you are now.'

Lydia sighed and gave him a self-deprecating smile. 'Leftover travel nerves, I guess,' she lied. 'You know how much I hate to fly. It takes a while to shake it out of your system.'

'Uh-huh. Well, you call if you need me.'

She frowned after him as he got into his truck and drove away, wondering if she and Otis didn't have a lot more in common than she'd previously thought.

As he turned the bend in her driveway, his headlights briefly washed over the thick woods that cuddled up to her yard and she saw a shadow; just a flash, really, and then it was gone. A deer, probably – the woods were filled with them.

# Twelve

It was almost midnight by the time Gino and Magozzi were ready to clear the scene at the Chatham. For all their hours spent going through Spencer's room and rental car, interviewing guests and staff and making phone calls, they had little to show for it. No one had seen anything – no terrified man running for his life, no crazed madman chasing him down the corridors, no upsetting disturbance at all. Spencer's rental car had been as clean as his room and his life from what they'd been able to gather so far. The unassuming, retired engineer from Woodland Hills had no next of kin that they'd been able to find and no police record – not even a speeding ticket.

They'd requested a rush on ballistics, but that wouldn't be in until the autopsy was complete. The lab would eventually process everything they'd pulled from the crime scene in the alley, Spencer's hotel room, and rental car, but that, too, was something they would have to wait for. Some homicides were obvious and had quick and clean endings, but this wasn't going to be one of them. A mugging was still on the table, but that had been ringing false all night.

In the unobtrusive space at the back of the lobby, Magozzi was pacing in small circles, which mirrored the same small circles looping around in his brain. He felt like he'd been waiting forever for Gino to finish a phone call. He had no real energy for physical or mental exertion, just an overabundance of coffee and nervous energy flooding his system.

There were no guests in the lobby at this hour and only a skeleton crew at the front desk. Jacob Amundson had kindly dropped off a plate of sandwiches an hour ago before signing out for the night, and it was time for them to do the same.

'Angela?' Magozzi asked when Gino finally shoved his phone back into his pocket.

'No, that was LAPD calling back. They dispatched the local PD to Woodland Hills to check out Spencer's house and try to track down next of kin. There was a break-in.'

'Jesus. The fates really had it in for Charles Spencer today.'

'No kidding. But it's nothing we haven't seen before. Dirtbags hang out in nice neighborhoods and watch for taxis. Somebody gets into a cab with a suitcase and it's a good gamble they're heading to the airport and they don't have anybody else in the house to give them a lift. The dirtbags hang around, case the place, make sure there's nobody else home, then make their move, ruin somebody's house and peace of mind, and get fifty bucks' worth of stuff on the black market if they're lucky. Anyhow, the cop I talked to said the B and E was a little weird. Every single room in the house was tossed, but nothing was obviously missing. TVs, electronics, a couple expensive watches sitting out on a dresser – they weren't touched. The only thing they think got lifted was a home computer.'

They both looked up when they heard the boisterous laughter of a couple entering the lobby. They were impeccably dressed and very tipsy. The woman was a little wobbly on her stiletto boots as she shrugged off her coat. The man grabbed her elbow gently to keep her steady and kissed her on the neck, eliciting a giggly trill. In this moment, they were having the time of their lives, and that made Magozzi happy after being steeped in darkness for most of the night. He hoped they realized just how precious life was.

'Come on, let's get out of here.'

# Thirteen

By the next morning the news was mildly abuzz
with two tragedies in one night. The gas explosion
in South Minneapolis was the first story, because it
was a dramatic cautionary tale and struck fear in the
hearts of all Minnesotans who hadn't gotten their
furnaces checked out before winter hit. Besides, it
was great art. Nothing like somebody's home shooting flames into the night sky, especially when the
owner was turning into a crispy critter inside.

Apparently, Magozzi thought, the old maxim 'If
it bleeds, it leads' no longer applied, since Charles
Spencer, who had certainly bled, only ranked second on the morning news hit parade, and the
coverage was minimal.

Magozzi realized his thoughts were trending cynical, but he hadn't had much sleep, the Mr. Coffee
in Homicide was taking forever to grunt out a new
pot, and he and Gino had a mountain of reports to
slog through.

After they'd left the Chatham well after midnight,
Gino had gone home to the warm arms of his wife,

Angela, and a plate of lasagna; Magozzi had gone home to a TV dinner and an empty, silent house. Both of them had worked their home computers for hours, but both of them had come up empty.

When Mr. Coffee gave a pop and a final, weary sigh, he filled two mugs and walked back to their desks, where he found Gino intensely focused on his computer screen, face scrunched up in what looked like befuddlement. 'What are you working on?'

Gino took the coffee and started dosing it with sugar packets, his eyes still fixed on his computer screen. 'Spencer's cell phone records. He was regularly calling a local number for the past three months – he called it three times yesterday alone. Happy happy joy joy, I'm thinking, we've got a person of interest.'

'Great. Let's go arrest him for murder.'

'Can't. He's dead.'

'What?'

'Yeah. Remember what the bartender at the Chatham said last night, that Spencer was mourning the loss of a friend? Well, turns out the number Spencer kept calling belonged to a guy named Wallace Luntz. So I look into Wallace Luntz, and guess what? He was the old guy who died in that gas explosion yesterday.'

Magozzi sat down and stared at the wall for a moment. 'That's weird.'

'Oh, it gets weirder. Here's the double-headed kicker. The ME's preliminary report says Luntz was dead before the house blew – bullet to the brain. And perk up your ears and listen to this. It's an audio transcript of a nine-one-one call Spencer made exactly seven seconds after his last call to Luntz. I just got it from the call center.' Gino pulled up an audio file on his computer and pressed the play key.

*Nine-one-one, what's your emergency?*

Home invasion at twelve forty Gleason Road! My friend is being attacked in his house, please send help . . .

*Are you at the location, sir?*

No, I was talking to him on the phone and he went to answer the door, and started screaming. Please, is help on the way?

*I have emergency vehicles en route to that address right now.*

Thank God.

'That's it,' Gino said, muting his computer. 'He hung up after that.'

Magozzi scraped at a piece of stubble on his jaw that his early morning shave had missed. 'You've gotta be kidding me. So Spencer was on the phone with his buddy, heard him getting attacked, and then the guy's house blows to kingdom come. And then Spencer ends up dead a couple hours later. What the hell?'

'That's exactly what I said to myself. These guys were connected, two friends who end up murdered on the same night? They had to be into something that made them targets, right? But the thing is, they were both dull as dirt – nice, older guys who worked average jobs until they retired.'

'Luntz, too?'

'Yeah. He worked for an iron foundry up north most of his life, then came down here to finish out his golden years. I talked to the arson investigator in charge of Luntz's case. Guy named Cory. They've been working the scene hard because they figured foul play from the get-go. The home invasion angle was the icing on the cake. The place was so hot, they're just getting in there now. They'll let us know if they pull anything besides charcoal out of the debris.'

Magozzi reached for his phone when it started skittering on his desk. 'Detective Magozzi here.'

There was a hanging silence, then a tentative female voice. 'Detective . . . my name is Lydia Ascher. The manager at the Chatham Hotel gave me your number. This is in regard to Chuck Spencer.'

Magozzi gave Gino a thumbs-up and put the phone on speaker. 'Are you a friend of Mr. Spencer's, ma'am?'

'Not really. We met on a plane yesterday and agreed to have lunch today, here at his hotel, but the manager told me to call you.'

'Are you at the Chatham now, Ms. Ascher?'

'Yes.'

'My partner and I would like to talk to you. We can be there in ten minutes.'

Magozzi heard her let out a shaky sigh. 'I'll be waiting in the lobby.'

Gino pushed himself up out of his chair and grabbed his coat. 'I got it. A geriatric love triangle. She killed 'em both. Now she's just toying with us.'

# Fourteen

Lydia Ascher was definitely not geriatric, not by a long shot. She was blond and blue and younger than they were by at least a few years, and well put together – really well put together – by some God who knew men were jerks but still passed out a brass ring every now and then just to make a bad day better.

Magozzi knew the type. Every man did. She was the head cheerleader in high school who would never give you a second look, but still, you went to every game just to watch her breasts move under her letter sweater when she raised up her pom-poms, making your heart go soft and other body parts do the opposite.

After the requisite introductions, she said, 'The murder here last night. It was Chuck, wasn't it?'

There was no way to sugarcoat a murder, so Magozzi just nodded solemnly. Besides, she'd already put two and two together. 'I'm sorry, Ms. Ascher.'

She took the news like any other person who was stunned by the sudden, violent death of an acquaintance – there was genuine sorrow and shock, but not the same variety as when it was personal. She was quiet for a long time, then looked down at her lap where her hands were curled in little balls. 'Do you know what happened?'

'It's early in the investigation. Anything we told you would be speculation at this point.'

'Yes, of course.' She shook her head. 'This is so sad. He was such a nice man, so excited to be in town visiting a new friend.'

Gino cocked an eyebrow at Magozzi. 'Wallace Luntz?'

She looked up. 'Yes, he said his friend's name was Wally. Does he know Chuck is . . . ?'

Gino winced, then explained the explosion, the 911 call from Spencer, and the fact that Wally Luntz had been shot by his intruder before his house had gone up like a rocket. That threw pretty Lydia for another, more significant loop – her face blanched and her eyes fixed on a distant point, like she was looking for answers to some confounding, internal mystery.

'Wally was murdered too?' she whispered.

'It looks that way.'

'Oh my God. This is horrible. I don't know what to say.'

'We're hoping you can help us fill in some blanks,' Magozzi prompted. 'Do you know why Mr. Spencer was in town to visit Wallace Luntz?'

'All I can tell you is what Chuck told me.'

After twenty minutes, Magozzi was beginning to think that Lydia Ascher was a beautiful distraction, but a dead end in the pertinent information department.

The whole hydrogen bomb thing was interesting – fascinating, actually – but she'd said it herself – it was old news, declassified in the eighties. Certainly nothing that would put a bull's-eye on a couple of second-generation men who were whiling away their retirement researching family footnotes to the Cold War fifty-plus years after the fact. And that was the extent of her knowledge about Spencer. If he and Wally had been laundering money for the mob or running drugs for a Mexican cartel, he hadn't shared that with his seatmate from L.A. to Minneapolis.

Magozzi flipped to a new page in his notebook. 'You mentioned that Mr. Spencer was trying to get in touch with other descendants. Did he?'

Lydia folded her lips together, and her brows tipped down. 'He told me Wally and some others had reached out to him through his website. It's called the Sixth Idea dot net. He showed a little of it to me on his laptop after we got off the plane.'

Magozzi made a note of the site's name and thought about the notable absence of any electronics on Spencer, in his hotel room, or in his rental car. 'So he did have a laptop computer with him?'

'Yes.'

'Thank you. I think we're just about finished here, Ms. Ascher. You've been very gracious with your time, we appreciate it.'

'I'm sorry I haven't been much help. And I'm very sorry for what happened. I hope you'll find whoever is responsible.'

Magozzi gave her a card. 'If you think of anything else, please call.'

'I will.' She stood and began to slip on her coat. Gino was quick to help her, because a happily married man had chivalry down to an art form. Magozzi would have gotten there maybe half a second later. He should have been a half a second earlier.

She shook their hands, then paused. 'You know, there's one thing I didn't mention. It's probably silly.'

'Nothing is silly, every detail can be a crucial one,' Magozzi reassured her, having trouble keeping his eyes off hers. *Good interview technique,* he thought. Yeah, right.

'Chuck and I had a cup of coffee after we got off the plane. There was a man in the café who just . . . well, he made me nervous.'

'How so?'

'Just a feeling. You know how sometimes people watch you, but they're pretending not to?'

Magozzi knew very well, because that's exactly what he was doing with Lydia Ascher, and probably what the man in the café had been doing, too. It was hard not to stare at a looker like her. 'Yes. So you think he was watching you.'

Her forehead crinkled. 'Actually, it seemed more like he was watching Chuck. In quick glances, you know?'

'What happened when you left the café?'

'He left after we did.'

'Like he was following you?'

'It crossed my mind.'

'Could you describe him?'

'I can do better than that if you have a minute.' She pulled a decent-sized sketch pad and a piece of charcoal out of the large tote at her feet and started sketching. There were few things that captivated people more than a truly gifted artist practicing their craft, and this woman was obviously gifted. Magozzi and Gino were both leaning forward, craning their necks to watch a human face come to life under her hand. Compared to the soulless, computer-generated police sketches, this was a Rembrandt.

'Wow,' Gino mumbled. 'You're pretty amazing.'

'Thank you.'

'Do you have one of those scary photographic memories?'

'Only when it comes to faces.' She pushed the drawing across the banquette table. 'That's what he looked like.'

Magozzi, a former hobby painter himself, picked up the paper and stared at the painstakingly detailed charcoal face, recognizing true talent; and at the same time, also recognizing that he didn't have any after all. He looked up at her. 'If this guy was in a crowd of a thousand, I could point him out in a heartbeat.'

Lydia shrugged uncomfortably. 'That's kind of you to say. I hope it helps.'

After Lydia Ascher left, Gino dragged his hands down his face, giving a preview of what he'd look like thirty years down the road. 'So, here's where we stand: we got a history lesson about weapons of mass destruction and a pretty incredible sketch of some guy who's probably a salesman from Omaha. What are you doing?'

Magozzi had his nose in his tablet computer. 'Trying to get on Spencer's website. These two guys had to be into something.' He kept punching keys.

'Anything interesting?'

'Yeah. The Sixth Idea dot net doesn't exist.'

'Try something else, maybe she gave you the wrong address.'

'I've tried a dozen different variations of it. Dot net, dot com, all caps, all lowercase. If there was a website, it's gone now.'

'That's a little funky.' Gino looked up and brightened when a waiter approached with a carafe of coffee and a tray of pastries.

'Compliments of the manager, Detectives.'

Gino rubbed his hands together. 'You just made my day.'

The waiter began pouring coffee into delicate china cups. 'There's a note from Mr. Amundson. He didn't want to disturb your meeting.'

'Thank you.' Magozzi opened the envelope that was tucked beneath a vase with a rose and pulled out a piece of cardstock. 'Huh.'

Gino had already eaten half a croissant and was eyeing something dusted with powdered sugar that looked deep-fried. 'What does it say?'

'The hotel computer geeks couldn't recover the surveillance video.'

'That tears it. We've gotta call Monkeewrench. Espinoza's the only guy we've got in-house who'd have a prayer of getting this technical shit done, and he's down in Florida having a hernia operation.'

Magozzi narrowed his eyes. 'He went to Florida for a hernia operation last year.'

'Yep. He says it's recurring.'

'So there's no doc between here and Florida who could handle it?'

'Not in winter. You want to call or should I?'

Magozzi grabbed his personal cell and punched number three on speed dial. Gino was number one. Grace was number two, and the Monkeewrench offices were number three. He thought about the order as the phone rang on speaker and what it said about his life.

Harley Davidson picked up on the second ring. 'Leo! We saw the news about the Chatham murder. Something we can do for you?'

'Actually, we need a favor if you and Grace can spare the time.'

'Oh goody. Is it illegal?'

'Not the first part, but what you find might change things.'

'Sounds promising. Fire away.'

Magozzi gave Gino a thumbs-up. 'Any chance you can get into a website that doesn't seem to exist anymore?'

'You got a name to go with that website?'

'Charles Spencer, Woodland Hills, California. The site name is the Sixth Idea dot net.'

Harley hummed. Nothing musical, more like a chant, something he often did while he was thinking. 'Is that the guy who bought it in the alley last night?'

'It is. We've still got a lid on his name.'

'Gotcha. Anything else?'

'How about calling up about an hour of security camera footage that mysteriously disappeared from the Chatham Hotel's server?'

'This is sounding better and better. Send the pertinents, we'll get right on it.'

'Is Grace there?'

'On her way as we speak.'

# Fifteen

Grace MacBride was getting better. She hadn't thrown caution to the wind just yet, but sometimes it seemed that she was positioning herself for the windup.

She no longer believed – as she had for most of her life – that every single person on the planet was out to kill her, but you had to be an absolute idiot not to realize that probably half of them were. By her count, she'd been up close and personal with at least six people who had actually taken a crack at it.

It wasn't the life of your average computer geek, but Grace wasn't average, and she was no idiot. This world was a dangerous place. The trick was identifying the good guys from the bad guys, and she'd been learning how to do that.

Not that Grace had totally lost her mind. She still wore her English riding boots most of the time, just in case there was some new maniac out there who wanted to slash her Achilles tendons; she still carried her Sig Sauer 9mm wherever she went, still maintained the elaborate security system on her property. She eyed the mailman with deep suspicion, and paid careful attention to all the signs of potential danger that most people were foolish enough to ignore. If she ever missed one, Charlie had her back.

Currently, Wonder Dog was sitting up straight and alert in the passenger seat of her Range Rover, tongue lolling out of his mouth in anticipation as she made the short drive to Harley's Summit Avenue mansion. The Monkeewrench offices were there, but Charlie's interest wasn't in their work with computers, it was in Harley's generosity with breakfast sausages. 'You're spoiled, you know that, Charlie?'

Charlie looked at her, wagged the stub of his tail and whined, as if to disabuse her of such a foolish notion. And Grace had to agree with him – he deserved to be spoiled, and he was always gracious when he accepted the many perks of his new life. When she'd found him freezing, cowering, and half-dead from starvation in an alley, she couldn't imagine anything in the world a human could do to make things right for him again. And yet he'd come around, just as she had. There were miracles in this life, like gaining the trust of a lost soul. She'd been one herself. And maybe she still was.

She pulled through the evergreen-draped gate into Harley's driveway, parked under the red stone portico that had once sheltered horses and carriages, and let Charlie out. He tore hell-bent for leather around the snowy yard, investigated the elaborate Christmas arrangements that adorned his front walk and steps, then revisited the yard to decorate a few tree trunks in yellow, contributing in his own way to Harley's seasonal décor, even though it didn't complement the color scheme.

Harley pushed open the big double front doors and stepped out into winter wonderland to greet them – he was a big, scary Father Christmas wearing biker leathers, jackboots, and a black beard that obscured his facial expressions, making him seem even more dangerous. And then the whole façade shattered when he crouched down, smacked his legs, and started murmuring ridiculous baby talk to Charlie while he gave him a doggy massage.

He looked up and winked. 'Hey, Gracie. Magozzi just called. They've got a job for us.'

'Something to do with the shooting at the Chatham last night?'

'Yep. Sounds pretty interesting, right up our alley. Missing security footage and a disappearing website. Come on, get your waiflike self in here while the cookies are still hot.'

'You did not make cookies.'

'Oh yes I did. Sister Carmella's famous Christmas spice cookies. I could have eaten two dozen of those things if she would have let me. Took me ten years to get the recipe off that old bat.'

Grace scolded him with a smile. 'You always said you liked Sister Carmella.'

'In the same way a hostage starts to like their captor. It was Catholic school Stockholm syndrome.'

Grace stomped the snow off her boots before she entered the marble entry foyer, which had been rearranged to accommodate a breathtaking twenty-foot spruce tree that was wearing more bling than a queen at coronation. This was the showpiece, but it wasn't the only Christmas tree in the house – he normally had four or five of them set up in various rooms, all decorated with different themes. Harley loved any holiday, probably because he'd never really had one as a kid.

And that was one of the extraordinary things about him – he'd had it as rough as any of them growing up, and she knew for a fact he'd never had a Christmas tree, had certainly never seen a present waiting for him under one in the multitude of foster homes he'd been shunted to before he was old enough to emancipate himself. And yet, as an adult, he'd never been bitter, had never shunned the things he had never had. On the contrary, he embraced them. In rather dramatic ways.

Grace suddenly wondered why she'd never put up a Christmas tree. She'd never had one growing up either. Maybe Harley had seen just enough magic at one point in his childhood to set his imagination soaring, and he was making up for lost time. She folded her arms across her chest and let her eyes travel up and down the pageantry. 'This is spectacular, Harley. You outdid yourself.'

He shrugged modestly. 'I added a few things this year.'

'Like a .50-caliber handgun?'

He stomped a boot in disappointment, but very lightly so he wouldn't scare Charlie. 'Oh, dammit, Gracie, you weren't supposed to see that yet. I hid everybody's presents in the boughs, and this big bad boy is so thick I figured nobody would find them until the needles started falling off.'

'I have a way of spotting firearms wherever they are. Besides, that's too big to miss.'

'Good point. Well, I figured a woman living alone shouldn't be without a savage knockout punch as a fail-safe.'

*A woman living alone.* The phrase hit Grace in a strange way, with no warning whatsoever. She'd always been alone, and had never imagined her life any differently. That was a trait she shared with Harley, Annie, and Roadrunner, which ironically had probably bonded them together as the tight family they were today. Maybe humans weren't meant to be solitary after all.

'And even if you never need it for self-defense, you could still use it to take out a few walls in your house with a couple bullets if you ever want to remodel,' Harley was saying. 'Merry Christmas.'

'I love it, Harley. Thank you.' She pecked his cheek.

'I thought it would tickle your fancy.'

'Are the cookies in the kitchen?'

'You got it. Bring the whole plate.'

Grace headed for the kitchen while Harley lingered at the tree, rocking back and forth on his run-down motorcycle boots, looking up at the spruce that stayed lit day and night, looking a little lost.

She paused at the kitchen door and sighed quietly. For the first week of Annie and Roadrunner's absence, it had been almost restful at the mansion without the boyish barbs that defined Harley's relationship with Roadrunner and the constant bickering between him and Annie. They'd gotten a lot of work done in the relative peace, and then he had become happily obsessed with Christmas decorations, like an empty-nest parent preparing for the return of collegiate children on holiday.

But after two weeks, when he ran out of rooms to decorate, he started down a dismal slope, and now it didn't feel to Grace like the productive peace of two partners; it felt like babysitting.

'I miss them, too,' Grace said.

He looked over at her sheepishly, then back at the tree. 'It's Christmas. Family time.'

'They'll be home in a few days. And then you and Annie and Roadrunner will be at it again, sniping at each other. Everything back to normal.'

Harley smiled and gazed up at the very top spire of the tree, which was still bare. 'I still can't figure out what to put up there for the final flourish. A star seems kind of obvious and pedestrian.'

'You'll think of something.'

# Sixteen

Annie Belinsky did a pirouette in front of the big baroque mirror in her hotel room, giving final approval to her wardrobe choice for the day's big meeting, which had been conveniently scheduled so as not to interfere with her daily afternoon excursion to Bergdorf Goodman. When in New York City during the holiday season, it was absolutely paramount to spend any and all free time at Bergdorf's, one of the best places on earth to Christmas shop, outside Bahnhofstrasse in Zurich.

She tugged at the lapels of her jaunty, velvet-trimmed tweed suit, which had been beautifully tailored overnight to accommodate her very generous proportions. Normally, anything without fur, feathers, or beads was absolutely unacceptable, but business meetings were an entirely different thing altogether, requiring a certain modicum of austerity. Southern belles, no matter how sartorially fearless, knew how to dress perfectly for any occasion.

She shot her snow-white French cuffs, arranged the cashmere scarf around her neck until it fell just so, then patted down her black bob before rapping on the door that divided the double suite she and Roadrunner shared. 'Roadrunner? Are you ready?'

'I'm ready, Annie. I've been ready for an hour.'

Annie opened the door with a flourish. 'What do you think?'

Roadrunner was sitting awkwardly on a velvet fainting couch that was several inches too low for his gangly six-foot-eight frame. His knees nearly brushed his ears. His eyes grew wide and he gave her a little smile. 'You look great, Annie. Kind of like Sherlock Holmes.'

She gave him a sideways glance and a fondly impatient sigh. The man wore Lycra biking suits all the time, what did she expect him to say about her finery? Besides, his genius mind was always far too occupied with things much more important than social graces, which was why they made such a great road team, as it turned out.

Annie could manipulate any situation with Southern charm and cunning, and Roadrunner was so technically brilliant he stunned any audience into silence when he spoke about his craft, even if he was wearing a Lycra biking suit. In fact, his complete oblivion to anything other than his work only enhanced his credibility in stuffy board-rooms, where people had certain expectations about appearances. He had the unadulterated innocence of a true savant, and in the end, Roadrunner always delivered the goods, goods that only he could conjure.

Grace and Harley, on the other hand, were so intimidating in their own distinct ways, they could chase demons out of a room just by being there, and some people found Grace's refusal to enter any space unarmed off-putting. Silly, but true.

'Come on, sugar. Let's get Grace and Harley on the line for a check-in before breakfast.'

'Morning, darlin'.' Annie laid her Mississippi accent on thick as molasses when Grace answered. It was amazing how quickly it came back to her after so many years away.

'Annie, how are you two?'

'Having a grand old time painting the town red. We're plucking up new clients faster than you could gather petals on the Rose Bowl parade route, and those petals might as well be money, because Roadrunner is nailing every single pitch. We have our last big New York City meeting this morning, and we head to Rochester tomorrow for our last appointment. And how about you? Staying out of trouble?'

'Trying to. Harley and I have the new software about thirty percent complete.'

'Hmm. I reckon that's about two months ahead of schedule. Maybe Roadrunner and I should stay on the road for a little longer.'

'Don't you dare,' Annie heard Harley blustering in the background. 'I got all the decorations up, and it's just me and Gracie here to enjoy them. It's Christmas, for God's sake. I've already got the prime rib dry-aging in the cooler.'

Annie winked at Roadrunner. 'Well, if I didn't know any better, I'd say you miss us.'

'Of course I do. Grace is way too nice to me and it's just wrong. Hey, I've gotta go, Leo and Gino just sent some stuff. Good luck, and we'll see you in a few days.'

Annie heard Harley's heavy footfalls receding. 'He sure gets sentimental around Christmastime, doesn't he?' she whispered into the phone.

'Yes he does. And you don't know the half of it – just wait until you see what he put in the foyer.'

'Well, now I'm intrigued. So you're doing a little something for our MPD friends?'

'They have a couple glitchy computer issues related to a homicide. Sounds like it'll be a piece of cake.'

# Seventeen

Max emerged from the subterranean world of public transit in his adopted homeland, leaving behind the rank, moldering smells left by the endless army of commuters whose boots had deposited snow-encased scraps of the city: flyers for a band showcase that reeked like stale beer, business cards for a new restaurant or boutique laced with perfume or a random droplet of coffee; a lost receipt or a greasy fast-food wrapper that had picked up a trace of dog crap along the way.

And even though such things were regularly cleaned up in New York subways, their scents lingered long after they'd been swept into a bin and removed. Most people didn't notice – they had long ago become inured to their own subway's funk and didn't perceive it as offensive. But Max had been cursed by a freakishly heightened sense of smell – as a young man in a confused and transitory Moscow in the days after the Berlin Wall had fallen, after the Cold War was over and anarchy ruled, his nickname had been Bloodhound.

But as bad as the smell was in this particular station, he remembered much worse smells from the underground in the former Soviet Union. There hadn't just been wet paper in those tunnels, there had been raw sewage, seeping into cracks and putrefying, along with the rat shit, and sometimes, one or two dead drunks who'd died from something – hypothermia, staph, a blackened liver steeped in cheap vodka – most people never knew, and never really cared to know, because it happened enough that it became part of day-to-day life.

More disturbing, those people eventually started not to notice the smell of rotting human flesh, as if a dead person in a subway was just one of life's many nuisances that somebody else would eventually clean up when it was convenient. Sometimes, it took a couple of days before the police finally cleared the corpses out, as if they were bags of trash to be carted off to the city dump, all in due time.

Max pulled his topcoat closed at the throat and shivered off the memories from a much darker time in his life; tried to push away the image of his own father suffering that particular fate, only to be unceremoniously tossed into some pile in a morgue, no doubt, and buried without a single word, or more likely cremated by the State, because that was so much more efficient in a world where efficiency was nonexistent unless dealing with the dead. He'd never been privy to the details of his father's death and disposal, but common sense and experience had led him to the conclusion that it had been grim.

With a great sigh of relief, he finally saw daylight and took the stairs up to street level two at a time until he could suck in the relatively fresher air of the city. Exhaust fumes he'd learned to handle long ago. The old Zhigulis and Fiats hadn't exactly had catalytic converters.

It had finally stopped snowing, and most of the day's accumulation had already been cleared, but a few flakes persisted, floating down from the heavens in a final good-bye, or maybe a final fuck you as the storm moved off to conquer the Atlantic and beyond. Max would be doing the same thing himself – very soon – after one last job.

He smelled Ivan the Terrible coming long before he emerged from the subway – the strong, revolting reek of Troika cigarettes, and the more comforting scents of gun oil and steel.

'*Privet*, Maksim.'

'You're still smoking those shit Troikas, Ivan? What's the matter with you?'

Ivan's laugh rattled like a badly broken piece of machinery, which he was. 'Old habits die hard, *tovarish*.'

'You miss the old days so much, you steep yourself in its stench?'

'This is a good life here, I will admit. Look at us both, living the American Dream. But we miss certain things about the old days, don't we? That's why you came here today. What is that Bruce Springsteen song? "Glory Days"? They're back, Maksim, for this short moment in time. History and our mother country call us into service once again, perhaps for the last time.'

'So you're not only clinging to your Troikas, you're clinging to your melodramatic Russian soul.'

'We will always be Russians, *tovarish*, whether you like it or not.'

Max grunted. 'History is not paying, so who is?'

Ivan seemed to relish letting the question hang. His cold, gray, soulless eyes actually sparked to life for a brief moment. 'This is a very important job, with rich rewards. And it comes from the *very* highest authority.' He let out his rattling chuckle again. 'From an old boss of ours, Maksim, so you understand what must be at stake.'

Max didn't know what was at stake – he never did, and he really didn't care. It wasn't his job to know details. The less he knew, the better. 'Tell me what I need to know.'

Ivan pulled a flash drive from an inner pocket of his coat. 'Details. Your flight is in three hours.'

Max palmed the flash drive. 'Are you joining me?'

'No, no. I have other business locally.' He smiled. 'But I'm certain you will enjoy your destination – the weather is just like Moscow.'

Max looked out the plane's window at the white, lake-pocked landscape below him. Minnesota was called the Land of Ten Thousand Lakes and from up in the sky, he could see it was an appropriate moniker. He'd never been to Minnesota before and he found it odd that his vocation would bring him to a quiet little city in the Midwest, one with such a wholesome reputation. But apparently it was the epicenter of something, because he had three targets here. Odder still was the nature of his assignment: according to the sparse details he'd been provided, his targets were to be protected at all costs – an unusual request for a career assassin to receive.

The conclusion was an obvious one – if Russia wanted these people kept alive, then somebody else wanted them dead, which meant they were of very high value and worth the risk of an ugly international incident if things went wrong. He would be the first one sacrificed if the situation necessitated it. Had he been the inquisitive type, he would have mentally pursued the matter further, but it wasn't his puzzle to solve.

When a flight attendant announced they would be landing in Minneapolis in thirty minutes, Max finished his Diet Coke and deleted the computer file he'd been reading and rereading for the better part of two hours. Undoubtedly, there would be more instructions to come, but the current ones he had memorized verbatim.

He had an unsettled feeling about this trip; the only thing that kept his mood aloft was the thought of seeing Vera again.

# Eighteen

Homicide was relatively quiet when Gino and Magozzi got back from meeting Lydia Ascher at the Chatham. Louise Washington and fire-haired Johnny McLaren were both at their desks working the phones, and Peterson the emaciated vegan was rooting around the snack table which was a mecca of junk food. Gino made a quick detour, gave Peterson a pat on his bony shoulder, then grabbed a couple of bags of cheesy puffs.

'Hey, Peterson. I thought vegans were supposed to be healthy.'

'Not necessarily. We just eat plant-based food and most junk food is plant based, so it's kind of a win-win.'

Gino scratched his chin, examining the potato chips, the tortilla chips, the Fritos, the Potato Stix, and the dizzying array of candy. 'Damn, Peterson, I never thought of it that way. You think if I stopped eating meat and dairy for a while and went on a diet of plant-based junk food, I'd get skinny like you?'

Peterson snickered. 'That's not going to happen. I've known you for four years, Rolseth. You'd rather smear honey on yourself and get eaten alive by fire ants before you gave up meat and dairy.'

'You're absolutely right, Peterson.' Magozzi dragged Gino away from the snacks and a potential vegan conversion. 'Let's get through some paper.'

Gino plopped down in his chair and started shuffling and stacking files, setting them up in piles that looked as precarious as the final stages of a game of Jenga.

Magozzi pulled Lydia Ascher's impromptu sketch out of his briefcase and put it in the printer to scan. Whether or not there was anything to it, it still belonged in the case files. 'So what do you think of Lydia Ascher?'

Gino shrugged, jiggling his computer mouse to wake up his machine. 'I think she's cute as a cloth-covered button and I'm positive she didn't have anything to do with Charles Spencer's murder. I'm on the fence about the spooky guy from the airport. I mean, Angela sees something weird about somebody every time we go anywhere and she's always right. Women are observant by nature, it's a survival thing. They anticipate, we react. You and I are only observant because we trained ourselves to be for our job. Plus, the situation kind of led Lydia there. A nice guy she met on a plane and has coffee with ends up murdered a few hours later. Her brain tries to make sense of it, so she remembers the guy in the airport café who gave her the creeps for whatever reason and a story forms subconsciously.'

Magozzi cocked his brow. 'Please don't tell me you're in therapy.'

'Hell no, it's just commonsense psychology... Oh lookie here. We got a report from Ballistics Dave, check it out.'

Magozzi abandoned the printer and went to his own desk, but Gino was already giving him a rundown by the time he'd seated himself in front of his own computer and pulled the report up for himself.

'Spencer bought it with a nine-millimeter and his friend Wally got his with a .45. Both guns are clean, riflings didn't jibe with anything on any registry.'

'Of course they didn't. We never get that lucky.'

'No, we never do, but now there's a possibility that we're looking for two shooters instead of just one. Great.'

'It could still be one shooter with two guns. But either way, it's weird. Seems like these guys were serious targets for no reason we can see.'

'Maybe the airport guy really was tailing Spencer after all.' Gino grunted, then picked up a call on his cell and put it on speaker. 'It's Cory from Arson,' he said. 'Hey, Cory, what do you know?'

'I know that Wally Luntz's house got blown to kingdom come because somebody rigged the gas lines from the outside. We found pieces of a device that looks like something you'd see in a war zone.'

'Jesus.'

'Yeah, there's no question it's arson. I heard he was murdered before the explosion. Is that true?'

'Yeah.'

Cory sighed through the phone. 'Wow. Somebody really wanted that guy wiped off the map. How's your shoulder, Gino?'

Gino sputtered. 'Where'd you hear about that?'

'We played broomball last night against Freddie Wilson's team.'

'Tell Wilson and Ames they're both dead men.'

Cory laughed. 'Hey, they weren't talking out of school or anything. In fact, Freddie said you were as graceful as a cat, you just didn't land on your feet.'

'That bastard. I hope you handed their asses to them.'

'Are you kidding? Nobody beats that team. We lost seven to one.'

Gino hung up and glared at Magozzi. 'What are you smiling at?'

'I'm thinking we didn't do so bad after all. A successful broomball future isn't out of the question.'

'We were behind ten to one in the first fifteen minutes.'

'We would have gotten better.'

Gino readjusted his chair position along with his bruised ego. 'I'm less worried about our future in broomball than I am about our future as detectives.' He opened up a file. 'Wallace Luntz. Retired iron foundry worker. Volunteered at his local public library. Delivered Meals on Wheels twice a week. No police record, no criminal associations, solid financials. He was a good neighbor and a model citizen, just like Charles Spencer. They both get shot in the head and Luntz's house gets shot up into the sky. What are we missing?'

'We're missing all the private information and deep dark secrets we would normally find on a victim's computer. And their computers are gone.'

# Nineteen

The only good thing about the long drive from Minneapolis to the country was the sensation that you were moving from some anxiety-ridden place of noise and crowds and traffic to someplace better. Lydia's jangled nerves finally started to still once she'd pulled off the freeway, and by the time she'd turned onto the wooded, snow-dusted back roads that would bring her home, she had calmed into a gentle sorrow for Chuck Spencer.

She hadn't really known him, but he'd been such a nice man. She'd never met his friend Wally, but surely neither one of them deserved such a senseless, brutal end. The coincidence of their murders on the same night wasn't lost on her, but that was work for the detectives.

She pulled into the aspen-lined drive and up to the house that had felt like home the first time the realtor had shown her the place. She stopped her car at the front walk and listened to the cold, peaceful silence of her woodland sanctuary. Here, deer romped and songbirds and wild turkeys feasted at her many feeders; fox patrolled for rabbits and mice, nature went on as nature always had, and people didn't kill each other.

She left her snowy boots on the braided rug by the door and ate a lunch of leftover chili and cheese, then went down the wooden staircase to the basement, where she kept useless and precious things.

The cupboard next to the washer and dryer held soaps, cleansers, and the meager remnants of her mother's legacy. She carried the box upstairs and placed it on the old oak table in her kitchen.

On top was her duplicate of the photo Chuck had shown her on the plane – eight men, including Chuck's father and her grandfather, standing next to a prop plane on some unknown tarmac with President Eisenhower – only her photo was a little different. On the back, her grandpa had written in flowery, old-fashioned script: *I am become death, destroyer of worlds*. A little creepy, but no revelation there. It was from the *Bhagavad Gita*, which she'd read some of in her college Hinduism class. And more interestingly, Robert Oppenheimer had quoted it in an interview when describing how he'd felt after witnessing the 1945 Trinity test in New Mexico of the world's first atomic bomb.

There wasn't much else in the box: stacks of old notebooks filled with scribbles and equations she would never make sense of – they might as well have been Egyptian hieroglyphics – and then, the book. She remembered what her mother had said from her hospital bed the night she died.

Remember the book in that box in the attic I showed you last year? Father gave it to me a long time ago and told me to memorize the part about the generator, that it was very important. I don't know why. Go get that box, Lydia. Get it tonight.

Lydia lifted the book out of the box. It was nothing but a worn paperback in the 1950s Cold War pulp fiction genre. She'd never read it, but it was something about nuclear Armageddon and the last survivors. Given her grandfather's occupation, it made sense that he'd given it to his daughter, perhaps as a cautionary tale or even as a survival manual.

The cover art was as atrocious as she'd remembered it – a comic book rendering of a scantily clad, buxom ingénue running from a conflagration. It had probably been a scandalous cover for the time. And how screwed up was that? She was sitting next to papers that in all likelihood amounted to a how-to manual on building the most destructive weapon ever conceived, and yet a cartoon of a half-naked woman had been unthinkable in polite society at the very same period in history.

She opened the book and ruffled the pages until she found the section bracketed in pink crayon, and in the top margin written in childlike printing by her mother when she was only nine years old: 'Memorize this. Never forget.'

Lydia read the marked material, which was nothing more than poorly written prose couching a tedious set of instructions on how to build a generator after the world had been nuked to smithereens. She closed the book and placed it facedown on the table. Obviously her grandfather had genuinely believed the world might end and he had wanted his daughter to be prepared. It seemed quaint now, that a generator had seemed like salvation in a post-Armageddon world. Then again, the world was more dangerous than ever, so maybe knowing how to build a generator wasn't such a bad idea. What if the power grid was attacked and went down? Or the Web?

She started when her cell phone rang, then relaxed when the caller ID flashed on her screen. 'Hi, Otis.'

'Hey, Lydia, how was your lunch?'

'It never happened,' she blurted out, feeling her eyes well and her throat tighten. 'Chuck was murdered last night.'

Otis was silent for a moment. 'Mind if I come over?'

# Twenty

Cheeton was a small Minnesota town so far north you could blow kisses to Canada. It was one of those inhospitable places where sane people would never choose to live, unless you'd been born here, and then you couldn't figure out how anyone would want to live anywhere else. You had to favor houses made of whole logs, the night howling of wolves in winter, and skedaddling out of the way when grumpy black bears came out of hibernation in the spring. The human population barely topped one thousand.

The folks up here were deep-rooted and what they used to call hardy stock, born and bred on the same land where their ancestors trapped beaver and fox a couple hundred years ago. They all took some sort of stupid pride in being able to stand the brutal winters and a growing season so short you could hardly get a radish to come up out of the ground before the frost settled in again.

It was barely December and the snowbanks were already piled at least ten feet high on the sides of the Klapton fire road, named for the family of five who had died in their cabin long before the single Cheeton fire truck had made it on the scene. You had to be a brave soul to live this far north in Minnesota, or maybe just an idiot.

Sheriff Ernie Fenster slowed his SUV cruiser once he hit the fire road. The snowplow had made a token pass to clear a single lane, but it would take a heck of a lot more work than that to make the road truly passable after last night's dump of the white stuff, and Andy wasn't going to be doing any more plowing today. His voice had been shaking pretty bad when he called it in, and that after driving all the way to his cabin and a landline before he remembered he had a radio in the truck.

*Tenth signpost in, Sheriff, right at the top of the northern bank. All you can see is one arm, sticking up out of the snow like he's waving at somebody, and even if I could have climbed up there, which I can't, not with my ticker, no way I was going to try and dig him out. Creepiest damn thing I ever did see.*

Ernie had already been pulling on his snowmobile suit, scrambling in the mess on his desk for the cruiser keys, and trying to raise somebody on the dispatch radio. No joy, so he scribbled a note to whatever deputy got into the office first and thumped his heavy boots straight for the door. He was breathing hard by the time he got there, what with all the heavy gear he was wearing to keep from freezing to death. *Look out your kitchen window, Andy. Has Ethel left for the office yet?*

*Hell no. Her car's still in her driveway, buried under an eight-foot snowdrift. I don't expect you'll be seeing her anytime soon.*

*Well, run next door, have her call the boys and send them out there as soon as she gets through. She knows all the numbers by heart, and I can't get anyone on the radio or the phone. Any chance that guy was still alive?*

*The arm was all black, Sheriff. Stands out pretty good against all the snow . . . and . . . the thing is, he was bare-ass naked from stem to stern.*

*If the arm was the only thing sticking out, how do you know he was naked? Andy? Andy? Are you still there?*

*Yeah. I never saw him, Sheriff. Swear to God. I was just scooping with the bucket and dumping it on top of the snowbank . . . and he fell out, all floppy and black way up there . . . oh dear Lord . . .*

Ernie pulled the cruiser to a stop at signpost number ten and looked up at the top of the northern bank of plow-pushed snow, already towering a good ten or twelve feet above the road. He couldn't see the arm. Andy would have had a better view from his higher perch inside the snowplow.

He sat behind the wheel of his idling SUV, savoring the blast of lukewarm heat on his legs when he kicked the fan up to its highest setting. Not that it did all that much good. Cold seeped into the car just about as fast as the heat blew out. Keeping the side window cracked wasn't helping, but ever since he'd found Artie Jensen dead from carbon monoxide poisoning in his locked-tight Grand Am, he'd no more sit in a car with the engine running than he'd pick his teeth with razor blades.

He glanced at the climate setting on the car's menu and saw that the outside temperature was below zero. What a pisser.

# Twenty-One

Overnight in Minneapolis, the temperatures had crashed down into stupid-cold territory. Such a thing was a rare occurrence in mid-December, but it happened every decade or so — a stern reminder from Old Man Winter that he was the boss and he'd do whatever he wanted to, whenever he wanted to do it.

'I hate this crap,' Gino muttered as he and Magozzi walked into City Hall early the next morning.

'What?'

'When it's so damn cold, the minute you step into a warm building, every inch of skin on your body burns like somebody dumped gas on you and threw a match.'

Magozzi subconsciously flexed his fingers in his cold-stiff leather gloves, feeling prickles in them as his sluggish blood started to move again. 'The first day of spring is only ninety days away.'

'God, I feel so much better now. Maybe I won't hang myself after all. Did you see the sun dog this morning?'

'What's a sun dog?'

'When it's so frigging cold, ice crystals form in the air and when the sun starts to come up, it creates a halo. Kind of like a subzero rainbow without all the pretty colors.'

'Why were you up that early?'

'You mean besides the fact that we're working a case? I've got a five-year-old, why do you think? I was stupid enough to get him a three-D Advent calendar, and every day you get to open up a little window in the calendar and there's a piece of chocolate inside. He gets up half an hour earlier every morning the closer to Christmas it gets.'

'You let him eat chocolate in the morning?'

'It's the only time I let him eat chocolate. Mornings on school days, then his sugar buzz is the teacher's problem, not mine.'

The Homicide room wasn't a madhouse yet, but it was still humming for such an early hour. Generally, murder ebbed a little during the holiday season, but there were still enough call-outs to keep everybody busy. Unfortunately, most of the suspicious deaths they got in December ended up being suicides.

Johnny McLaren was situating himself at his desk, shrugging out of his parka and revealing an epically bad, striped sports coat. Nobody really knew if McLaren's astoundingly poor wardrobe choices were intentional or not, and nobody really wanted to know, because any answer would destroy the mystique.

'Hey, Johnny, what's up?' Gino asked as he passed by on his way to the snack table.

He smiled and rattled a waxed paper bag. 'I've got Cronuts and there's one with your name on it.'

Gino stopped in his tracks, reversed his course, and gave McLaren a melty smile that people usually got from watching a cute kitten or puppy video on YouTube. 'You've gotta be kidding me. Where did you get those?'

'Kiosk in the IDS tower. They just started selling them.'

'You are the man. You ever try one of these, Leo?'

Magozzi held up his hand. 'They're all yours. Crossing a croissant and a donut is like breeding a zebra to a goat – it's a complete abomination.'

McLaren snickered. 'Suit yourself.'

Magozzi looked down at his phone – the call he'd been waiting for was coming in. 'Hi, Grace.'

'Magozzi. I finally got into the surveillance footage from the Chatham Hotel. You and Gino need to see it and I'm uncomfortable sending it over the wire.'

'We'll be right over.'

Grace had no concept of time when she was working – hours seemed like minutes, and sometimes it was the other way around. Getting lost in an abstract world that was far less dangerous than the real one she inhabited was like taking a vacation. Harley, Annie, and Roadrunner understood this – anybody else would probably question her sanity, as if the real world were all there was.

It didn't surprise her to see that the sun had risen when she finally looked up from her computer. The office was quiet except for the faint hum of the machines. Harley and Charlie were absent and she'd never even noticed their departure.

A few minutes later she heard the elevator rising to the third-floor Monkeewrench office in Harley's mansion. Instinctively, she put her hand on her Sig. Just in case.

'Hey, Gracie.' Harley clomped into the office hugging large bags of takeout. Charlie was close on his heels, his nose busy with the scent of food. 'You were really in it deep and the dog's stomach was growling, so I thought I'd order in.'

Grace sniffed the air. 'The German place down the street?'

'Yeah. Best sauerkraut and sausage in the world. Did you hit the jackpot while I was gone?'

Grace pushed back from her desk and retied her loose ponytail. 'I finally hit something. There was a breach in the Chatham server all right. My first guess was that somebody came away with some credit card numbers.'

Harley set the bags down on his desk and started unloading foam containers. 'If it was a credit card job, why the blackout on the video feed?'

'That was the weird thing. This wasn't an amateur job, and usually attacks like this are pretty surgical. They go for the data and that's it. This one covered more ground, including all the camera feeds in the hotel, so I started on the floor where Charles Spencer had a room.' She arched a brow at him, which was just about as self-congratulatory as she ever got. 'Fortunately, the attack didn't delete the actual surveillance footage, it just disabled the playback.'

Harley gave her a big, white grin that spliced his black beard. 'You are a genius. So what's the upshot?'

'The upshot is some excellent film of a couple men with guns outside Spencer's room. I'm running it through our facial recognition right now. Gino and Magozzi are on their way.'

Harley whistled. 'Who the hell was this Spencer guy and what was he into?'

Grace shook her head. 'That's the kink. By all accounts, Charles Spencer was about as vanilla as you can get.'

'He was obviously a somebody, and I'm guessing whoever tried to wipe the surveillance did a damn fine job of making his website disappear, too. I've been banging my head against a brick wall for hours trying to recover Spencer's website, and man, it's pissing me off.'

'You'll get it. You always do.'

Harley grinned. 'Damn right I will.'

# Twenty-Two

Harley always saw them coming. He had about a hundred automated cameras on his property, two of them focused on the unbreachable gate that blocked the driveway.

'Gino Rolseth,' Gino barked into the hidden intercom, and recognizing his voice imprint, the gate opened. 'That thing gives me the creeps,' he told Magozzi, slouched in the passenger seat, tired, hungry, and frustrated that the hours were ticking away on their chances to solve Charles Spencer's murder.

'Every house in the world is going to have this kind of security one day. Monkeewrench is a glimpse into the future.'

'Whatever,' Gino grumped. He didn't want to live in that world. He wanted his kids to grow up in a neighborhood like he had, when doors were seldom locked and everyone looked out for one another.

Charlie was tap-dancing at the front door when they entered the mansion, frenetically alternating his affections between Gino and Magozzi, making sure they were both equally hairy. Suddenly, everything seemed a little bit better.

Aside from Charlie, the canine welcome wagon, the entrance to Harley's place was dominated by a monster Christmas tree that Gino barely noticed. His primary focus was always on the circular foyer table, hand-carved out of some kind of wood you weren't supposed to be able to buy anymore. Every time he and Magozzi came here, that gazillion-dollar table held some kind of food and, almost always, some kind of booze. It was close to noon today, and the food was beer-simmered brats with sauerkraut, German potato salad, and a lovely mini keg with steins crowded under the tap, waiting for something dark and luscious to come forth.

Were they on duty? Yes. Did Gino give a shit? No.

'Thanks for the grub, guys.' Gino entered the third-floor loft with a dot of whole-grain mustard decorating his lower lip and a beer stein worth more than his retirement clutched in his right hand.

'Gino, you son of a bitch,' Harley bellowed as he thumped across the floor. He wrapped Gino in a bear hug that smelled like old leather. 'Good to see you, buddy, it's been a while. You get enough to eat?'

'I want to live here, Harley.'

'Anytime, my friend. Anytime. What do you think of the tree?'

'What tree?'

Harley laughed, then turned to Magozzi and clapped a hand on his shoulder. All his life, this massive man had held back affection from all but the family of Monkeewrench, but over the years he had developed a deep fondness for the two cops who had wormed their way into his experience-hardened heart.

Grace spun in her chair, gave a little smile, and wagged her fingers at them. Magozzi noticed she was back in her uniform of safety black, and her eyes were a vivid blue against her winter-pale skin.

Harley clapped his hands together. 'Come on, I know you guys have a lot on your plates, so let's get to it.' Harley led them across the maple floor toward Grace's workstation. 'I'm still working on trying to recapture Spencer's website. Somebody went to a lot of trouble to try to wipe it, just like they tried to wipe the surveillance footage. That's weird enough, but weirder still, whoever's behind it covered their tracks pretty damn well. I'm not saying there aren't tracks out there, it's just going to take some time. We're dealing with fairly high-level stuff here, so I figure there's gotta be something real juicy about

Spencer and his website – something that'll crack your case wide open, like the site was a front for a Darknet drug emporium or something like that.'

'That would be good,' Magozzi said.

'In the meantime, Gracie's got good stuff for you. Give the nice detectives a peek at your handiwork.'

Magozzi decided to test the new waters of day-time touch and put both hands on her shoulders. She didn't flinch – a very good sign. 'What have you got for us, Grace?'

She swiveled her chair around to face her computer again, all business, but the warmth of his hands was distracting. 'I think I have a picture of your killers.' With a couple of mouse clicks, she called up the recovered shot of the two armed men outside Chuck Spencer's hotel room door. Gino and Magozzi both took a sharp breath, then looked at each other.

'Lydia's man from the airport,' Gino murmured, and Magozzi nodded.

'She was right – Spencer was being followed. He was a target.'

'Yeah, and odds are, Luntz was, too.'

Grace looked up at Magozzi, her brows tipped in question. 'Who's Luntz?'

'Wally Luntz. A new friend of Spencer's. They were going to get together last night, but Luntz took a bullet to the head, too. Right before his house blew up.'

'The gas explosion in South Minneapolis?'

'Arson says it's no accident.'

Harley spun around in his chair. 'Whoa. I think you better start at the beginning.'

Magozzi and Gino told Grace and Harley about Lydia, about her plane ride with Spencer, his planned meeting with Wally Luntz, and the stunningly realistic sketch of the man Lydia thought was watching Chuck in the airport coffee shop.

Grace's face went perfectly still. The only indication that she wasn't a wax model of a human was the faint, shifting crease between her brows. 'That's a monumental coincidence that two people with such exclusive family histories got seated next to each other on a plane.'

Magozzi shrugged. 'We think that's all it was – a monumental coincidence. We interviewed her yesterday. She doesn't know anything, she just showed up at the Chatham to have lunch with Spencer like they'd planned. She had no clue he'd been murdered the night before.'

'Well, this whole thing is monumentally *weird*,' Harley said. 'Can't you guys ever get a normal homicide?'

'Apparently not.'

'What about the hydrogen bomb stuff? You think there's anything there?'

Magozzi shook his head. 'It's been declassified for decades. Besides, that was a long time ago. Nobody's going to get killed over Cold War artifacts sixty years after the fact.'

'Yeah. You're right. Okay, I'm going to put everything you have into the Beast and while that's working, Grace and I will get Spencer's website up, and that's a promise.'

The Beast was a parallel processing miracle of Monkeewrench design that could sort through massive amounts of data, scour the Web, and find connections humans could easily overlook – if the Pope was connected to a South African penguin, it would eventually find out how. 'We really appreciate that.'

'And send us any new information you get,' Harley said, rising from his chair. '*Anything*, no matter how insignificant it seems. The Beast has a big appetite and the more we feed it, the faster it works. Kind of like me.'

Gino bent over and squinted at Grace's monitor one last time. 'Can you run this through facial recognition for us?'

'We already did. These men don't exist, at least on the Web.'

# Twenty-Three

Alvin Keller had been diagnosed with Lou Gehrig's disease a decade ago, and he'd been waiting to die for a very long time. Now he was eighty-seven, almost completely paralyzed, and his ability to speak was worsening by the day. Soon, the doctors told him, he would be unable to swallow, and then, unable to breathe. Decisions would have to be made.

*You should have shot yourself in the head years ago, when you could still raise your hand that high.*

But now it was too late; he couldn't do it himself, and no one would help him, certainly not his dear wife of sixty years. And that was the basest survival instinct at work – no matter how aware you were that you wouldn't live to see a cure; how aware you were that a horrendous disease would eventually trap your perfectly cognizant, brilliant mind in such a sorry, degenerating vessel, it was still impossible for him to relinquish life. It was a cruel irony; or perhaps in his case, cosmic punishment for the things he'd done. At least the end was near – that much he knew.

Alvin had heard that at the end of your life on this earth there would be hallucinations, but he hadn't ever imagined they would be as vivid as this one. She was a beautiful woman, dressed in fur and jewels, standing in the middle of his living room. Her face remained placid as she reached into her pocket and withdrew a gun.

Ah! This was an amusing twist, tailored precisely by his own imagination. His beautiful hallucination had suddenly turned into his angel of death: his savior. She knew he welcomed the end – of course she did – for his own mind had conjured her. Alvin let out a halting sigh, closed his eyes, and smiled.

Eventually he opened his eyes again. The beautiful woman was still there, the imaginary gun was rising in her hand, but behind her was now a man who had appeared as suddenly and silently as she had. He was looking straight at him with a forefinger pressed against his lips.

Suddenly, the woman's head exploded, and Alvin felt pieces of something ping against his face. This, he hadn't expected from a hallucination, nor had he expected the man to sit beside him on the sofa and gently wipe away whatever had settled on his face with a cloth. It all felt so real. He closed his eyes again and heard the male hallucination say, 'Bring the van to the back, Vera.'

Vivian Keller's arthritic joints complained bitterly as she eased out of her old Ford Taurus with a single grocery bag. The cold was the greatest plague to her condition, and on wet, snowy days like this one, it was torture to even get out of bed. But her suffering was nothing compared to poor Alvin's.

She entered her tiny kitchen quietly and didn't announce her arrival, because Alvin was most certainly asleep and she didn't want to wake him. The medications kept him out of sorts most of the time, and the doctor had told them both that sleep was good.

She unloaded cans of Campbell's Scotch Broth and a loaf of bread, and set the soup on the stove to warm so it would be ready for Alvin when he woke up. Then she dutifully washed the can in the sink and removed the labels, not because she cared anything about recycling but because it postponed entering the sad, depressing realm of a husband dying slowly and painfully.

Finally, she went into the living room, pausing in the doorway to let her eyes adjust. The room was dim with the shades drawn, because the medications made Alvin's eyes sensitive to light. But she didn't need much light to see what was on the floor.

Vivian started screaming.

# Twenty-Four

Gino had just pulled out of Harley's driveway and was heading west on Summit Avenue when Dispatch called and sent them to a homicide scene in the Longfellow neighborhood.

'First responder is on scene. One definite homicide, one missing, possibly kidnapped.'

'Pam, is that you?' Magozzi asked.

'Yes, Detective. Magozzi, right?'

'You got it. And we already have one, possibly two connected homicides on our plate. No way we can take on another.'

'There was just a multiple in Uptown and everybody else is on call-out until they get things sorted. Chief Malcherson wants you to do the preliminary on this one and secure the scene until he can cut somebody loose and assign them. He'll send your relief in under an hour.'

'Oh, great,' Gino grumbled, jumping onto the freeway. 'My head's already a mess.'

An ambulance wailed past Gino and Magozzi as they pulled up to a small one-and-a-half-story brick house in a neighborhood filled with clone structures, erected in the post-World War II boom of returning veterans with modest incomes in need of housing for their new families. Demographically, it was split down the middle, divided between elderly people, many of whom were probably the original occupants of the houses when they'd been new over half a century ago, and young families just starting out in life, drawn in by the reasonable prices of two-bedroom, single-bath real estate. Not exactly a hotbed of homicide.

Gino squinted through the windshield at an approaching uniform who was trailing crime-scene tape behind him as he finished the job. He looked vaguely familiar and very young, even underneath the concealing bulk of his cold-weather gear. 'We know that kid, don't we?'

Magozzi flipped through his mental photo gallery of players from crime scenes past. Unfortunately, the photo gallery didn't have captions with names. 'Looks familiar.'

Gino rolled down his window. 'Afternoon, Officer.'

'Hi, Detectives. Brady Armand. I was with Officer Bad Heart Bull when we found those kidnapped Indian girls last fall.'

Gino nodded, pulling the memories front and center. Brady and his partner had found four little girls alive when they'd all expected the opposite. 'That was one great day in the middle of a really rotten case.'

'Yes sir.'

'You were the first responder on this scene?' Gino was scouring the street for other squads and saw none.

'I called in for backup, but it's going to be pretty slow and pretty lean, what with the Uptown situation. Sounds messy, and there are a lot of conflicting reports coming in.'

'Same on our end. We already have two active cases on our docket, so we're just temps here – Chief Malcherson requested that we do a prelim and preserve the scene until he can pull somebody to take over. What can you tell us?'

Brady stomped his feet on the snowy sidewalk, trying to keep warm. 'We have kind of a strange situation here.'

Magozzi got out of the car and noticed a curtain flutter closed in the front window of the neighboring house, which was decorated to the nines with outdoor Christmas lights and a massive inflatable snowman that was almost as big as the front yard it inhabited. 'Strange how?'

Brady was consulting his notebook. 'Elderly female home-owner – Vivian Keller – returned home from a quick trip to the corner market and found a dead stranger on her living room floor. Her husband, Alvin, is missing and he's really sick. ALS, I think she said. And that's about all I could get, because she was pretty much on the verge of hysteria and was having chest pains. You probably saw the ambulance on your way in.'

Magozzi nodded. 'So chances are her husband didn't go anywhere on his own.'

'Definitely not, according to the wife. He was almost totally paralyzed.'

'Any of the neighbors offer up anything?'

Brady jerked a thumb toward the snowman next door. 'An old guy named Knute Viestad came out when I got here. He's the one who called it in. He was watching TV when he heard Vivian scream, so he called nine-one-one. He thought maybe Alvin had finally given up the ghost, but he's pretty frail himself, so he stayed put inside just in case it was something else.'

*Smart*, Magozzi thought. Because it had been something else.

'Anyhow, he said he didn't see or hear anything before that.'

Gino's breath made frosty balloons in the frigid air. 'We need to find Alvin Keller. Get a BOLO out right now. He's not just a vulnerable, he's a witness.'

'You got it.' Brady headed for his squad at a jog.

Gino and Magozzi gloved up and took it slow up the front walk of the Keller house and the three concrete steps that led to the front door, which was slightly ajar.

Magozzi pushed open the door with the familiar dread of viewing yet another dead body. As a young homicide detective, he'd always thought that the dread would mellow eventually, but it never had. Which, in retrospect, was probably a good thing, because it kept the senses honed and on high alert; it helped you notice things you might not if your endocrine system wasn't gushing adrenaline like Old Faithful gushed water.

Inside the house, it was dim and breathless and redolent with a pungent artificial air freshener. It was clean and neatly kept, but the furnishings were from another era – the eighties, Magozzi figured – and they showed a lot of wear and tear: a rip in the faded upholstery here, a few dings in a coffee table there, some bald places in the carpet that bore the fairly fresh tracks of a vacuum. It had aged right along with the owners, which made him sad, thinking of Vivian Keller in the hospital and

Alvin Keller, who was God only knew where. This had the potential to be a really tragic situation for more than just the baffling corpse on the floor that lay not far from the front door.

'Holy shit, this is twenty kinds of weird,' Gino said, looking down at the woman. She was fairly young, mid-thirties at most, black pantsuit beneath a fur coat. Diamonds sparkled around her neck. She definitely did not belong in this threadbare world of the Kellers. It was like she'd been dropped here from outer space.

Gino and Magozzi circled the body, befuddled by the incongruity, then simultaneously crouched down for closer examination. 'Entry wound to the back of the head. Small caliber. And lookie here, praise the Lord, we got us some evidence for a change,' Gino said, pointing to a discarded handgun lying on the rug a few feet from the body. 'Ruger .22. Just a wild guess, but she probably didn't shoot herself in the back of the head.'

Magozzi frowned. 'Third-party shooter. Who left their gun behind at a crime scene?'

'Could be her gun. It's a nice personal security pocket rocket for a lady of wealth and taste. Ballistics is going to be interesting.' He touched her throat to check for a pulse he knew wouldn't be there, then started going through her pockets.

'Nothing. No ID, no makeup. And look around – there's no handbag. Women don't go anywhere without a handbag.'

'Well, if she was robbed, the robber has an IQ of about four, because she's wearing a shitload of cash in diamonds alone.'

Gino pulled back the cuff of one of her fine leather gloves and exposed a bejeweled Swiss watch which racked up the dollar signs on an already expensive inventory of personal effects. 'Look at this, Leo. And her clothes sure as hell didn't come from Target, and that coat is chinchilla. Seventy grand at least. She so doesn't belong here, so why is she here?'

'That's the question of the day.'

'She's still wearing her gloves.'

Magozzi lifted a shoulder, contemplating a small detail when there were so many bigger, mystifying details to worry about. 'Yeah. So maybe she just got here before she was shot. Or maybe she wasn't planning on staying at all, asking for directions or something. Or she had poor circulation, or warts she wanted to keep covered. I think that goes in the pending bin for now. We've got bigger questions.'

'Ain't that the truth.'

Magozzi stood up and stepped back, worrying his lower lip with his teeth. 'Seriously? Seventy grand for a chinchilla coat?'

'Oh, yeah. Adjusting for inflation, of course.'

'Tell me why you know this.'

'I know this because I used to hang out with Donnie Bergstrom in the fifth grade, and his dad had a bunch of chinchillas in cages in the basement, and they were so soft and cute, we used to go down and play with them until we got yelled at to leave the animals alone. So one day, Donnie and I go downstairs and the chinchillas are all gone. I asked where they went, and Donnie told me his dad killed them when they got big enough, because the pelts were worth a fortune, which explained why Donnie had a big house and a foosball table, and real-live arcade games. I spent the whole night crying my eyes out.'

'That . . . really sucks.'

'Not as bad as this sucks, Leo. We've got a woman dressed to the nines with a goldmine of swag on her person nobody bothered to take, no signs of sexual assault that I can see, shot to death in the home of an elderly couple, and a possibly kidnapped, terminally ill old man. You want to take a stab at that?'

Magozzi looked around the small house, reminded again that these were not people of means. 'If Alvin Keller was kidnapped, it wasn't for ransom. Besides, this won't be our case for long.'

'Thank God for small favors.'

Magozzi tipped his head, studying a faded, framed print of the Last Supper on the far wall while he waited for Gino to march out one of his crazy theories, but he wasn't talking. It was actually disappointing. 'Are you speculating or sleeping?'

'I don't like the timeline. I mean, how long does it take to go to the corner market?'

'Probably not very long.'

'Exactly. So this rich lady pops into an unlikely place. A jealous ex is following her, confronts her in a stranger's house, then the jealous ex maybe kidnaps the only witness, or kills him, and right now he's on the way to a body dump, all during the wife's trip to the store. Yep. Happens all the time in Weirdville.'

'We don't really know if she was a stranger. Vivian didn't know her, but maybe Alvin did. Bottom line, we need to get her ID'd and we need to find out more about Alvin and Vivian Keller.'

Brady came in through the front door, his cheeks red from the cold. 'BOLO is out. Backup is on

144

the way. I'm going to get back out there and start talking to people.'

'Good work, Brady.' Magozzi looked out the front window and saw a few timid rubberneckers in full-on winter regalia gathering on the sidewalk. 'Start running plates on the cars parked on the street, too. Our victim got here somehow.'

'Sure thing, Detectives.'

Gino pulled out his cell and started dialing. 'I'll get on the cab companies, see if she was a fare. You'd remember somebody like this lady.'

While Gino made his call, Magozzi checked in with Hennepin County Medical Center to see how Vivian was doing. The nurse put him on hold, so he wandered around the house, looking for something, anything.

There were no pictures of kids or grandkids, which probably meant that Vivian and Alvin didn't have any. There was a curio cabinet in the tiny dining room that had porcelain figurines of cats and dogs, but no signs of any current pets. He found an address book that was in a kitchen cabinet next to an ancient, wall-mounted rotary phone that probably had antique value by now. No answering machine.

In the same cabinet there was a staggering number of prescription drug bottles and printed pharmacy drug information sheets coldly detailing how every single one of them could cause anything from dry mouth and dizziness to sudden death, and every other really shitty side effect you could imagine in between. He checked the blue pill keepers that had compartments for every day of the week. They were loaded for the next six days, and both Vivian and Alvin had taken their morning doses. Nothing out of place.

Gino walked into the kitchen just as Magozzi found a grocery store receipt and the Campbell's Scotch Broth withering on the stove. 'What's that smell?'

'Soup's on. Vivian came home from the store, put the soup on the stove, then found a dead stranger. And you're right about the timeline being short. Time stamp on this receipt places her there less than an hour ago. Three cans of soup and a loaf of bread and the store's four blocks away.'

Gino peered into the pan and turned off the burner. 'Campbell's Scotch Broth. Huh. I didn't even know they still made it. My grandpa ate that for lunch every day of his life.'

Magozzi had almost forgotten he'd been on hold with HCMC, and when the nurse finally came back on the line, he put it on speaker for Gino to hear.

'Detective Magozzi?'

'Yes.'

'Sorry to take so long. Vivian Keller arrested en route to us. She's in ICU.'

Magozzi thanked the nurse and hung up. 'Poor lady.'

'Yeah,' Gino said morosely. 'Come on. Let's go talk to Mr. Snowman next door while we wait for our relief.'

# Twenty-Five

Knute Viestad was indeed frail, as Brady had mentioned, and leaned heavily on one of those high-tech canes as he opened the door a crack, keeping the security chain bolted. He could have been eighty or a hundred, Magozzi couldn't tell.

'Are you the police?' he asked in a reedy voice.

'Yes sir. Detective Magozzi and my partner, Detective Rolseth.'

He closed the door, unlocked the chain, and opened the door. 'Come on in.'

'Thank you for speaking with us, Mr. Viestad.'

He hobbled to the sofa and sank into it, gesturing to two easy chairs. 'Please, have a seat. It's Alvin, isn't it?' He looked away as his eyes started misting with tears. 'The minute I heard Vivian scream, and then heard the sirens . . . dang, I knew this day was coming.'

Magozzi and Gino stole a quick glance at each other, and Gino took the lead. 'Sir, Mr. Keller is missing. His wife came home from the store and he was gone.'

Mr. Viestad's hands started to quiver on the top of his cane. 'I . . . I don't understand. Alvin couldn't have gone anywhere on his own. Where's Vivian?'

'She's in the hospital, Mr. Viestad, she had quite a shock.'

His mouth groped around a hundred questions, his eyes bobbled in confusion as he tried to follow an impossible story line, but he remained mute.

Magozzi knew how he felt – this *was* an impossible story line, and Mr. Viestad didn't know the half of it yet. 'Did you know Alvin and Vivian well?' he asked, hoping to get him refocused.

That seemed to bring him to a happy place. 'We've been friends for nearly twenty years. They sure did look out for me when my Ruth died in oh-nine. Don't know what I'd have done without them to help me get through.' His happy place suddenly disappeared and he bowed his head shamefully. 'But I didn't look after Vivian, did I? When I heard her screaming, I called nine-one-one, but to be honest, I was afraid to go to her.'

'You did the right thing, Mr. Viestad. Nobody should walk into potential trouble.'

'That's exactly right,' Gino seconded, and Knute looked up, his lips trembling.

'Thank you for that, Detectives. But what happened to Alvin?'

'We're trying to find that out, sir,' Magozzi said gently. 'Did the Kellers have any children?'

He shook his head.

*Shit*, Magozzi thought, praying to God he wasn't going to have to call a bus for another elderly person today. 'Mr. Viestad, we found a woman in the Kellers' home. Young, expensively dressed. She was murdered.'

Poor Knute looked like somebody had just whacked him on the head with a cast-iron frying pan. 'Murdered?' he finally peeped.

'She was shot. You didn't hear anything?'

'I was watching TV and the only thing I heard was Vivian screaming.'

'Could she have been an acquaintance of the Kellers?'

The old man shook his head decisively. 'Oh, no. They didn't see anyone. All their old friends, the ones still living, anyhow, live way up north by the Canadian border. But at this age, nobody goes visiting anymore, not with that new Sipe or Skype or whatever it's called. And with Alvin so sick and all, they pretty much stayed put and didn't have anybody over, except me and the Meals on Wheels lady, but she's not a young woman. Mercy me. I just don't understand this . . .'

'Skype?' Gino asked.

Viestad looked up. 'Sure. Alvin tried to show me how to run the dag-blamed thing, but that's all Greek to me.'

'So he Skyped with friends?' Magozzi asked, wondering how they could have missed a computer in their initial walk-through.

'Oh, yes, that kept him busy and his mind off his troubles. He always said how much he missed it up there. He worked at a foundry there for years before he retired.'

Magozzi lifted his head abruptly. 'What kind of foundry?'

'Iron foundry. They made train cars, farm implements, things like that. American Iron Foundry, I think it's called.'

Magozzi scrawled down *Wallace Luntz – foundry?* in his notebook.

'We didn't see a computer in the house,' Gino said.

Viestad frowned. 'Can't miss it. It's a big ol' rig, one of them fancy new ones, sitting right on the table by the sofa. That's where Alvin spent most of his time.'

Gino let out a deep breath and pushed up out of his chair. 'Mr. Viestad, thank you so much for helping us out.'

Knute Viestad stood slowly. 'I hope I have helped you out. Do you know where they took Vivian?'

'Hennepin County Medical Center.'

He nodded. 'Thank you. And if there's anything more I can do for you . . . you got any more questions, any way I can help with Alvin, I'm always here. I don't go anywhere either.'

'This is just sad all the way around,' Gino muttered as they did another walk-through of the Kellers' house, looking for a computer that wasn't there. 'And weird. Every new piece of information just fogs up the picture. What are we supposed to believe? That some home invader or jealous ex walked in, shot a woman, left the bling and the gun, and then saw the computer and thought, hey, that's a nice unit. I'm going to throw it in my car, and while I'm at it, why not throw in an old dying guy, too. Shit. I'm not seeing any happy endings here.'

'Didn't you say Wally Luntz used to work at an iron foundry, too?'

Gino paused and started fiddling with his phone, pulling up his case notes. 'Yeah. American Iron Foundry, Cheeton, Minnesota.'

They reentered the living room – the fur-clad corpse on the floor was as startling the second time around as it had been the first.

Magozzi wandered back to the kitchen cabinet where he'd found the address book earlier. Most of the entries were faded, written in an elegant cursive hand trained back in a time when penmanship had been important. Under *L*, he found a newer addition, written in the shaky script of an elderly person. 'Wally Luntz,' he read the entry out loud. 'It's a newer entry, a recent contact. Chuck Spencer's name and number are in here, too.'

Gino looked up, his brows creeping toward his hairline. 'That connects our two homicides with Alvin Keller, and maybe the dead woman on his living room floor. We just bought ourselves another case, buddy.'

Magozzi closed the address book and noticed the cover for the first time. *American Iron Foundry, Cheeton, Minnesota,* was imprinted in gold letters on the front. He held it up for Gino to see. 'We sure as hell did. Call Chief Malcherson and let him know. Technically this is our case now, but ask him if he'll approve a tandem with whoever shows up to relieve us.'

Gino was already dialing. 'I hear you. While I'm talking to the chief, get the chinchilla and the diamonds before anybody else shows and call your fence.'

# Twenty-Six

Cheeton Sheriff Ernie Fenster had an Iron Range accent and apparently a lot going on in his small-town office – Magozzi could hear plenty of background noise when the sheriff finally picked up.

'Sheriff, this is Homicide Detective Leo Magozzi out of Minneapolis. Do you have a few minutes?'

'Absolutely. How can I help you, Detective?'

'We've got a couple homicide cases down here and a possible kidnapping of a vulnerable adult that have some connections, so we're chasing down every lead. Two of our victims used to work in Cheeton, at the American Iron Foundry – Wallace Luntz and Alvin Keller.'

The sheriff slurped something liquid. 'Well, that's real interesting. Our county plow driver found a dead local stark naked in a snowbank yesterday, and he worked for AIF, too. Of course, most everybody up here does.'

Magozzi felt a little jolt of optimism, but he kept it on a tight leash. When you worked Homicide, you learned that there were endless opportunities for promising leads to disintegrate like flash paper. 'Do you have a cause of death yet? Hypothermia?'

'Might have been, but the bullet hole in his head didn't do him any good either.'

*Bingo.*

'Should get the ME's report sometime today,' the sheriff continued. 'He had to thaw out before they could start cutting. Darn shame. A young guy, thirty-five, name of Ed Farrell. I didn't really know him – he transferred from an AIF plant out East somewhere a couple years ago – but by all accounts he was well-liked and excelled at his job. I spent a lot of time at our plant interviewing people yesterday, and nobody had a bad word to say about him. I also broke his wife's heart, and she didn't have anything bad to say about him either. Poor woman. First she learns her husband's been murdered, then she goes home after identifying the body and finds her house ripped apart.'

*Bingo, part two.* 'Burglary?'

'Actually, it looked more like vandals. Every room was trashed, drawers dumped, closet emptied, like that, but the only thing she noticed missing right off the bat besides the computer was a box full of family stuff.'

'Valuables?'

'No, nothing like that, just some old family photos.'

'Any suspects?'

'Nope.'

'What can you tell me about American Iron Foundry, Sheriff?'

'Just that it's been around darn near forever. They used to do piecemeal work, like most metal fabricators. Car parts, train cars and tracks, all kinds of ironware, like that. If you were born in Cheeton, chances are you'll end up working there one day, just like your daddy before you. My own worked there his whole life and never had a complaint except for during WW Two. They had a lot of government contracts back then to manufacture support equipment for the boys abroad, and from then on things got real high pressure real fast.'

'How so?'

'The government sent in their people to manage and refit the place, and what does the government do best?'

'Uh . . . not much?'

The sheriff chuckled. 'You got that right. They'll take a perfectly good company and screw it into the ground because they're nothing but a bunch of overeducated nincompoops who've never had a real job or a bottom line in their lives.'

Magozzi smiled, trying to remember the last time he'd heard the term *nincompoop*.

'Anyhow, it caused a lot of friction, but that's old news. Things really changed about fifteen years ago, though. The bottom dropped out of the iron business, so AIF merged with a new outfit. They took over the foundry and started retooling things again. Ed Farrell was part of the latest transition team. That's what they call folks now who barge in and turn a perfectly good place upside down.'

'You said they used to do metal fabrication. They don't anymore?'

'Oh, sure they do, but like I said, the bottom of that market dropped off a while ago. This new company expanded operations and built a new plant. For the past decade or so they've been manufacturing computer equipment and processing chips for Silver Dune Technology. Turns out you need a lot of water to manufacture computer chips, and guess what we've got a lot of in Minnesota?'

'Water. Makes sense.'

'We're better for it. The chip division's pumped more money into the local economy than the iron foundry ever did. A new era, you know?'

Magozzi looked out the Kellers' lace-flounced living room window and saw a Crime Scene van pull up to the curb where Gino was working his phone, followed by two squads and an unmarked that disgorged Johnny McLaren and a new promotion named Russ Tamblin. 'Our victims retired from the foundry years before Ed Farrell came to Cheeton, so there's probably nothing there, but I thank you for your time.'

'You're very welcome. And say – maybe we're both chasing the same rabbit, maybe we're not, but I'd be happy to send you what I've got, if you'd oblige and do the same.'

'I was just about to ask that very thing,' Magozzi said, thinking that Sheriff Ernie Fenster was a guy he wouldn't mind having a couple of beers with, as long as it wasn't on the Canadian border in the middle of December. 'Did you get a slug from your victim?'

'The doc did. Sent it off to BCA. I'll let you know if we get a hit.'

As Magozzi hung up, Gino poked his head through the front door. 'The chief, McLaren, and Tamblin are all on board for a tandem on this one. I called Monkeewrench to let them know about Keller and the iron foundry so they could add it to the Beast's search in progress. They said they're getting close to recovering Spencer's website, so let's get our new partners up to speed, then head over to Harley's. Did Cheeton pan any gold?'

'Maybe. They had a homicide yesterday, another worker at our favorite foundry, shot in the head and stuffed naked into a snowbank in the middle of nowhere. Ed Farrell. Double *R*, double *L*. And guess what? His house was trashed, but the only things missing were his computer and a box of family photos.'

Gino was still for a moment. 'Just like Charles Spencer and Alvin Keller, only the Keller place wasn't trashed.'

'Maybe they found what they were looking for right away.'

Gino looked off to the side for the space of a few breaths, then nodded. 'I'll call Harley back, tell him to punch Farrell into the Beast.'

# Twenty-Seven

Vera Kushner looked up from her computer at the nurses' station when she heard the front doors of Meadowbrook Memory Care open. A handsome, well-dressed man approached her, a warm smile on his face. He was making direct eye contact with her, which she suddenly realized was so very unusual in this day and age, when most everybody was constantly fixated on their phones. Somehow, when she hadn't been looking, meaningless interaction with electronic devices had usurped meaningful interaction with real, live human beings. She was getting too old for this world.

Vera hesitated a moment before shifting into her 'Welcome to Meadowbrook!' demeanor. This facility was small, and even though she hadn't worked here long, she knew all the family members who visited their loved ones regularly. She'd never seen this man before. 'Good afternoon, sir, how can I help you?'

'I'm here to see my uncle. Arthur Friedman.'

'Oh, of course. Mr. Friedman is one of my favorite patients. Have you visited with us before?'

His smile faded. 'Unfortunately, no. I didn't even know Uncle Art had Alzheimer's until last week.' He shrugged uncomfortably. 'Family rift and all. You know how that goes.'

Vera knew exactly how things went. Meadowbrook was expensive, the residents wealthy, and it wasn't unusual for family vultures to suddenly show up in the end stages in the hopes they'd get written into a will at the last minute, which was so stupid. The people she cared for weren't legally competent to change their wills, and didn't they know that? And yet they kept coming for some scrap, some little handout that would never happen. It made her furious, but she kept her composure, because she wasn't here to judge.

'What is your name, sir, so I can check you into our system?'

'James Friedman. Jimmy. At least that's what Uncle Art always used to call me. I hope he'll remember me.'

Vera forced a sympathetic smile. 'Your uncle has good days and bad days, but he is in an advanced stage of the disease. If you haven't seen him for a while, his condition might come as a shock.'

The man nodded solemnly. 'Thank you for telling me that. Is he in good health?'

'We try to keep him as healthy and as comfortable as possible, but as mobility becomes more and more limited . . . well, it can be challenging.'

'Yes, of course. I see.' He tipped his head curiously. 'Do I detect a hint of an accent?'

'You have a sharp ear, Mr. Friedman. I thought I'd completely lost my accent after all these years.'

'It's very faint. Where are you from originally?'

'Ukraine. Now, if you'll just follow me.'

Vera led him to Suite Six and stopped at the door. Mr. Friedman was in bed, just staring at a far wall. He didn't even acknowledge a presence in the room, which broke her heart. He was having a bad day. 'Hello, Mr. Friedman. You have a visitor, isn't that exciting? It's your nephew, Jimmy.' She adjusted his pillows and blanket and wiped the spittle at the corners of his mouth.

Mr. Friedman just continued to stare right through her, as if she were a ghost. There were rare times when his eyes sparked with life and cognizance, but those moments didn't last. For the most part he was a dark silhouette of the person he'd once been, a person she would never know, but wished she could. 'I'll get you a plate of cookies, Mr. Friedman. Oatmeal raisin today, your favorite.'

She excused herself and heard Jimmy say, 'Hi, Uncle Art. It's Jimmy.'

When Vera returned with cookies and a glass of milk ten minutes later, Mr. Friedman was sleeping. His nephew was holding his hand, talking quietly to him.

'Is this normal for Uncle Art?' he whispered.

'I'm afraid it is, and I'm terribly sorry. Your uncle isn't often cognizant anymore.'

'Really?'

'As I mentioned before, he's in the very late stages of the disease.'

He sighed and shook her hand warmly. 'Thank you for your compassion for Uncle Art. He's obviously in good hands.'

After Jimmy Friedman checked out and left, Vera logged off her computer, then dug her cell out of her purse and made a call. It was answered on the first ring. 'He had a visitor, Max. Mr. Friedman's nephew, but as we know, Mr. Friedman was an only child.'

'Sloppy, sloppy work. Did you recognize the idiot?'

'No, but I bluebugged his phone.'

'Did he question him?'

'He tried, but gave up quickly. Mr. Friedman's Alzheimer's saved him.'

Max snorted. 'For what kind of life, the poor bastard?'

'How is our other friend?'

Vera heard Max sighing on the other end of the line. 'Sadly, he passed away before we could speak. His heart, I think.'

# Twenty-Eight

There was no food or booze sitting out on Harley's foyer table when Gino and Magozzi arrived – a clear indication that it had been all work and no play at the mansion. Charlie was notably absent, too, as was Grace when they entered the third-floor office.

Harley was at his computer station, robotically dipping into a bag of Doritos with one hand while he worked his computer mouse with the other. He'd heard them coming, gave a backwards wave, but didn't break attention from his screen. 'Hey, guys, pull up some chairs. Grace and Charlie are out for a walk but they should be back soon.'

Magozzi looked around the office, at the empty bags of chips and various other junk food containers in Harley's wastebasket; Grace's wastebasket was empty, save for an apple core and an empty bottle of orange juice. Some people ate through stress, other people starved through it.

Harley rubbed his hands together and finally spun around in his chair. 'Okay, we finally recovered Spencer's site. It was a bitch, but we did it.'

Magozzi rolled a chair next to Harley. 'Who took it down?'

'Don't know yet, but it's somebody who almost knows what they're doing. Grace and I will figure it out. In the meantime . . .' Harley toggled up the home page of the site. 'The background is the old black-and-white photo of eight men and President Eisenhower that Lydia Ascher told you about. The website is directed to the descendants of these men who worked on the hydrogen bomb. It's basically a trip down memory lane for a pretty exclusive group of people. Lots of historical factoids, family anecdotes – interesting stuff, but nothing earth-shattering.' Harley navigated to a different page where there was a diagram with names.

'Looks like a family tree,' Gino said.

'That's exactly what it is. On the left are the names of those eight men, and on all these branches shooting out from the main bracket are names of some of their descendants. Spencer was trying to fill in the tree.' Harley started pointing out names one by one. 'Chuck Spencer, son. Wally Luntz, son . . .'

'Alvin Keller, are you kidding me?' Gino jabbed his finger at the name on the screen, earning a solemn look from Harley.

'Yeah, how about that? Your missing Alvin Keller – he was one of the original eight physicists. Not exactly the retired iron foundry worker he was playing in his retirement. And check this out, the dead guy in the snowbank in Cheeton, Ed Farrell – he was a grandson. If I were you, I'd do a welfare check on these other names, because it looks like somebody is trying to take out everybody on this family tree.'

Magozzi blinked at the screen and felt the muscles in his shoulders tighten. 'Lydia Ascher isn't on the tree and she's a descendant.'

'Spencer's website was an outreach, and Lydia Ascher never signed onto it, never even knew about it until she met Spencer on the plane. There are probably a lot more descendants out there who don't have a clue Spencer's site existed.'

Gino folded his arms across his chest. 'So there's some kind of a hit list on people who visited the site? And maybe all the descendants? That doesn't make any kind of sense.'

'Well, here's something interesting – Spencer's website was called the Sixth Idea – it's basically why he launched the site in the first place, as a general query about something he'd found in his father's old papers called the Sixth Idea. And he got a lot of responses from site users who'd found references to it in old documents *their* bomb-building parents or grandparents left for them after they'd kicked the bucket. It was like they were all on a treasure hunt, looking to solve an old mystery.'

Gino frowned. 'So what's the mystery? What's the Sixth Idea?'

'Nobody knows, according to the chat room threads we've read so far. Alvin Keller, the one guy who would know, said it was a myth – Cold War scare tactics and saber-rattling. So we put the Beast on it, and there is no such thing as the Sixth Idea. But there *is* a Third Idea – it was the code name for the Soviet Union's development of thermonuclear weapons, aka the H-bomb.'

'Jesus,' Gino grumbled. 'If the H-bomb was only the third idea, I don't even want to think about what the sixth idea is.'

Harley shrugged. 'The hydrogen bomb was the ultimate Armageddon tool, and that's one of the reasons it got scrapped by the U.S. and the Russians after the tests. I'm going with Alvin Keller – the concept of a Sixth Idea was just a myth, a Cold War scare tactic. Make your enemy think you've got something bigger and badder, and eventually you'll get yourself a nonproliferation treaty and a test ban.'

Magozzi shook his head. 'Well, most of the people who were talking about it on Spencer's site ended up dead under very suspicious circumstances. And Keller's missing.'

'All I can tell you is the site is totally innocent, at least to the users. But maybe it's not so innocent to somebody else.'

# Twenty-Nine

It was noon by the time Lydia finally left her art room in the lower level of her house. On paper, the space was considered a basement, but in actuality it was anything but. The east wall was all glass, looking out over the lake, and in the morning the light was spectacular. It was her favorite spot in the whole house.

She had a stack of contract work to start on, but this morning her lazy hand had started sketching what it wanted to instead of what her many clients had ordered. The freestyle session had produced something very unexpected. She thought about taking it down from her easel and putting it in her portfolio labeled RANDOM SKETCHES, then decided to leave it up. She wasn't quite finished with it.

Lydia turned on her stool for one more look out at the frozen lake before going upstairs for lunch, smiling at the inch of snow that had decorated her little woods while she hadn't been looking.

She made a cup of tea, put some chicken soup on the stove to heat, then sat down at the kitchen table. Her grandfather's paperback was still sitting there, just where she'd left it. She picked it up and examined the cover again, then her brain stumbled, stopped, and rewound back in time.

'What's this, Mom?'

Alice chuckled and sank cross-legged like a little girl on the hard wood floor of the attic. 'Father — your grandfather — was a very organized man. He planned everything far in advance. He was only thirty-five years old when he died, but already he had this special box set aside for me.' She nudged the old dusty cardboard box toward Lydia as if the moment had great import. 'This is it.'

Lydia lifted the top flaps and peeked inside. 'What is all this?'

Alice shrugged. 'His work files, old photos of people I don't know, notebooks full of math and equations I'll never understand. Apparently in our family, real intelligence skips a generation and, honey, you're the lucky winner. Maybe you'll be able to make sense of it — or maybe there's nothing to be made sense of. Maybe they're all just old mementos.'

Lydia frowned, then giggled as she pulled out a battered paperback with a buxom, half-dressed woman screaming and running from a fire. 'One of these things is not like the others.'

'Father did love those torrid old pulp fiction paperbacks. I think it was his only escape from his work.' Alice's face went very still. 'But there are some unusual things about this one.'

'Like what?'

'He gave it to me two days before he died and swore me to secrecy. It was mine and mine alone. I never told anybody, not my mother or brother or sister. When I got older, I realized how strange it was that he would give me such a book when I was only eight years old.'

Lydia frowned. 'That is strange. It looks kind of . . . racy.'

'The cover was, at least for the time. But the subject matter was deadly serious and about as dark as it gets. This was no bodice ripper. But that's not the only puzzling thing about it. Notice, there's a title and the author's name on the front cover.'

'Yes . . . *In Case of Emergency* by Thea S. Dixid.'

'But there's no copyright page.'

'So what does that mean?'

'This wasn't published by an actual publishing company. And there's no record of this book ever existing. No author named Thea S. Dixid, no title *In Case of Emergency* ever copyrighted.'

'Are you sure?'

'I was a librarian for most of my life. I know how to look up books. I think Father wrote it himself and had it bound.'

'Really? Why do you think that?'

'Because it's filled with places I remember. There was a five-and-ten-cent store in the book –'

'A what?'

Alice chuckled. 'You know, a dime store. Ben Franklin?'

Lydia shrugged helplessly.

'I loved that place. I can still see the front door and the little brass bell hanging from it to announce customers. And the address painted in gold letters and numbers on the glass. Five-six-five Main Street. There was a tiny chip in the number six.'

'Good memories?'

'Wonderful memories. The store had a big plastic hand in the window with all the fingers spread out and every nail painted a different color. Exactly the way it was described in this book. There was a little soda fountain in there with a sign taped to the mirror behind the counter: WE HAVE VANILLA LEMON PHOSPHATES.' She looked at Lydia. 'That was in the book, too. And that was where Father took me every Wednesday afternoon after school, back when we were still happy.'

'What made you all unhappy?'

'When Father started working for the government. Started working on the bomb.'

'Where was that?'

'Olean. Our last year there, before we started moving around.'

'Olean, New York, where Grandpa's buried?'

'Yes. Like I said, it was the last place we were happy. It was one of those little Americana towns that existed in such a narrow slice of time, where boys built their own soapbox cars with their dads for the annual derby down a big hill. All the veterans marched in the Fourth of July parade on Main Street and everyone in town came. I saw two Civil War vets march in that parade when I was little.' She smiled. 'Father grew up near there. The family mausoleum was there and that's where he wanted to be. Had it in his will, Mother said. Everything arranged in advance.'

'I thought' – she hesitated for a moment – 'that there were no remains after his plane crashed.'

'True. It was a memorial service primarily, but he has a nice plaque on a drawer in the family vault. I went to visit it once, years ago. Only once. Father is in my head, nowhere else . . .'

Lydia sparked back to the present when she heard her forgotten soup boiling angrily on the stove. She pulled it from the burner, left it to cool, then went back to the book and started reading from the beginning.

After an hour she'd come across all the passages her mother had mentioned, about the five-and-dime and the Fourth of July parade, and of course the section about building a generator. The rest of what she'd read was tedious, really. Her grandfather may have been a genius physicist, but he hadn't been a very good fiction writer. Why he would self-publish such a dark book and insist his daughter keep it a secret was a mystery she would probably never solve. If there was a hidden meaning somewhere in there, she couldn't see it.

She looked out the window and was alarmed to see almost white-out conditions. The morning weather had mentioned a system that would be moving through today, but this was looking serious. She decided to make the fifteen-mile drive to the grocery store and stock up in case the weather really meant business.

She picked up the phone and dialed Otis.

'Big storm coming, Lydie,' he answered.

'It looks that way. Listen, I'm going into town for some supplies. Do you need anything?'

'Thanks, but I'm all set.'

'Well, I'm cooking dinner – I'm thinking pork roast and applesauce – I hope you can make it.'

'If you're cooking, I'll be there, even if I have to walk through two feet of fresh snow.'

Lydia smiled. 'I'll be back in a couple hours. See you then?'

'With bells on. Be careful on the roads.'

Otis hung up and set the receiver back into its cradle and stared out the window. The same white SUV he'd seen passing by on the road fifteen minutes ago was slowly heading past his driveway again in the opposite direction. It wasn't unusual to see vehicles he didn't recognize on this tiny little back road, but this one troubled him for some reason – it seemed like it was trolling, looking for something.

'Paranoid old fool,' he muttered to himself. His whole life, he'd never worried a single minute about himself, but ever since Lydia had moved in next door, he'd taken it upon himself to look out for her. A single city woman, living all alone out in the country, it just seemed like the right thing to do. Maybe he'd go over to her place a little early, take a look at that cabinet and the leaky faucet she'd asked him to repair. Keep an eye on things.

He was halfway out the door when he turned back to grab his shotgun out of the front closet. You could never be too careful. Besides, his horses hadn't settled down one whit – probably the storm, but maybe not.

# Thirty

The flakes were large and intricate, like the ones you cut out of folded white paper in grade school. They were softly wet, melting the moment they floated against your skin, so large that Charlie kept leaping upward to catch them in his teeth.

'You're humiliating yourself,' Grace told him. 'No dignity, none at all, and that vicious little Chihuahua is watching you from across the street.'

Charlie sobered immediately. He was inexplicably terrified of little yapping dogs he could have gobbled up in one bite, and there were a lot of them in this neighborhood, which was why Grace liked to take him for walks here.

*You have to build his confidence,* Magozzi kept telling her. *Let him meet other dogs, go to off-leash dog parks where he can discover his dogginess. Don't laugh. He's getting better and better at trusting people, but he hasn't figured out that he isn't a person. Every species has a right, a need, to socialize with other members of the same species.*

She looked up at the fat white snowflakes spinning down out of the sky and wondered whether he'd been talking about Charlie or her.

But now the Chihuahua across the street had been cosseted in its owner's mink-clad arms and hustled home to something wonderful, like a warm fire and caviar, and Grace and Charlie had the street to themselves again.

She was smiling when she got back to the upstairs loft at Harley's. Charlie had dusted her in the race up three flights of stairs, of course, and had already happily washed every face in the room and settled into his chair, right next to Grace's computer station.

It was the first time since she'd met Magozzi that she hadn't commanded and monopolized his attention the moment she walked into a room. He and Gino were behind Harley at his station, all of them focused on his monitor. Everybody greeted her, but none of them took their eyes off the computer.

'What is it?' she asked, putting her hands on Magozzi's shoulders. For her, it was a daring, amplifying response to his earlier public display of affection, but the caseload was clearly taking its toll on him, and even she was beginning to appreciate that a little human touch could make things better, if even for a moment.

Harley swiveled his chair to look at her, his face dark. 'We've been looking at some of the descendants of the eight men in that photo with Eisenhower, starting with the twenty-five who signed on to Spencer's Sixth Idea website. Sixteen of them are dead from natural causes – cancer, heart attacks, car accidents, like that – but the rest were all homicides, all in the few months since Spencer's website was activated. They were all regular visitors to that site and they were all talking about the Sixth Idea.'

Grace was seldom caught off guard by man's inhumanity to man – she'd seen enough of it personally to carve cynicism deep into her psyche – but these murders touched another chord that almost smothered her voice. 'Nine murders,' she whispered. 'Nine people died because they visited Charles Spencer's website and talked about the Sixth Idea?'

'We're spitballing here,' Gino replied. 'But this is just one more coincidence in a long line of coincidences in this batshit case. Chuck Spencer and Lydia Ascher, two descendants of eight men who worked on the H-bomb, miraculously seated next to each other on a plane? What are the odds?'

'And then Wally Luntz, another descendant about to meet his Internet buddy Spencer, murdered the same night as Spencer was murdered?' Magozzi interjected. 'And then there's Alvin Keller and Ed Farrell, and now this? I'm not real big on conspiracy theories, but we'd be idiots to look the other way on this one.'

Grace spoke carefully, quietly. 'Harley and I read every entry on that website. None of those people even knew what the Sixth Idea was or if it even existed at all. Why would they be killed for something they knew nothing about?'

And that was the big question. Magozzi, Gino, and Harley were watching her like soldiers staring at a grenade with no pin, waiting for it to explode in their faces.

'It has to be the government, Magozzi,' she said finally. 'Who was involved with developing the H-bomb? The scientists working on it and the government they worked for.'

Funny that she had addressed that specifically to him. He had the strange feeling it was a loyalty test of some kind and had a terrible feeling that he would fail.

'Why hasn't anybody put these murders together before now?'

'Because the victims were scattered across the country,' Magozzi said. 'Without Lydia Ascher and her freak encounter with Spencer on the plane, and more importantly, without you and Harley recovering the website, we wouldn't have pulled it together either.' Magozzi looked down at his phone when it started chiming. 'It's McLaren. I'll put it on speaker.'

'Hey, Leo, are you guys still with Monkeewrench?'

'Yeah, what's up?'

'What's up is we printed the dead lady in the chinchilla coat, and I think we just went a little further down the rabbit hole. The prints popped right away on NCIC, but they've got a federal cover on them. Access restraint.'

Magozzi let out a puff of air and looked at Grace. 'Which means anyone from the DOD to the FBI doesn't want anybody to know who she is.'

McLaren cleared his throat. 'Exactly. But I happen to know a guy who helps me out with stuff like this. He got me a name to go with the prints – Natalia Smirnova, a Russian national.'

All the eyes in the room were fixed on Magozzi's phone. 'Who is she?' he asked.

'Don't know. He couldn't pull any more information from where he was sitting. But I thought maybe if you had a name, you might be able to dig a little deeper, if you know what I'm saying.'

Magozzi knew what he was saying. This was the sort of thing Monkeewrench excelled at. 'Thanks, McLaren. Any word on Alvin Keller?'

'Haven't found him yet, and your tip line is dead empty. The news is twenty-four/seven on a blackout in Boston, and a missing elderly man doesn't get a lot of coverage when you've got a bunch of stuck elevators in a big city.'

'That's bullshit. Boston's in the middle of a blizzard, which they have like every twenty minutes. It's winter, for Christ's sake. There are blackouts all over the place. In the meantime, Alvin Keller is out there somewhere with a rapidly expiring life expectancy. Call the TV stations. Tell them their lack of coverage is facilitating the death of a helpless, sick old man and we're going to make sure everybody knows it.'

'I'll give it my best shot, but the news cycle has kind of been dry for a while, so they're trying to spin Boston in with the blackouts in Detroit and Fort Collins last week. You know how it goes. There haven't been any plane crashes or terrorist attacks or Ebola cases lately, so they need a new way to scare people into thinking they're going to die any minute. For now, it's the power grid collapsing. In an hour, it might be thyroid cancer or rickets.'

'Christ.' Magozzi's phone started clicking and his screen flashed on and off. 'McLaren, my phone's on the fritz again, so we'll catch up with you at City Hall.'

Magozzi clicked off and tapped his phone screen in frustration. 'Damn thing. Whoever named these things smartphones should be drawn and quartered.'

Harley got up out of his chair and held out his hand. 'Give it to me. Your phone, too, Gino.'

Gino reluctantly passed his phone to Harley. 'Why?'

Harley raised his eyes. 'Didn't you hear that clicking?'

# Thirty-One

The assassin was already here, so it was fortunate that the target Max was here to protect didn't happen to be home. There was always a way into any building, no matter what its security. This one was no different, but easier, because the man Max was following had already done the initial work and was leading the way. The alarms had been disabled with the snip of a phone line, ingress obtained – rather flawlessly, he had to concede – and all that remained was to follow silently, unseen, unfelt, undetected. There was no question this man was smart, young, and well-trained, but his youth would work against him. Brawn, agility, passion – none of those things could match the calm precision that came with maturity and experience, something Max had amassed in great measure over the past few decades.

He could smell adrenaline as the man sought out a place to conceal himself comfortably while he waited for his quarry to return.

It was a fast job. Unsavory, of course, but quick and silent. He had some disposal choices here, unlike this morning's job in the city, and as he pondered the efficacy of each one, he smelled somebody else behind him. He ducked, spun, and saw a door opening, a shotgun rising up in the gloom of the basement. Max had no choice but to fire.

He stood over each of his kills for a moment, taking deep breaths to slow his heart. Murder didn't bother him; to have been taken unaware disturbed him greatly, but that was for later contemplation – the larger issue at hand was that he now had two bodies to deal with. The story line had changed, and he would have to adapt. As he pondered his options, his nose picked up another scent, the scent of exhaust, and he heard a garage door creaking open above him. Suddenly, all his choices were gone.

# Thirty-Two

Lydia didn't know how long she'd been holding her breath, but when she finally turned into her driveway, she let it out in a great, shaky rush. Her knuckles were sore from her death grip on the steering wheel, and she felt a trickle of nervous sweat rolling down her spine.

*Note to self: don't ever drive in a snowstorm again, you idiot.*

It had been all fun and games on the way into town, like driving through a postcard. Pretty, fat white flakes tumbled from the sky and frosted the evergreens, scarlet cardinals flashed through the woods like sparks of fire, and deer and turkeys appeared by the roadside, scavenging whatever forage they could find before it was buried under the gathering snow. That should have been her first clue – watch the wildlife, they know a hell of a lot more about the weather than you do.

By the time she'd left the general store, the roads had deteriorated in a big way – the wet snow she'd enjoyed on the drive in had quickly accumulated on the tar and turned to wicked, slippery ice. She'd almost lost control of her car a few times, and with sketchy cell coverage in this part of the world, a careless maneuver could launch her into the ditch, where she'd probably be waiting a very long time for a stray passerby to notice and help.

But she was safely home now and could look forward to a cozy fire in the hearth, preparing a nice meal she and Otis would enjoy together, and the wicked sense of a snow day, when the weather forced you to stay at home and do absolutely nothing but enjoy life.

She hooked her parka over a peg on the coatrack, then turned as she always did, to what she'd seen the first time she entered this house. A wall nook next to the front closet where she'd placed a spider plant with graceful green and white arms rising from the roots and flowing like the splash of a waterfall down toward the tile floor. The leaves shuddered in the heated puffs of the register that blew warm air up into the foyer, welcoming her home.

Lydia took one of those deep breaths that let everything else go, because this was sanctuary; but her shoulders tightened a little, because that deep breath had pulled something different, something alien, into her nostrils. A faint, subtle scent that didn't belong in her house.

She stopped by the spider plant, looking into the obviously empty kitchen. Everything was as it should be – her coffee mug sat by the sink next to a plate with toast crumbs, waiting for washing. Everything was in its proper place, and yet there was that strange scent.

Chuck's murder had put her on edge in some deep part of her psyche – why else would she slip her hand into her purse and pull out her little gun, thinking that damn, she had to get a bigger one.

Silliness, really. She crept through the kitchen, the gun slipping on the sweat of her right palm, and then she stopped, focusing on the oak table with its bamboo placemats and the artful arrangement of pine and holly circling the frosted yarn snowman that had been her mother's from the time Lydia had been a child – part of Christmas, part of her life – and suddenly things from the past and present seemed to clash and crash into each other in a strange way she couldn't make sense of.

*Prickle, prickle.*

*Oh, come on,* she told herself. *There's nothing out of order here. Just your wild imagination.* But still, there was that strange smell.

She followed it to the open stairs that led to the basement and thought, hey, she was impressively brave. Here she was, an insecure, uncertain, probably insane person pretty much terrified by a weird smell.

It was stronger here, floating up from the lowest level of her house, totally unfamiliar and somehow wrong. She should call someone – 911, maybe.

*Hello, there's a strange smell in my basement, I'm here alone with a gun in my hand . . .*

No, that was nonsense. It was broad daylight, nothing wrong here except my stupid nose, so I can walk down these open-backed stairs and look around and everything will be in its proper place just like it was upstairs. Yep, the pool table with its pretty green felt and the dartboard on the wall, and oh my God. Otis lay in a pool of blood right there in front of her, a cylindrical hole in the middle of his forehead.

Half an hour later, Lydia was sitting on the sofa next to a Deputy Terry Harmon while other deputies covered her yard and the scene in the basement. It was utterly surreal – her basement was now a crime scene and Chuck and Otis, two people she'd known personally, had both been shot to death in the span of forty-eight hours. What were the odds of that?

*They weren't connected to each other in any way except you – you're the common denominator.*

Lydia tamped down the ridiculous inner voice, the part of the human brain that always tried to explain the inexplicable, tried to connect random events and put a neat bow on them. The truth was, Chuck had probably been the victim of a mugging – the sinister man she'd seen at the airport had been a creation of her overactive imagination. And Otis had probably surprised a burglar. If she hadn't invited Otis over for dinner, he would probably still be alive; and if she hadn't decided to go shopping in the middle of a snowstorm, she would probably be dead.

*If, if, if.* She took a deep breath, trying to shake the feeling that something very bad was starting to coalesce around her.

'I'm sorry about Otis,' Deputy Harmon was saying. 'I know he was a neighbor and a friend.'

'Yes, he was. Thank you.'

'Did you recognize the other man?'

Lydia's brain stuttered to a dead stop. 'What do you mean, the other man?'

'The man in the laundry room.'

Lydia's world started to spin, but it was a slow spin. 'I . . . I don't understand. I only saw Otis.' Her hands found each other between her knees, and started twisting together. 'There's a man in my laundry room? Is he dead, too?' She knew it was a stupid question, but it just came rolling off her tongue anyhow.

'Yes. Lydia, do you think you can come downstairs with me? Just in case you can identify him?'

Well, yes, of course she could go downstairs and look at a dead body she didn't even know was there. All part of a normal day.

She let Deputy Harmon lead her downstairs by the arm. She pinched her eyes shut as they passed Otis, and she suddenly realized she would never, ever be able to work in this formerly beautiful space again. She could never do laundry again, she probably couldn't even live here. No, she definitely couldn't live here.

She let her mind obsess over finding a new house and selling this one, but all too soon, she was standing in the laundry room over a dead man who also had a hole in his head, just like Otis.

'Lydia? Are you all right?'

No prickles – just an all-encompassing, black sense of dread. 'The man from the airport,' she whispered.

# Thirty-Three

In the hour since Harley had commandeered their phones, Magozzi and Gino had been working Monkeewrench's secure landlines, following up with local law enforcement on the other murder victims in other states. Grace was still trying to trace the source of the cyberattacks on the Chatham server and Spencer's website, and Harley had been largely silent at his desk, all his attention focused on their cell phones.

'Bingo,' he finally barked. 'You guys are clean now, but you had ears on you, and pretty impressive ones at that. We're not talking some drive-by bluejacker looking for your personal information. Whoever it was went through your carrier, and believe me, that is hard to do, unless you're the NSA.'

'Jesus,' Gino murmured.

'Hey, it could be a good thing. It's one more path for Grace and me to follow. But here's the deal – no telling how long you stay clean. This isn't amateur hour.' He smiled and turned over their phones. 'Of course, I took the liberty of uploading a new firewall that will make anybody who tries to hack you deeply sorry they did, but that's beside the point. You could have infected the whole MPD communication network, or maybe that's where you got your bugs in the first place. Either way, call Chief Malcherson, tell him you've been compromised and that the department needs to do a deep security sweep and clean up the system.'

Gino stared down at his phone like it was a mortal enemy. 'Sure thing. Should I tell the chief we're considering the possibility that the government is behind it, and by the way, we also think they're assassinating innocent people who pay their salaries?'

Harley shrugged. 'Our government, somebody else's government, Chinese hackers, terrorists – at this point it doesn't really matter. Safety first.' He reached under his desk and pulled out a lockbox. 'Answer your calls on your regular cells, talk to Angela and ask her what she's making for dinner, but use these temporarily for more sensitive conversations.' He tossed them two cell phones. 'Burners. Untraceable, unhackable.'

Magozzi looked out the window at the worsening snow that was now blowing sideways. Forty-eight hours ago they were investigating a simple shooting in a downtown Minneapolis alley; now they were using burner phones and spinning government conspiracy theories.

'Guys?' Grace called from the other side of the room. 'We got something from the Beast.'

Harley rolled his chair over to a printer that was spitting out pages. He read and reread them, then passed them over to Magozzi and Gino and went to his computer.

'What is it?'

'A BOLO on an Arthur Friedman, an advanced Alzheimer's patient who supposedly wandered out of his care facility, but I have my doubts about that.' He started typing furiously on his keyboard.

Magozzi frowned down at the photo of Arthur Friedman and the list of pertinent details. 'What do you mean? And why would the Beast spit out a "Be on the Lookout" for some Alzheimer's patient?'

'Because we linked the Beast to Spencer's website so it could access all the data there and make any connections. See here?' He tapped his screen. 'Arthur Friedman is one of the original eight physicists, the only other one alive besides Alvin Keller. If Alvin Keller is still alive.'

'Shit,' Gino muttered. 'Somebody took them both – two sick old men, goddamnit. I'm going to make some calls and turn the fire up on this.'

Magozzi started when his cell rang from its cradle in his sweaty palm. 'Unknown caller.'

Harley rubbed his hands together and returned his attention to his computer screen, making a few quick strokes on his keyboard. 'Goody. Answer it, I'm monitoring you right now. If it's legit, call them back on our landline.'

'Magozzi here.'

The voice was timid, quaky, frightened. 'Detective Magozzi. This is Lydia Ascher. I met with you and Detective Rolseth yesterday at the Chatham.'

'Of course. Ms. Ascher, can I call you back at the number you're calling from?'

There was a slight hesitation. 'Can you call back right away? Because there are two dead men in my house, and one of them is the man in the sketch I drew for you yesterday. The sketch of the man I thought was following Chuck Spencer in the airport.'

Magozzi was instantly focused, alert, totally wired. 'Are you alone?'

'No, the police are here –'

And then there was another voice talking to him, a Deputy Harmon, giving him a concise cop summary of what had happened.

'I'm on my way,' Magozzi answered in a rush of breath. 'Jesus Christ, don't leave her alone, Deputy. I'll explain when I get there.'

# Thirty-Four

Magozzi and Gino had left Harley's minutes after Lydia's call, but there was no rushing the drive, which had been hampered by snow-covered roads that deteriorated the farther north they got.

Magozzi was white-knuckling the steering wheel of the sedan; Gino was white-knuckling his travel mug of coffee as he stared out the passenger window, unconsciously redistributing his weight around in his seat to compensate for every shimmy or slip of the car.

'This sucks,' Gino finally complained. 'How many times have we caught a case in winter and ended up driving north through shit weather to follow a lead?'

'At least it's not an ice storm.'

'Where are the snowplows? I haven't seen one snowplow since we left Harley's. And by the way, what the hell are we walking into? The man from the airport wasn't at Lydia Ascher's for tea and cookies, I can guarantee you that. Jesus, Leo, we caught him on tape, standing outside Spencer's hotel room with a gun right before Spencer bought it in the alley. And he had a partner. I'm a little worried about Lydia's life expectancy right now.'

'I hear you.' Magozzi made a turn onto a curvy, tree-crowded lane. Under normal circumstances it would have been charming, but now it seemed like an oppressive physical representation of where they were at right now with their cases – lost in the middle of a claustrophobic, twisting labyrinth that maybe didn't have an exit sign at the end.

'Why do people live out here?' Gino mumbled, straining against his seat belt as he looked through the windshield.

'Because they can. It's pretty. Isolated. Quiet.'

'Yeah, and mostly safe, until you find two dead guys in your house. People still get killed outside the city limits.'

'This is something different.'

'You're telling me.'

Magozzi pulled into a snowy driveway. Through the trees he could see the confetti of flashing squad car lights. They were confronted by two deputies with guns drawn – one at the driver's side, one at the passenger's side – before they could open the car doors, which made them both feel a little better about Lydia Ascher's safety. Magozzi and Gino held their badge cases up to the windows and their car doors were opened simultaneously.

'Glad to see you, Detectives. Would you please step up to the sidelight windows on either side of the front door, and then stop?'

Another layer of protection, Magozzi thought, knowing they had Lydia somewhere close, where she could look out unseen and confirm their identities before they gained entrance. After a moment Lydia Ascher opened the front door. A deputy stood beside her. Magozzi had always thought that he and Gino presented a benign and comforting presence to most they encountered, but this woman was frightened. It made him feel guilty for no reason.

'Thank you for coming, Detectives,' she said. 'This is Deputy Harmon, you spoke with him on the phone.'

The niceties were brief, and once Lydia was sitting on the living room sofa with another deputy, Harmon led them down wooden steps to the basement level. As they made the descent, their heads swiveled, taking in everything around them, finally focusing on the dead man next to the pool table near the foot of the staircase.

'Otis Ferringer, Lydia Ascher's neighbor and close friend,' Harmon explained. 'She took it hard, figures he walked into something when he came over for dinner and it's her fault.'

Gino's eyes were busy. 'He comes to dinner toting a shotgun?'

He gestured at the Winchester still clutched in the dead man's hand.

It was the first time Deputy Harmon broke cop character, looking off to the side and swallowing. 'Otis carried that Winchester everywhere, never shot at anything except skeet or to put a wounded animal out of its misery. Lived here his whole life, kind of a legend to the locals, you know? And he took care of Lydia from the day she moved here.'

'And the other DB?'

Harmon led the way to the laundry room where the man depicted in Lydia Ascher's sketch was lying on his side in a small pool of blood. It was beyond creepy, seeing the drawing of a man not brought to life but to death, right before their eyes.

'Don't know who he is. No ID, no personal effects except for this nine-millimeter Ruger lying on the floor by his hand. It wasn't discharged and neither was Otis's shotgun. It looks like a small caliber brought them both down, but we haven't found a third weapon or any shells or casings. I did a year in the Cities before I came back home, saw a bit of this kind of thing. But never here. I took this post to get away from that shit.' He stopped abruptly, startled by his own language. As a rule, cops didn't use vulgarities beyond their own circles. 'Excuse the language, Detectives. I'm way out of my league here.'

'No problem,' Magozzi reassured him. 'Seems like we're poorer for losing you, Deputy Harmon.'

'Nice of you to say so.'

'So we have a missing shooter.'

'Yes sir, which means we've still got some dead-eye out there and frankly, it's got us all on edge. Spooked, actually. We do domestics, DWIs, and roadkills. Nothing like this.'

'BCA is on the way?' Magozzi asked.

'En route, along with the local doc who covers suspicious deaths until the big boys get out here. Doesn't happen often.'

'Deputy, we have good reason to believe that this incident is connected to several other homicides. Technically, this is your ball game, your jurisdiction. Understand, we have nothing solid that would stand up in court to justify our gut instincts here, but we think Lydia Ascher was the intended target, and may still be a target.'

Harmon blinked at him. 'Jesus. So she's not safe?'

Gino's brows crowded together as he shook his head. 'We believe she needs to be put in protective custody as soon as possible. Does Jefferson County have that capability?'

Harmon had been struggling with nerves since they'd arrived, but for the first time he exuded a little bit of confidence. 'Sheriff Gannet is ex-military. He ran a protective detail unit in Iraq for three years. First thing he did when he got sworn in was implement an emergency response protocol for every single thing that could possibly happen, from protecting a witness to a dirty bomb detonation. A lot of the force and the county commissioners thought it was a little over the top, but I guess the sheriff's smarter than all of us put together. I'll let him know right away.'

Magozzi let out a breath. 'She's in good hands, then.'

'You bet. There's a little motel across the lake that caters to the summer fishing crowd, then closes for the winter. We've done training drills there. It's easy to cover from all angles, and we'll pull in Highway Patrol to help out. Listen, I should check in with my men and call Sheriff Gannet. Holler if you need anything.'

'Thank you, Deputy.'

Magozzi followed Gino toward the staircase, then stopped at the entrance to another room that had a huge bank of windows looking out onto a woods and a snow-covered lake beyond. He looked past a birdfeeder down to a long dock with a weathered, snowcapped wooden bench at the end.

He saw himself on that bench with a fishing pole in one hand and a beer in the other, and wondered what the hell he'd been doing with his life. This wasn't a Lake of the Isles mansion or one of those Lake Minnetonka mega-million show-offs. It was just a plain house, and all he thought of was that he could afford this, he could live like this, and what the hell had he been doing in the shabby remains of his ex-wife's choice of habitat in the middle of the city?

Grace had been absolutely right to call him out on that, just as he'd been absolutely right to call her out on the very same matter. They were both stuck in tiny, suffocating houses with ugly, suffocating histories – little time warps of negativity that had long outlived their usefulness.

And this was a revelation he'd never seen coming – maybe he and Grace really did have some common ground, something he'd never even dared to hope for.

He looked around the room and saw an easel, tablets, and a table covered with art supplies.

'Don't tell me there's another dead body in there.'

Magozzi looked over his shoulder with a funny smile. 'Check this out, Gino.' He stepped aside and gestured to the sketch pad on the easel. Gino saw his own face staring back at him, precisely, perfectly rendered in charcoal.

'Well. Isn't that something. Think she has a crush on me?'

Magozzi nodded. 'The only possible explanation.' He walked back to the laundry room and Gino followed. 'You do realize we have a pattern emerging here.'

Gino rocked back and forth on his heels. 'Of course I do. Chinchilla lady at the Keller house. She was there to kill Alvin Keller, one of the original H-bomb scientists.'

'We don't know that for sure.'

'Pretend we do. So, somebody stops chinchilla lady with a .22 before she can kill Alvin. Then, at our very own feet, at this very minute, we have airport guy. He was here to kill Lydia – pretend we know that. Somebody stopped *him* with a .22. Coincidence? Hell no. What we've got here are two sets of killers – one set is trying to kill the descendants, and the other set is trying to save them, and don't even ask me who the players are because it's as obvious as a black cat on a snowbank and you know it. Chinchilla lady sealed that up and slapped a bow on it. Americans, Russians. Mini Cold War.'

Magozzi looked down at the airport guy. After listening to Gino's tangled reasoning, looking at a dead body was almost restful. 'So you're saying the Russians are trying to kill all the descendants. And probably the last two surviving original scientists.'

'Of course. The Russians are always the bad guys.'

'And they're killing them why?'

'Well, I haven't quite thought that through, but let's face facts – the original scientists, the architects of the Sixth Idea, whatever it is, all worked for the U.S. government and lived here unmolested for the last sixty years. So did their families. Then, suddenly, the Sixth Idea appears on the Web courtesy of Charles Spencer, and somebody starts bumping off the kids and grandkids of these guys and stealing their computers and papers. Are the Americans killing their own citizens? Of course not. So that leaves the Russians – they want the Sixth Idea, and they'll do anything to get it.'

Magozzi tried to grimace away a growing headache. He wanted to curl up in a ball in the corner, but when Gino was on a fishing expedition for mermaids, you had to throw in a courtesy line. 'How is killing everybody with any possible knowledge of the Sixth Idea going to help the Russians get it?'

Gino cocked a brow. 'Excellent question. So let's change things up and say the Russians and the Americans have the Sixth Idea. That means we're looking at a third party. The ayatollah of Crazy-stan heard about the Sixth Idea and he's pulling out all the stops to get in on the action. Who wants Crazy-stan to have the Sixth Idea? Nobody. Safer to kill everybody who might know something than to let things get into the wrong hands.'

'So the Russians and the Americans are killing everybody?'

'No way. Remember, the Russians are the bad guys. And there's some brave American operative out there with a .22, operating in the shadows, saving the day, saving Alvin Keller and Arthur Friedman and Lydia Ascher from getting kidnapped and brought back to Crazy-stan for torture. Or killed by the Russians to shut them up.'

'Gino.'

'What?'

'You're kind of going off the reservation.'

He lifted his shoulders. 'Just thinking out loud.'

# Thirty-Five

Max sat in his SUV across the lake from Lydia Ascher's house, watching the police fan out across her property. The onslaught of emergency vehicles had been relentless – he was impressed by the rapid response and strong presence of this rural force. Lydia Ascher would be safe tonight.

A few hundred yards away, three ice fishermen were huddled in the openings of portable fish shacks, ignoring their lines as they gawked at the dramatic spectacle across the lake. They hadn't noticed his presence, but even if they had, this vehicle would disappear soon, and so would Max.

He put the SUV in gear and gently eased off the shoulder and onto the small stripe of snow-covered tar that encircled the lake, taking one last, wistful look at the fishermen. He hadn't thought about it in years and years, but as a young boy, during better times for his family, Max had spent a lot of time ice fishing on the Moskva River with his father. They would sit outside on overturned buckets in the bitter cold, pulling carp and bream and pike out of the slushy holes in the ice. Sometimes they would roast them over scraps of wood right on the snowy riverbank while they drank tea from an old steel thermos and gnawed on black bread. If there was a surplus of fish, they'd bring them home for his mother and grandmother to pickle. He'd especially liked the pickled pike.

Good memories, he realized, and decided that once he settled in at his Montana ranch for good, he'd buy all the best gear and start ice fishing the two lakes on his property. Why hadn't he thought of that before?

# Thirty-Six

Lydia was dwelling in a strange limbo between numbness and panic and she couldn't still her mind, especially now that she was alone. Well, she wasn't alone exactly – the deputies were just outside and the Minneapolis detectives were downstairs – but without any immediate distraction, she was fixating on the man from the airport. It was no coincidence he'd been here in her house. That meant he'd followed her or hunted her down somehow, and why was that? The conclusion seemed obvious: he'd been following Chuck, had probably killed him, and Wally, too, and she was next. And what did they all have in common? They were all descendants of the men who'd worked on the hydrogen bomb. Otis had just been in the wrong place at the wrong time.

The problem was, if you grew up in a great family, in a great town, with virtually no crime, in a great country where most everyone still put their hands over their hearts when a flag was presented, you just weren't prepared for people you'd never met trying to kill you.

She remembered her mother's stories about the weekly drills in her grade school, when duck and cover was preached over and over again. Duck under your desk, cover the backs of your little heads so the big, bad atomic bombs won't hurt you. And then, after a successful drill, the little darlings were praised for their obedience and rewarded with a film show.

In the fourth grade, they showed us wonderful, child-appropriate films in the grade school's plush auditorium. Films like the *Green Grass of Wyoming*. It had horses and sweet families and cute young men. There was a wonderful new film every Thursday.

But when we moved up to junior high, they must have decided we were old enough to terrify because they only showed films in the classroom with clickety-click projectors on portable screens. It was the same film over and over. A blinding explosion, wooden structures blasted and disintegrated by a rush of fiery wind, trees bent to the ground, just like the buildings, just like the little goats tethered beside them. There one minute, gone the next.

'Duck and cover,' a stern narrator pronounced, and the film shifted to a classroom of youngsters under the fragile wooden desks, hands laced over the backs of their heads, perfectly safe.

Her mother had covered her eyes when she'd finished telling Lydia the story, and tears leaked through her fingers. She'd been in her fifties then, still quaking with the terror of a child who had been taught that there were terrible people in the world who would heedlessly bomb ten-year-old girls fresh from recess.

Until now, she hadn't thought much about that tale of her mother's childhood, a childhood cut short by the atom bomb and the pervasive horror of the Cold War. How must it have felt to her mother, an innocent child, waiting for immolation? Perhaps just like she felt now, trying desperately to make sense of strangers willing to kill.

The last thing she needed was coffee, and yet here she was, walking to the kitchen to pour herself a cup. It didn't make any sense, but it was something to do, something to keep her mind and hands moving and occupied. Small tasks. Pour the coffee, add cream and sugar, stir vigorously. Wipe the counter while you're at it, and water the poinsettias . . .

She jumped a little when she heard footsteps on the basement stairs, and her mind started playing a black-and-white horror movie of zombies, slowly dragging themselves up the stairs to eat her flesh.

But it was just Deputy Harmon. 'Ms. Ascher, I have to go outside, but Detectives Magozzi and Rolseth will be up shortly. Will you be all right?'

Lydia nodded. 'Yes. Thank you.'

Once the front door had closed behind him, she started pacing in tight circles, her eyes darting from corner to corner as if she would find answers there. Or maybe zombies.

'Ms. Ascher?'

Lydia spun around and saw Detectives Magozzi and Rolseth standing at the top of the stairs. 'He was here to kill me, wasn't he?' she said.

Magozzi's thoughts started cycloning. Where the hell did you start? How did you tell someone they might be on some phantom's hit list? 'We can't dismiss it as a possibility. We just saw the security footage from the Chatham Hotel the night Mr. Spencer was murdered. The man in your basement, the man from the airport, was caught on film, standing outside his hotel room door with a gun.'

She raised her eyes to his and as young as she was, he saw in that moment that she had grown up, and sadly, grown old. Perfect childhood, perfect life, perfect certainty that this world would always be that way, suddenly swirling down and out of her eyes like water following a drain.

He recognized what he saw in her empty stare as what he had felt at his first homicide scene years ago. A deadening shock as he'd looked down at a tiny child, dead by his mother's hand. That was the day the world had stopped making sense. And for Lydia Ascher, that day was now.

Lydia sank down into a chair at the kitchen table. 'What's happening, Detectives? Tell me everything.'

And Magozzi and Gino did, because she deserved to know. And amazingly, things came out a lot smoother than Magozzi imagined they would, in part because she'd been in on it from the beginning and knew the backstory.

Unfortunately, all of it was too incredible to comprehend at this point, no matter how you told it, and as traumatized as she was by the nasty surprise she'd found in her basement, Lydia seemed to switch off halfway through the telling. Her eyes went blank and she looked down into her empty coffee cup, just shaking her head. But she came back to life when they started telling her about Ed Farrell's murder in Cheeton, the other victims who were either murdered or missing, and the connection they all had to American Iron Foundry.

'American Iron Foundry is where my grandfather worked. And where Chuck's father worked, only not in Cheeton – they were both on the East Coast. New York and New Jersey. Maybe other places, too. From what I know from my mother, the government manufactured bomb components in plants scattered all over the country. So this is about the bomb after all?'

'Actually, we think it's all about the Sixth Idea.'

'So somebody wants me dead. The same people who probably killed Chuck and Wally and the man up in Cheeton. Because of something I know nothing about.'

'That's all speculation, but we're erring on the side of caution. For obvious reasons.'

'And you have no idea who wants me dead, or who killed the others?'

'We're working around the clock to find out. So are a lot of other people, both law enforcement and private individuals.'

She let out a weary sigh and started worrying a yarn snowman that was sitting on top of the table. 'This is hopeless. Because *I don't know anything*. And neither did Chuck. Or Wally.'

Magozzi saw a single tear splash down onto the oak table and felt his heart squeeze. He and Gino were both as frustrated as she was. The only difference was, nobody was trying to kill them. At least not yet. 'Ms. Ascher, this is overwhelming right now, but it's anything but hopeless. You have a lot of evidence in your basement that might help us . . .'

'Like what?'

'Ballistics, for one thing. And the man from the airport. If we can identify him, we're halfway there.'

'And what if you can't identify him? What if ballistics doesn't tell you anything?'

Gino clasped his hands together and leaned across the table, and Magozzi let him take over. He was the father of a teenage daughter, a blue-ribbon husband, and he was ultimately more qualified than he was to comfort a woman in distress. 'There is an end to this, Ms. Ascher, you have our word. And we're going to keep you safe until we get to that end. In our line of work, you gather puzzle pieces until you can envision the finished picture, and now we have some more pieces to work with. Maybe it's the same with your drawing. Like you get the eyes right, but you can't figure out the mouth until you draw an ear or an eyebrow, and then the whole face comes together, just like that.'

Lydia cocked her head at Gino. 'You have a unique perspective, Detective Rolseth.'

Magozzi was watching in amazement. With a lame metaphor, Gino had calmed and engaged her.

The man had lessons to teach. 'Ms. Ascher, you mentioned you had some old papers and photographs that belonged to your grandfather that were similar to the material Charles Spencer showed you on the plane. Perhaps we could go through those with you and see if something grabs our attention.'

'Of course. It's in a box right behind your chairs, Detectives. But there's probably nothing there you haven't already seen in Chuck's paperwork.'

'We never found Mr. Spencer's paperwork. Almost all of his personal effects were stolen, except for a small suitcase in his hotel room.'

'Oh. I didn't realize. Let me get it for you.' She walked around the table and froze, her gaze fixed on the floor. 'It was right there,' she said, pointing to an empty corner.

'Maybe you moved it?'

Lydia shook her head slowly. 'No. No, definitely not. It was there when I left the house today, I'm positive. Somebody stole it. And it obviously wasn't the man from the airport.' She abruptly leaned between them both and started frenetically shuffling things on the kitchen table, oblivious to the fact that she was inappropriately situated between two strangers, bumping and jostling them.

She calmed down when her hand found an old paperback. 'This is all I have left,' she mumbled.

'One of your favorites?' Magozzi asked after a skeptical glance at what was clearly a dated pulp fiction romance. His very own aunt, ostensibly a prude of the highest order, had kept a treasure trove of these novels under her bed, which Magozzi had found as a precocious eleven-year-old, and received a sound beating with a flyswatter for his trouble. God, he had hated that woman . . .

'No,' Lydia interrupted his reverie. 'This was in the box my grandfather left to my mother in his will. All those journals with formulas and equations and then this.' She held up the book. 'A cheap paperback of nonsense. It's baffling.'

She told them what her grandfather had told her mother – to hide the book, to keep it from the eyes of all others, and then pass it on to her own children.

Magozzi closed his eyes, let his mind ramble wherever it wanted to go. 'Someone took the box of journals.'

Lydia looked down at the table, watching her fingers move aimlessly across the wood-grained surface. 'Apparently.'

'But they missed this.'

Lydia exhaled a long breath. 'I was curious about it, so I took it out of the box.'

'So they saw the box filled with all the journals and never realized this book was part of it.' He wasn't making a case, just thinking out loud.

'Maybe.'

'It looks like a book you were reading – like a lot of books people read, then lay on a table or chair to pick up later.'

'This one is a little different.' And then Lydia told them about what her mother had said; about the five-and-dime, the real places her mother had known and lived in, and that she thought her father had written the book.

'Do you mind if we take this along? We have some friends who might be able to make sense of it.'

Lydia nodded. 'Please. Take it.'

Gino looked out the window where Deputy Harmon and a few other officers were gathering around a squad car. 'Ms. Ascher, we need to speak with Deputy Harmon for a few minutes. He's arranging a safe place for you tonight. Around-the-clock protection until we can figure this thing out.'

She let out a shuddering sigh of relief. 'I never even thought about where I'd spend the night. All I knew for sure was that I couldn't stay here.'

'They'll do a good job. We'll make sure of it.'

'Yes. Thank you, Detectives.'

Lydia's yard was bordered with a dense woods shouldered with white pines which were soughing in the wind. It was a cold sound with a brutal accompaniment of icy pellets smacking against any piece of exposed skin.

Deputy Harmon was getting out of his squad when Gino and Magozzi approached. His face was red from the cold and he kept shifting his weight from foot to foot. 'The sheriff is getting everything set up at the motel, Detectives.'

'You mind if we take a look before we leave?'

'Hell no. You see something we missed, we welcome the input.'

They all turned when they heard a vehicle coming down the snowy drive.

'BCA,' Gino said. 'Deputy Harmon, we'd like to stick around until we can get prints on the John Doe.'

'No problem.' He looked anxiously toward Lydia's house. 'Is Ms. Ascher all right?'

'She's fine, but you might want to let her know BCA is about to take over her house.'

'You got it, Detectives.'

Gino smiled a little as he watched him jog up the front walk. 'I think Deputy Harmon's smitten.'

'Nothing more powerful than the bond between a white knight and a damsel in distress,' Magozzi said and then cringed, because it had come out sounding a lot more cynical than he'd meant it.

'Speaking from experience?'

'Nope. Grace may have been running from killers half her life, but she's never been a damsel in distress. And I've never been accused of being a white knight.'

'Are you kidding? You're the second best cop on the force after me. Truth, justice, the American way.'

# Thirty-Seven

Zero studied the faces of his four numerically named colleagues. A week ago, those faces had been animated with confidence and excitement. Today, their expressions were a grim mélange of despair, desperation, and fear. Zero felt all those things, too, but anger trumped every other emotion. Although they were all equals in this legacy venture, he was first in command and things were suddenly starting to fall apart – under *his* watch. How had such a thing happened with unlimited resources and the finest talent at their disposal?

Since it was inconceivable that his own leadership ability was the issue, he placed the blame squarely on the shoulders of the other men. He folded his hands together tightly on the table and tried to keep his voice even as he addressed them. 'We have a monumental disaster on our hands, gentlemen. We've lost two people in the field and two physicists have disappeared into thin air. Lydia Ascher is still a liability, even more so now that she's involved with the two Minneapolis detectives working with Monkeewrench on the murders of Spencer and Luntz. We've all heard the audio from their conversations – they're getting too close for comfort. Of course, we're dead in the water now in that regard, because the detectives aren't using their cell phones anymore, and I wonder why?'

Three, a skinny, fussy man with a wispy mustache, spoke up. 'Monkeewrench. They found our wiretaps –'

'Of course they did. That was a rhetorical question,' Zero snapped. 'For now, forget about Monkeewrench and the detectives. The only thing we need to worry about is keeping this project safe and out of the hands of maniacs. You all understand what is at stake.' He paused, letting that sink in before he continued. 'We need to fix this and fix it fast.'

'Who is killing our people?' Two spoke up. 'We weren't anticipating outside interference, and aside from keeping our systems secure, that's our biggest problem right now.'

Zero nodded, reluctantly conceding the point – high-level assassins were difficult and dangerous to retain, and even more difficult to replace, and their roster was down by two. 'We need to find out, and we need to take care of it. And we need to stay invisible while we do it. We're in crisis management mode now, and we goddamn better do this right.'

# Thirty-Eight

There was a time long ago in Harley Davidson's life when he'd never aspired to be wealthy or successful or educated – all the things he was now. At sixteen, he'd never aspired to anything except finding a family, and that meant earning the right to fly colors as a Hells Angel, riding free on the open road without a care in the world, surrounded by a band of brothers – a family, for the first time in his life.

But his brothers in the Angels hadn't turned out to be the kind of family he'd had in mind, and the love wasn't unconditional – there were serious strings attached, prices he wasn't willing to pay. If it hadn't been for an old biker named Del, he probably wouldn't be alive right now, hacking into an Interpol server – all in the name of justice, of course. And even if he had survived, without Del, he probably wouldn't have gone to college in Atlanta, wouldn't have found his *real* people – Grace, Roadrunner, and Annie.

He hadn't thought about Del in a long time. But it seemed appropriate this Christmas, especially with half of Monkeewrench missing, which for some inexplicable reason was hitting him with melancholia. He'd always thought he loved the holiday so much because it was the perfect time to go way over the top and spread his embarrassment of riches. But it really wasn't that at all. Sure, Roadrunner could be a real pain in the ass sometimes, especially when they were working on a program together; and Annie was a supreme diva who loved to punch his buttons whenever the opportunity presented itself. But they were his family, his only family, the kind that did give you unconditional love, and he missed them being together as a unit.

'Harley? Are you busy?'

'Oh, hell yes, I'm over here committing all sorts of egregious cybercrimes that could put me in prison for a long time. What's up, Gracie?'

'I'm doing an autopsy on the malware that took Spencer's website down. It's the same variant that corrupted the Chatham's server.'

Harley got up from his chair and covered the distance to Grace's computer station in a few Herculean strides. He crouched down and stared at her screen for a few minutes, then popped back up. 'That's a Stuxnet hybrid, like the one that wiped out a bunch of Iranian nuke centrifuges a few years back. A totally surgical virus.'

Grace looked up at him. 'And a virus that originated with our government. Of course, the Stuxnet genie is out of the bottle now and anybody can riff off it.'

'Sure. So what's the timeline on the virus?'

'The infection started not too long after Spencer's website went live. He was on somebody's radar a few months ago. But the Chatham's server didn't get compromised until the day he was murdered.'

'Jesus. Spencer was a dead man walking. They gave his computer cancer, put it in remission, and when the time was right, they killed the website. And him along with it.'

'And his friend Wally Luntz. And they tried to kill any video evidence that would indicate Spencer's murder was anything but a simple tourist mugging gone bad.'

'So who is "they"?'

Grace sighed. 'I still can't trace the source.'

'Goddamnit, this is turning into a real ball of vipers –' Grace and Harley both looked up abruptly when an angry alarm went off on Harley's computer. All their computers had very specific alarms – gentle pings or bells or chimes to indicate new incoming information, new connections made by the Beast, and a myriad of other harmless activities their computers engaged in while they weren't being monitored by their users. And then there were the loud, angry klaxons that warned them whatever they were working on was putting their system in peril of a potential security breach. It was a safety measure they'd put into place to conceal their illegal intrusions.

'Shit, that's my Interpol hack,' Harley huffed, running across the room and initiating a self-destruct on the program he had executed.

Grace dashed after him, and the thirty feet of maple flooring between their stations seemed like a football field. 'Are we secure?'

Harley let out a heavy sigh. 'We're good. Safe.' He reached over to his printer, which was spitting out paper. He scanned the pages for a few moments, then passed them to Grace. 'Natalia Smirnova's Interpol file.'

# Thirty-Nine

So what do you think?' Gino asked as Magozzi hopped into the sedan.

'Jefferson County pulled out all the stops. I don't think we could have done much better.' He gestured at all the squad cars surrounding the motel, at the policemen and-women making rounds of the property, inside and out. 'Nobody in their right mind would go anywhere near this much police presence. Plus, the media's going to be all over this place in a heartbeat, which is another great deterrent. They might not know what the story is, but twenty-some cop cars surrounding a little cinder-block motel is going to grab some attention.'

Gino nodded and made a careful turn onto the highway. The roads had been cleared, but there was still an icy sheen of snowpack that the salt hadn't eaten away yet. 'Yeah. Lydia's going to be okay. The only problem is, Jefferson County — hell, no county — can keep this kind of thing up for long. We've got a bigger problem, and that's hanging the sun on this thing, because until we do, our happy hunters are still out there hiding in the dark and our fair heroine is under grievous threat.'

Magozzi arched a brow at him. 'Good God, what cable channel are you watching now?'

'No channel. Helen's reading *The Mists of Avalon*. Aloud.'

Magozzi grinned. He loved these little glimpses into Gino's home life. 'Well, except for the first part, which was all cop speak, it was kind of poetic, Gino. It's bad, but still.'

'Yeah, well, exhaustion has a tendency to warp my mind.'

Magozzi grabbed one of the cell phones Harley had given them. 'I'll call Monkeewrench and let them know we're going to drop off Lydia's book. Maybe they have something new for us.'

Harley answered on the first ring.

'Magozzi?'

'Hey, Harley, I've got you on speaker. Gino and I are heading back to the city.'

'Stop here on the way in.'

'We were planning on it.'

'Good. Drive safe and see you soon. Bye.'

When Magozzi hung up, Gino gave him a sidelong glance. 'You've never had such a short conversation with Harley in your life.'

'Something's up.'

Once they hit the freeway, the roads cleared up. The plows had been busy and the snow had finally stopped. Still, it took them a good hour and a half to drive to Harley's.

Magozzi and Gino had become inured to the spectacle of the Summit Avenue mansion over the years, but no matter how many times you'd seen the place decked out for any given season, the Christmas pageantry always took your breath away. Especially at night, when thousands of tiny lights twinkled in the trees like a galaxy of stars.

They didn't have to knock; Grace and Harley opened up the big double doors and ushered them inside. Magozzi didn't like the way both their eyes were coursing the yard beyond the front steps. He also didn't like the fact that Harley was wearing his weapon. Grace was never without her gun and he and Gino were used to that, but Harley didn't possess her level of paranoia and rarely carried. Especially in his own house, which was more secure than most banks.

'Come in, guys,' he said, closing and locking the doors behind them.

'What's wrong?' Magozzi asked, looking directly at Grace. Her blue eyes were dark and vigilant and decidedly troubled.

'Is Lydia Ascher all right?'

'She's in protective custody.'

Grace's posture relaxed, but only slightly. 'Good. Let's go sit.'

They followed Harley to a sunken seating area lined with bookshelves that were crammed with everything from priceless volumes to paperback fiction. He poured four glasses of wine from a decanter and sank into a leather sofa. 'We found out a little bit more about Natalia Smirnova, your chinchilla lady. McLaren already told you she was a Russian national – we found out she was former KGB, only they don't call themselves the KGB anymore. Interpol registered a death certificate for her three years ago, but no record of who filed it. And that's all we could get on her before we had to sever our connection and cover our tracks, but we'll keep working on it. So what was an ex-KGB agent doing in Alvin Keller's house?'

Magozzi stared down at the garnet red wine in his glass. It reminded him of blood, which made his stomach churn. But still, he took a sip. You never turned down wine at Harley's because you might never again in a lifetime get a chance to sip a rare vintage like the ones he always offered. 'She was either looking for something or she was there to kill him. Or maybe she was there to kidnap him.'

Nobody said anything for a long time. A grandfather clock in the corner of the room gently ticked down the minutes.

'How far do you want to take this?' Grace finally asked quietly.

Magozzi looked at her abruptly. 'I don't want you or Harley to take any more risks. Period. This is starting to blow up.'

Grace narrowed her eyes at him. It was about as emotional as she ever got. 'And we don't want you two taking any more risks, but it's what we all do. Everybody in this room is going to follow this through to the end, you know that, Magozzi. Whoever is behind this will go down. Hard.'

'Amen,' Harley said, getting up to refill his glass. 'In a big-ass fireball. This is total bullshit. The way I'm seeing things now, innocent people are getting killed so a bunch of limp-dick bureaucrats can try to get their hands on some nuclear Viagra. Fuck them. Did you get any IDs on the two vics at Lydia Ascher's house?'

'One was her elderly neighbor. He went over there for dinner and walked into a bad situation. The man from the airport is a John Doe. No prints on file.'

'Shit,' Harley mumbled. 'You got *anything* new we can work with?'

Magozzi suddenly felt the bulge of Lydia's paperback in his coat pocket, the last thing left of her family legacy that hadn't been stolen. 'Might be a long shot, but yes.'

# Forty

Lydia was sitting in an interior room in the Lady Slipper Motel that adjoined one of the guest rooms. The artist in her saw the potential of the space to become a cozy little library nook, but the current owners were using it for storage, which made sense. Visiting hunters and fishermen, the lifeblood of business here, didn't want or need a cozy little library nook.

It didn't exactly qualify as luxury accommodations, but it had some unused furniture, including a twin bed, a door that locked, and no windows, which was the height of luxury if you were hiding from bad guys who wanted to kill you.

Come to the posh, cinder-block Lady Slipper Motel and stay in our fabulous Presidential Suite, which boasts the ultimate safe room. Spare towels, bedding, and a housekeeping cart are included in the price!

There was a part of her that found her current situation ridiculous. Of course nobody was trying to kill her. She hadn't done anything wrong.

She didn't know anything about any Sixth Idea, didn't even possess her grandfather's documents anymore. She'd met Chuck Spencer on a plane, had coffee with him after the flight, big deal. And the spooky man from the airport was dead, there couldn't possibly be an army of killers out there waiting to take his place. That was preposterous.

But on the flipside, she could connect the dots, just like the detectives had. Chuck had started some kind of a chain reaction, and innocent people were dying. People just like her. People with her same family history.

Deputy Harmon was right outside the door in the guest room, and hadn't moved from his station since they'd arrived, which made her feel safe. He'd been with her from the beginning, and she trusted him, and he'd also let her keep her gun, which scared the hell out of her. Wasn't that a just-in-case admission that maybe, just maybe, someone could get past her protector and burst into her sanctuary? Of course it was.

'Are you okay, Lydia?' he asked through the closed door.

'I'm okay, Deputy Harmon. How about you? Security detail is kind of boring, isn't it?'

Harmon was in an uncomfortable chair positioned between the door and a dresser. The room was dark except for the faint glow of the bathroom light leaking under the closed door. 'Keeping people safe is never boring.'

'You're doing a good job so far.' Her hands were restless and she suddenly wished she'd brought a sketch pad. She'd seen enough of Deputy Harmon today to draw him blindfolded. 'Do you think this is all a little overkill? I mean, we don't know if I'm really a target.'

'You hit it – we don't know, which is all the more reason to take every precaution. The Minneapolis detectives were right about that.'

'But what happens tomorrow? Or the next day? I can't stay here forever, and neither can you and all the other officers who are watching over me tonight. I'm not the only person who lives in this county.'

Deputy Harmon had been so focused on keeping Lydia safe in the here and now that he hadn't really thought about what would happen next. She was right – most of Jefferson County's force was here tonight, but their job was to serve and protect everybody, not just one person. This was a temporary measure, but what was the long-term plan? He'd have to ask Sheriff Gannet about that. 'We'll do what we have to do to keep you safe, Lydia, I promise.'

Lydia smiled. She didn't have any answers right now – nobody did – but she did feel certain about one thing: Deputy Harmon was a devoted cop and a sincere and lovely man. She found herself wondering if he was married, which seemed totally inappropriate under the circumstances. 'Thank you for that.'

'It's getting late. Do you think you can sleep?'

'Are you serious?'

He chuckled at that. For all this woman had been through today, Lord, how resilient – brave, a little funny, and just as sweet as she could be.

Suddenly his eyes shifted to the drape-shrouded window. Moonlight was coming in through a tiny gap in the drapery, laying a white stripe across the room. Just a sliver, really, but how the hell had he missed this in his pre-check of the room?

Because it hadn't been very dark then, he forgave himself. The moon hadn't risen yet. But it had now. Shit.

He crawled on his belly like an inchworm to where the drape pull hung. It was just a foot out of his reach and he had to rise from his crouch to tug at the cord to close the curtains tight.

'Deputy?' Lydia whispered. 'Is something wrong?'

*

Nearly half a mile across the lake, beyond the houses on the shore, across a road and then up onto a small, snow-stuffed hill, the man lay on his stomach. The sniper rifle was secure and rock-steady on its tripod, which had been no mean feat in this goddamned, freezing white place that was uninhabitable compared to his New Mexico home. The sooner he completed this task perfectly, the sooner he would be back in the southwestern sun.

Pinpointing the correct motel room had been difficult, but not impossible. This small-town, rural community had an impressive police force that covered all the bases they could imagine, and they'd done a damn fine job of it. He hadn't expected that.

And then, through the amazing scope of his amazing rifle, he saw draperies move and the man shadow behind them.

'Deputy?' Lydia whispered again, a little louder, but her query was interrupted by a sharp crack-ing sound that almost stopped her heart and sent her scrambling to the back of the room. And then she heard Deputy Harmon cry out, followed by the sound of something, surely him, hitting the floor.

*You stay in this room no matter what happens, and if something goes wrong, which it won't, make sure the door is locked and don't come out until you hear my voice telling you it's clear, understand?*

*Yes, Deputy Harmon.*

*Because if a bad guy made it in here by some miracle, the first words out of his mouth would be that he was a Jefferson County deputy sheriff, here to take care of you, maybe move you someplace else, who knows? Don't believe him. You wait to hear my voice. And if somebody tries to break into the room, you shoot through the door. Period. Because it won't be one of ours. Every officer on duty here knows where you are and that you're armed.*

Remembering every word of that warning lecture replayed in her mind in less than a second. It was the movie equivalent of 'Don't open the door at the top of the stairs.' Everyone knows not to open the door at the top of the stairs, but all the stupid heroines did it anyway, to their peril. Not Lydia.

Her conviction had been so strong, she'd thought, but then she'd heard Deputy Harmon cry out, and her conviction vanished in an instant. When he didn't answer her strident whisper, she opened the door, saw his crumpled figure beneath the window,

238

and scrambled over there on her hands and knees, because you didn't just sit cowering in a storage room when someone was in trouble. You threw good sense to the wind without ever considering consequences.

There was blood on the carpet under his head, but not too much. She'd seen too much blood when her mother had fallen down the basement stairs and fractured her skull on an uneven ridge of concrete. Lydia had been eight years old then, not nearly old enough to know what to do, but by some grace of God, she knew enough to grab folded towels from the laundry basket and slip them under her mother's head. Everyone had thought she was so smart, trying to staunch the bleeding like that, but the truth was, she was trying to soak up the blood puddling, a lot of blood puddling, on her mother's scrupulously scrubbed basement floor so she wouldn't get mad at the mess.

Deputy Harmon wasn't bleeding so profusely, so she ignored his head wound for the moment, raced to turn on a bedside lamp, then back to his side. She pressed a button on his shoulder unit, hoping someone would hear her, and said with surprising calmness, 'Officer down. Deputy Harmon has been shot.'

There was an instant response to her call from outside. Lights and noise; sirens blaring; men shouting; pounding, running footsteps in the hall. Lydia poked her head up just enough to peer out the window, and then there was a second cracking sound and the window dissolved, sending a shower of tiny, relatively harmless pieces of safety glass into the air. In a flash, she had the sudden, horrible realization that those shots had been meant for her, and if she wasn't safe here with all these police surrounding her, where would she be safe?

*Nowhere,* she thought as she threw herself over Deputy Harmon's unconscious body. The caretaker in her did it to protect this wounded man from the flying glass; the survivor in her did it to avoid getting shot.

Max was standing on a sheltered, snowy hill a half a mile across the lake from the Lady Slipper Motel. He wasn't supposed to be here, but as he'd been driving away earlier, past the gawking ice fishermen on Lydia Ascher's lake, a few things had rung false about one of the men. He'd made a last-minute decision to stay on and watch him, and the decision had ultimately been a fortuitous one.

He decided to leave the sniper's body – it would be just one more mystery for the local police to try to solve, although this would certainly end up as another cold case, because Max didn't make mistakes. But the rifle he would take. It was American made, a very fine Barrett with a Swarovski scope, and it would most certainly come in handy at the ranch.

# Forty-One

Magozzi didn't even remember crawling into bed, which meant he'd been asleep before his head hit the pillow. He slept hard and dreamlessly, but at some point during the night, jagged little vignettes started gnawing away at the edges of his subconscious. In one of them, he was in Donnie Bergstrom's basement as Gino had described it, staring at rows and rows of cages where chinchillas sat, staring at him with big, sad brown eyes. And then the chinchillas started scurrying in their little prisons as a klaxon sounded.

Magozzi jolted awake and tried to reorient himself in the dark. The klaxon from his dream was actually his phone – one of the burners Harley had given him – and it was ringing relentlessly on the bedside table. He squinted at the screen, but couldn't bring his vision into focus. 'Magozzi, here.'

'Detective, this is Sheriff Gannet from Jefferson County. I'm calling you from one of those phones you gave me. With all due respect, I thought you were being a little paranoid today, but I'm grateful for it now.'

Magozzi sat up and felt his stomach knot up. 'Sheriff, is something wrong?'

'You could say that. Somebody took a couple shots at Lydia Ascher's motel room.'

'Jesus. Is she all right?'

'She's unhurt, but Deputy Harmon caught a bullet. Got real lucky – it just grazed his scalp. We recovered the bullets in the room. They were NATO rounds, Detective. Fire came from a hill across the lake, where we found an empty tripod and a man in winter camo, shot in the back of the head. No rifle. Whoever killed him must have taken it.'

Magozzi was out of bed, looking for jeans, a T-shirt, his brain, anything that would be useful. 'Jesus. A sniper?'

'Couldn't be anything else. Detective, I don't know about you, but we're in over our heads here. You saw our setup at the motel – nobody could have gotten within five hundred yards of that place. But how were we supposed to anticipate a sniper?'

'No way you could have anticipated that. Were you able to ID him?'

'No, I'm sorry to say. Prints didn't pop up anywhere, there was nothing on his person. I sent my men out to look for abandoned vehicles – the guy had to get here somehow, right? But that hasn't turned up anything either. He either teleported here or he had a ride.'

Magozzi finally found a discarded pair of jeans and struggled into them. 'Sheriff, the weapon that killed the sniper – any guess on the caliber?'

'That's another thing – looks like a .22. The same caliber that killed the two men in Lydia's basement. What the hell are we dealing with, Detective?'

'We don't know exactly, but the picture's starting to fill in. Sheriff, tell me one thing – is Lydia safe for now?'

'As safe as she can be. She's in the hospital, and we have a real heavy presence on her floor, and outside at all the entry points. But the thing is, we had that motel covered seven ways from Sunday and that didn't work out so well. Do you have some alternatives in mind? Because whoever is after her means business. The only thing on our side right now is that Lydia Ascher apparently has some homicidal guardian angel with a .22 out there keeping her alive, and they obviously know something that we don't. Like the fact that there was a sniper waiting to take a crack at her.'

'Agreed. Let me make some calls and I'll get back to you.'

Magozzi heard the sheriff let out a heavy sigh. 'When this is all over, you owe me a pitcher of beer and a full briefing.'

'You have my word.'

'I appreciate it.'

Magozzi hung up and stared down at the phone. The sheriff was a sharp guy – by all appearances, Lydia did have a guardian angel out there somewhere. Maybe the same guardian angel who had killed an ex-KGB agent in Alvin Keller's living room with a .22.

The morning sludge was still thick in his head, and it took him a few moments to realize that he couldn't pull up his contact list on his phone because it *wasn't* his phone, it was the burner Harley had given him. His personal phone was down-stairs, which seemed like miles away, and so was his archaic address book – the kind you actually put entries in with an ink pen. Or maybe he'd thrown it away, deeming it a useless, redundant artifact, he couldn't remember.

There had been a time when he'd had Chief Malcherson's private number committed to mem-ory. There had been a time when he'd had a lot of things like phone numbers committed to memory. But like everybody else in the world, smartphones and computers had eliminated his need to retain any information.

He suddenly felt like an intellectual cripple. Electronics had the allure of granting power and superiority until you didn't have them anymore. Then you became the digitally challenged version of somebody who couldn't feed themselves when a natural disaster shut down the local grocery store for a couple of days and Domino's wasn't delivering.

He dialed one of the few numbers he still did have memorized because he'd called it endlessly over the course of so many years, but Gino's personal cell went straight to voice mail. He thought twice about leaving a message, didn't do it because what if Harley was wrong and someone had figured out how to tap into burner phones? – then got angry with himself because paranoia had absconded with his peace of mind over the course of twenty-four hours. It had happened just like that. In the deepest, darkest, most selfish part of his mind, he realized that he'd always been impatient with Grace MacBride's paranoia, even though she'd had good reason – she'd spent ten years of her life running from a nameless, faceless killer. Now he felt nothing but empathy.

Gino called back immediately, his voice croaking with interrupted sleep. 'Leo. What's up?'

'Somebody took a couple shots at Lydia tonight. A sniper, who got a .22 slug to the back of his head for his trouble, which probably saved her life. No prints on file, no positive ID.'

'Shit.'

'We've gotta talk to Malcherson ASAP. This thing is running off the rails. Meet me at Pig's Eye.'

'Yeah. Okay. Give me half an hour.'

# Forty-Two

The Pig's Eye Diner was open all night, and did a brisk business after two a.m. bar close. But an hour before sunrise, the inebriates were long gone, and Magozzi, Gino, and Chief of Police Malcherson were the only customers.

Meeting with the chief in any environment other than his perfectly ordered, spotlessly clean office was disturbing. He was starkly out of place in a greasy spoon with paper napkin dispensers and plastic condiment squeeze bottles sitting on Formica tabletops. The ripped vinyl upholstery in the booth they inhabited was an affront to his finely tailored suit; in fact, it probably wanted to jump off his body and catch the next flight back to Milan.

Malcherson was a solid, stoic third-generation Swede whose coloring reflected his heritage – intense blue eyes and blond hair that was just starting to gray at the temples. It suddenly occurred to Magozzi in his predawn delirium that maybe the blue and yellow colors of the Swedish flag had been selected to reflect the genetic traits of its people.

The man was normally unflappable, but once he and Gino got to the juicy part of the narrative that involved an ex-KGB agent with a federal access restraint on her fingerprints and a dead sniper, he unraveled in his very special Malcherson way, which meant he set down his fork, abandoned his ham and cheese omelet completely, and stared silently down into his coffee mug for a long time.

'Impressive that you were able to ascertain the dead woman at the Keller house was ex-KGB when there was a federal cover on her fingerprints and you had absolutely no access to her identity,' he warned them. 'I'm not going to ask how you obtained this information, but I trust you will omit this detail from your reports.'

'Yes sir,' Magozzi reassured him, hearing the subtext loud and clear. Malcherson knew damn well the information could have only come from Monkeewrench. They'd all walked this gray line together before. 'We can't prove it definitively, so it won't be noted in our reports. We just told you because we wanted to emphasize the urgency of the situation.'

Malcherson's shoulders had been riding his earlobes for a while, and Magozzi was happy to see them drop slightly. Everybody's asses were covered.

'The first priority is Lydia Ascher's safety,' he finally said. 'MPD doesn't have the manpower or the facilities, and we can't trust the postulation that she has some sort of protector out there, watching over her.' He looked up, and his bloodhound face seemed even more challenged by gravity than usual. 'This chain of events has become bigger than the sum of its parts. I have to inform Special Agent in Charge Shafer. Whatever your private opinions about the FBI are, they are well-versed in witness protection. And if there is some kind of . . . international angle, it should be addressed on a federal level.'

'No argument from us, sir,' Gino said.

'In the meantime, we still have three unsolved homicides in our immediate jurisdiction, possibly multiple killers, two missing elderly men, and not a single piece of conclusive evidence.'

Magozzi wasn't sure if that was an accusation, a dismissal, or a neutral statement of fact. 'We're hoping ballistics and crime-scene analysis from Lydia Ascher's house will yield something positive, sir.'

'I'm not assailing your deductive or investigative skills, Detective Magozzi. I've read every single one of your reports thus far, and you've taken what little information the scenes have yielded and gone as far as you possibly could. And that fact, combined with these recent developments, makes it extremely difficult to contrive a theory that doesn't involve some sort of larger conspiracy. Especially in view of the fact that not only were your phones compromised, the entire MPD communications system was.'

Gino's jaw dropped. 'Jesus . . . Jeez.' He quickly corrected his language because profanity was absolutely unacceptable to the chief. 'Sorry, Chief, but this is kind of unbelievable.'

'All of it is unbelievable, and extremely troubling.'

Magozzi's scrambled eggs suddenly felt like a ball of barbed wire in his stomach. 'This all started with Charles Spencer, and the only reason I can think of to monitor us and MPD is because we're working all the connected cases. Like somebody wants to make sure we don't solve our murders. And frankly, they're doing a pretty good job so far.'

Malcherson tapped his fingers on the table in a measured cadence. 'I have our IT people trying to trace the intrusion, but they haven't had much luck so far.'

'Monkeewrench is looking into the same angle – the attack on our personal phones, on the Chatham's server, and the one that took down Charles Spencer's website. Apparently, it's all pretty sophisticated.'

Malcherson pushed his coffee mug away, stood, and laid a twenty on the table. 'I'll be in touch, Detectives. If I were you, I'd expect an FBI debriefing in the near future. Was I clear when I told you to omit any speculative evidence from your reports?'

Magozzi nodded. 'Crystal clear, Chief.'

'Indeed.'

Gino watched him walk out the door, then put his head in his hands. 'Oh, God. Another FBI debriefing. Isn't that why we took vacation this month, because we were so traumatized by the last one?'

'I don't want to wait for a formal debriefing. Let's call Agent Dahl right now.'

'Dahl is pretty high up on the food chain to be dealing with witness protection.'

'I'm not talking the witness protection aspect, I'm talking about this whole big mess. This is sensitive, and we have no idea who's involved. If Shafer decides to put a lid on this locally and go straight to Washington, we don't have a prayer of getting any answers.'

Gino squirmed in his seat, dragged his hand over his prickly brush of hair. 'Dahl's not going to put his neck on the chopping block for us. I mean, he's a decent guy who actually has some ethics, and probably the only Fed I really trust, but still . . .'

'It would have to be totally off the record. He's closer to the devil than we are, and he has access we don't. At least authorized access.'

'So you're going full-blown conspiracy and assuming the U.S. government has something to do with this.'

'Hey, you already went there. I'm just following in your footsteps. But the fact of the matter is, chinchilla lady had a federal access restraint on her prints, and according to Interpol she died three years ago. I want to know who submitted her fake death certificate and why.'

Gino's gaze lingered over his empty, egg-yolk-smeared plate, then to Malcherson's unfinished omelet. Magozzi could tell he was tempted, but civility got the better of him. 'Okay. Call Dahl. I'll get us some sticky buns and coffees to go.'

That was the great thing about Gino, Magozzi thought as he watched him walk up to the diner's service counter. His whole world could be crashing down around his ears, but he always managed to stay grounded in life's simplest realities, starting and ending with family and food.

# Forty-Three

Grace was settled in her bedroom at Harley's, but sleep had been impossible – she'd managed to doze, but fitful, disjointed dreams kept waking her. Fortunately, the Beast never slept; unfortunately, even it had its limitations – if there was no information for it to find, it hit a dead end just like humans did. And it seemed like the Sixth Idea was the deadest end of all. So far, they hadn't even come close to identifying any of the players, all of whom were clearly comfortable operating in the shadows.

She rolled over and clicked on a bedside lamp. Charlie lifted his head briefly, but in the next minute he was snoring again. Lydia's paperback was lying on the table next to her – she'd read most of it, but there was nothing notable about it except for the fact that Lydia's grandfather had most likely written it and self-published it, and this was probably the only copy in existence. So why had he placed such a great deal of import on it and asked that it be kept secret? It could have just been a personal indulgence, a simple vanity project, but if that were the case, you'd think he would have wanted his daughter, or the whole family for that matter, to know he was the author.

She picked it up and stared at the cover. *In Case of Emergency.* It was an ominous title, or maybe it was a message, because if there were ever an emergency in Lydia Ascher's world, it was happening now. It used to be a common capital-lettered phrase on a lot of things. IN CASE OF EMERGENCY was on glass cases in every multistory building, right next to the elevator. You didn't have to read through multiple lines of tiny print in many languages to know that in case of emergency, you pulled the alarm lever or broke the glass or pushed the red button in an elevator. Lydia's grandfather probably didn't think of that phrase as simply an intriguing book title. Maybe it was direction for those who came after him.

*In case of emergency, break this glass. In case of emergency, push this button. In case of emergency . . . read this book.*

The author's name was unusual, too, and a strange choice for a pseudonym. Thea S. Dixid. A dixid was a water midge.

Grace closed her eyes, but all she could see was the book cover, as if it had imprinted on her retinas.

At some point she eventually fell asleep, but what seemed like moments later she lurched up in bed, her eyes wide in the dark. *In Case of Emergency by Thea S. Dixid.*

Thea S. Dixid. Scramble the letters and you got Sixth Idea.

She grabbed her phone off the nightstand and dialed Magozzi.

'Grace.'

'Listen, Magozzi, we need Lydia Ascher here. I think her Armageddon book is some kind of a key after all, and she's the only one in the world who might be able to decipher it.'

'Not a chance, Grace. A sniper took a couple shots at her tonight while she was in protective custody.'

'A *sniper*?'

'Yeah. Sheriff said they had over thirty men guarding her, making sure nobody got close, so the bastard fired from across the lake over half a mile out. Whoever is on the other end of this isn't just trying to kill Lydia, they're dead set on it.'

Grace was shaking her head, even though no one was there to see it. She knew what it felt like to be hunted. She knew what it felt like to run with no clear finish line in sight, no big red arrows telling you THIS WAY TO ABSOLUTE SAFETY. Her heart ached in a very intimate way for this woman she'd never even met. 'Is she safe now?'

'Jefferson County still has her, and the sniper is dead, but Gino and I just met with Chief Malcherson. He's going to arrange a safe house with the Feds. Now, what makes you think Lydia's book might be a key?'

'The author's name – Thea S. Dixid. If you scramble the letters, it spells Sixth Idea. And the title: *In Case of Emergency*. I'm hoping that it's some kind of a message and her grandfather embedded something in the actual text, maybe anticipating events like the ones happening now. Has Lydia read the book?'

'I don't know. I'll ask her.'

'She needs to read it word by word and make note of anything – *anything* – that gives her pause or strikes her as unusual. Any tiny detail might be able to help us, which will help us help her.'

'We'll pick up the book and get it to her as soon as we can.'

'You and Gino have enough tails to chase. Bring her here.' She said it without hesitation.

'Absolutely not. She's a target, Grace, and anyone near her is in the line of fire. I don't want you or Harley anywhere near her. Her neighbor bought it just coming to her house for dinner, and a Jefferson

County deputy was wounded tonight. He's lucky to be alive.'

Grace held her tongue. But only for a few moments. She understood that there was some knee-jerk, biological compulsion for men to protect women, no matter how capable the woman. She appreciated the sentiment, but she also resented it, at least in this particular situation. 'And so is she. You ask the FBI if they have anything within an hour of Lydia's current location that can come close to the mansion's security. My guess is they don't. You do know all of Harley's windows and doors are bulletproof, right?'

'I . . . Really?' he stuttered.

'The perimeter of the property is covered by motion detectors and surveillance cameras that have infrared capability and can read the thermal signatures off everything in their sight lines up to a mile away. If someone is hiding in the bushes or in the alley, we'll see them. There is a biometric keyless entry that incorporates voice, facial, and behavioral recognition. And there's a panic room that would blow James Bond's mind. Twenty-five hundred square feet that looks like a suite at the Four Seasons. And that's only the half of it.'

'When did Harley do all this?'

'Right after we moved the Monkeewrench offices here. He's been upgrading ever since. We're the safest place in the world, Magozzi.' She heard him sigh.

'I believe you. But nobody in law enforcement is going to put civilians in danger, no matter how impressive your security.'

'Which is stupid. The Feds could put a team around Harley's just as easily as they could their own facility, which is just going to be a house that doesn't have one-tenth of what we do. In the end, they rely on agents with guns to protect witnesses. We rely on technology. Combine the two and you have a perfect security setup, at least for the short term, until the Feds can arrange something.'

Grace waited for Magozzi to respond, and the longer he took, the more her impatience flared. 'This is an innocent life we're talking about, and this is her best chance, at least for now.'

'This is an impossible choice, Grace. You know that.'

'Of course I do. But it's not your choice to make. It's not ours, either, it's Lydia's. Call Chief Malcherson and let him know what we're offering.'

# Forty-Four

Magozzi hung up with Grace just as he was pulling off the sloppy, snow-packed street into the City Hall parking garage, not quite sure what had just happened. Grace MacBride was a walking conundrum – wildly unpredictable, paranoid, antisocial – and at the same time she was steady, brave, and deeply caring. If you walked on her rug, you knew it might be pulled out from under your feet at any moment, with a single exception – if you were a victim of violence or persecution or both, Grace became downright empathetic. She'd lived through it all, and he sensed and feared that maybe her only true connection to others was a shared experience of trauma. What that meant for their relationship was that unknown $x$ in an algebra equation.

He shut off the car as Gino nudged his old Volvo into the empty parking space next to him. Neither of them seemed to be in much of a hurry to jump out of their warm cars – in all probability they were both in some sort of sleeping wakefulness. Or maybe it was waking sleepfulness.

Magozzi pinched his eyes shut and squeezed the bridge of his nose. It was always a bad sign when your internal dialogue started to turn into indecipherable babble with made-up words and psychological conditions.

He finally got out of his car and lifted his face, letting the cold air smack him up a little bit in the hopes his brain would switch off idiot mode.

'I need one of those sticky buns, Gino. I'm not going to be able to function without sugar and caffeine this morning.'

Gino gave him a half-smile. 'Really? Jeez, you're getting old. You've gotten at least five hours of sleep in the past forty-eight hours, what more do you want?'

Magozzi begged with his hand palm-up. 'The bun, Gino. That's what I want.'

Gino passed him a white waxed bakery bag that was about half a pound lighter than it had been when they'd left the Pig's Eye Diner. 'I already ate mine.' He explained the obvious weight discrepancy.

'Did it help?'

'Oh, yeah. I'm so wired I could run a marathon right now.'

'Grace called on the way over here. She thinks that book of Lydia's might be some kind of a clue from the grave.'

'What kind of clue?'

'The author's name spells Sixth Idea.'

'Seriously? That's not a coincidence. It can't be.'

'Right. Especially if her grandfather wrote the book. Grace is hoping it's a road map of some kind.'

'A road map to where?'

'The Sixth Idea, I guess. Or at least some answers. She wants to bring Lydia to Harley's and work with her to figure it out.'

Gino shoved his gloved hands into the pockets of his bulky, olive drab parka. 'And I suppose you told her a sniper tried to take her out tonight, and that anybody a mile away from Lydia Ascher is in the crosshairs?'

'Of course I did.'

'And let me guess – she doesn't care about any of that.'

'It's more calculated than that. She said Harley's place is safer than anything the Feds can come up with, at least in the short term, and after she gave me a rundown, I believe it. Did you know he has bulletproof windows and doors and a panic room?'

Gino tipped his head curiously. 'Didn't know, but it doesn't surprise me. So what did you tell her?'

'She asked me to call Malcherson and present the offer to the Feds. But ultimately, it's Lydia's choice.'

'Christ. You ever notice that for a woman with bars on all her windows, she jumps into dangerous situations at the drop of a hat? You ever think she has a death wish?'

'I think she has motives we'll never understand.'

'So what are you going to do?'

'I promised her I'd call Malcherson.'

Gino looked away and nudged a chunk of dirty snow that had fallen off his wheel well with a wet plop. 'Shit. Did Dahl call you back yet?'

Magozzi shook his head. 'I called from a burner phone. Maybe his supersecret Fed phone blocks unlisted numbers.'

'Or maybe he doesn't want to talk to us. Last time he got involved with us, we dragged him up to an Indian reservation in northern Minnesota during the worst blizzard in fifty years to sort through the bodies of a bunch of dead terrorists.'

'There is that.' Magozzi shoved his hand in the pocket of his overcoat when he heard his phone buzzing. 'Malcherson,' he told Gino. 'Chief, have you met with Shafer yet?'

'I'm on my way. Are there any new developments I should know about before I speak with him?'

'Well, actually, sir, there is. Monkeewrench wanted me to run something by you.'

Malcherson grunted. 'I certainly hope it doesn't involve MI6.'

Magozzi opened his mouth to answer, then snapped it shut. On rare occasions, the chief toyed with humor and sarcasm, but Magozzi wasn't sure if this was one of those occasions – he was never really sure – so he answered straight, like always. 'No sir, nothing like that.'

He told the chief what Grace had told him, and not once did he interrupt with questions or protests or challenges – he just listened, processing and carefully considering the information as it was fed to him. Malcherson was probably one of the last critical thinkers alive.

'I will mention this to Special Agent in Charge Shafer,' he finally said once Magozzi had finished. 'But as you pointed out, the decision ultimately rests with Ms. Ascher, and she should be informed of every possible choice before she makes that decision. Let me find out what the FBI has to offer and if they would even provide support outside one of their facilities. There are also policy and legal implications at play here.'

Magozzi hung up and looked at Gino. 'He'll call us back.'

McLaren was already at his desk when Magozzi and Gino slogged into Homicide. He looked particularly undone this morning, his red hair showing deep, ragged furrows where his fingers had been dragging through it, a clashing, weirdly knotted red and green plaid tie hanging loosely askew around the collar of his wrinkled shirt. 'One single frigging break on the Alvin Keller case,' he greeted them dourly. 'And no thanks to the news – Miami just had a blackout, so for sure we've got a global catastrophe on our hands, no time for reporting on a boring missing person.'

'What's the break on Keller?'

'Someone just found his body in Curtis Park. But nothing on Arthur Friedman.'

# Forty-Five

This is not a park,' Gino groused, shoulders hunched, hands jammed in his parka pockets, watching his silly little loafers slog through four inches of newly fallen snow.

'Of course it's a park. See the sign? Curtis Park. What's your beef?'

'Parks have plowed sidewalks. Trimmed trees. Lakes and paths and shit. Look at this place. See those dead brown vines choking the trees to death? Woodbine, the northern kudzu. Every homeowner knows you rip those things out when they're babies or they'll kill your trees and maybe kidnap your children. And look at my loafers. They're going to rot by lunchtime and I'll probably freeze my feet off and have to walk on my ankles for the rest of my life.'

'You have boots in your locker. And free will, which for some reason you decided not to exercise this morning.'

'Thanks for the sympathy, Leo, but you don't get it. I'm a married man. When you get married,

266

you lose all free will and rely on your wife to make sure you're dressed properly for the weather and occasion.'

'That's pathetic. Do you lose all cognitive function when you get married, too?'

'Pretty much. At least when it comes to dressing yourself.'

'I'll make you a cheat sheet – snow plus loafers equals cold, wet feet. Proceed to locker for appropriate attire before venturing outside.'

Magozzi couldn't tell if Gino was amused or annoyed; maybe a little of both. But it didn't really matter – Gino would air his complaints about anything, anytime, no matter what, and Magozzi would continue to parry with his limited scope of influence. It was a perfect symbiosis.

They finally found the bench, deep into this five-acre pretend park. A mastodon patrolman guarded the bench and the dead man on it with a stoic stance and a fiercely protective countenance that would have frightened pit bulls. High school wrestler, Magozzi thought. Long torso, massive arms, short, powerful legs, and so gung-ho and new to the job he was still in that phase where you thought you could actually make a difference. In stark contrast was the frail body of Alvin Keller, oddly covered with a blanket, a towel tucked beneath his head.

'Excellent catch, Patrolman Snyder.'

'Thank you, Detective Magozzi. My pleasure to serve.'

He sounded like a veteran, and probably was – lately, they'd been the best additions to the force in a long time. 'Do you have anything for us?'

'Yes sir. This is exactly how I found him. I recognized his face from the BOLO. Doesn't look like foul play, but I didn't touch anything or move the blanket.' He took a long look at the man on the bench. 'He looks like he was sick.'

'He was dying of ALS.'

Snyder's face darkened and he took a deep breath. *He knows the disease,* Magozzi thought.

'He almost looks . . . peaceful. Maybe he came here to die.'

Gino walked to the other side of the bench. 'Under normal circumstances, I'd agree with you, Officer. But this man was almost totally paralyzed, and probably kidnapped. Taken from his house and away from his wife of sixty years.'

Patrolman Snyder dropped his head. 'I'm sorry to hear that. It's strange, though. There was some respect paid here. Why would a kidnapper take the time or care? And why would he put him in a public space like this, almost pose him?'

'Maybe the kidnapper wanted him to be found.' Magozzi looked at Gino. 'He was in bad shape. Heart attack, maybe.'

Gino got closer to the body and lifted the blanket. 'No signs of foul play under here, either. I think you're probably right about the heart attack, Leo. Poor guy must have been terrified.'

Magozzi took a long look at Alvin Keller's very, very white face. The pallor of death accentuated the deep furrows that old age and disease had carved there. And maybe some very dark, unspoken secrets had contributed to those furrows as well.

He looked down at his phone when it started chirping. 'It's Chief Malcherson. Excuse me, Officer Snyder.'

Gino stayed with Snyder while Magozzi retreated out of the wind beneath a small clump of birch trees. He'd always thought birch trees were some of the most beautiful things in the natural world, with their chalk-white trunks studded up and down with almond-shaped black eyes. But at the moment those black eyes seemed to be staring at him, accusing him. 'Chief.'

'Detective Magozzi. I just spoke at length with Special Agent in Charge Shafer. He was very alarmed by recent developments.'

'I'm sure he was. Are the Feds getting involved?'

'Not officially, at least not yet. But he promised to do everything possible to provide support in the meantime.'

'Like a safe house for Lydia Ascher?'

Malcherson cleared his throat. 'Ultimately, yes. But she's not a federal witness yet, Detective. There is strict protocol.'

Magozzi felt blood creeping up his neck to his face. 'Oh. I get it. Just a little too much red tape to save a life, better luck next time. So what's this support he's offering? Is he going to crochet us a safe house out of all that red tape in his spare time?'

Malcherson cleared his throat. 'I was candid with him, Detective. He knows what's at stake, and he knows there is a larger issue at hand that has to be investigated. Delicately. And he has access to certain channels that we don't.'

'That larger issue being his career?'

'Detective,' Malcherson warned.

'I'm sorry, Chief, but it really bothers me that Shafer acts like he's God until it inconveniences him to be omnipotent, then he's just some clueless schlub in a big office, wearing government shackles and playing dumb and helpless.'

'Those weren't my exact words to him.'

Magozzi was a little nonplussed – sometimes it was easy to forget that Malcherson had been on the job for a long, long time before he'd stepped into the muck of political life, and his allegiance would always lie with the men and women serving under him. He'd never really left the trenches. 'I owe you an apology, Chief. Paul Shafer has always rubbed me the wrong way, and I'm pretty sure he feels the same about me.'

'No harm done, Detective. Now, more importantly – Monkeewrench's offer to shelter Lydia Ascher. I am not remotely comfortable with that, and I certainly can't condone it.'

'I feel the same way, but as private citizens, it's their call. And it's Lydia Ascher's call. And with the Feds bailing, it's her best shot at this point.'

'I know this is a difficult situation for you, Detective Magozzi. Please, talk to Monkeewrench again, and all of you think this through very carefully before you make the offer to Ms. Ascher, because she would be a fool not to accept.'

'I will, sir. And if we do end up bringing her to Harley's, do we have your permission to request some off-duty volunteers to cover the neighborhood?'

'That won't be necessary. MPD and St. Paul PD will provide twenty-four-hour coverage if this comes to pass. It seems both our departments have a year-end budget surplus.'

Magozzi flexed his hands in his frozen gloves and smiled at the black eyes on the birch bark, because they were smiling back at him now. The budget surplus was absolute bullshit; for all he knew, the chief would be paying overtime out of pocket. 'I appreciate that, Chief.'

'Call me when Ms. Ascher makes her decision.'

Magozzi stared down at the Call Ended message on his phone's screen, then heard crunching snow behind him as Gino bravely slogged through it in his ruined loafers.

'What did the chief have to say?'

'The Feds are out for now, and they're not offering a safe house to Lydia. That bastard Paul Shafer is stonewalling. Protocol bullshit, he said, which is ass-covering bullshit in plain English.'

Gino folded his arms across his chest. 'You've gotta be kidding me. Since when does Shafer turn down a date to thunder in on his white steed and save the day?'

'I think we might be underestimating this whole thing. When Shafer doesn't dive in headfirst, that means he's positioning himself. He sees a career maker or a career breaker, and he wants to be on the right side of it when things go down.'

'So the chief told him enough that his ears are pricked. You think Shafer knows something?'

'I think Shafer's on a hunting expedition right now.'

'What does the chief think about Monkeewrench's private safe house offer now that the Feds are out?'

'He hates the idea as much as we do, but said he'd provide additional police support if that's the way it goes. Twenty-four-hour coverage around Harley's place. Even Shafer offered to provide additional support, whatever that means.'

Gino looked up at the dirty gray sky that promised more fits and spurts of snow to brighten everyone's day. 'So is that what we're going to do?'

Magozzi followed Gino's eyes up to the sky. 'There are no good choices anymore, Gino, only bad ones.'

# Forty-Six

Lydia flailed awake in the most embarrassing way – her numb, stiff limbs spasmed as if they were trying to claw their way out of a nightmare, and she felt the dreaded trickle of sleep drool drying on her chin – one of the greatest horrors of nodding off in public. The chair she'd fallen asleep in should be classified as a torture device, along with the hospital food she'd eaten earlier, but by God, she was still alive. And so was Deputy Harmon, who was snoring peacefully in the bed beside her chair. She didn't see any drool on his chin.

There had been absolutely no question that she would stay at his bedside overnight and keep vigil, even though his wound wasn't critical. He'd stayed by her side ever since she'd called 911 yesterday, and he'd never left it until the ambulance took him away from the motel. No conscious decision necessary. He was stuck with her until he walked out of this place on his own.

However, in the light of day, she was beginning to question the benefit of her loyalty. Deputy

Harmon had been shot because of her. Wasn't she putting him in danger again, along with everybody else in the hospital? She suddenly realized that she was a liability to anybody around her.

She hadn't cried yesterday – not over Otis, not over the bizarre fact that she was marked for death – most likely, she'd been in shock. But finally, she felt tears dripping down her cheeks and she brushed them away with the back of her hand.

'You're going to be okay,' she heard Deputy Harmon's groggy voice.

She looked up at him and smiled through her tears. 'And so are you. How are you feeling, Deputy?'

'My name is Terry.' He gave her a lopsided grin. 'Hurts like a son of a gun, but I'll make it through, and so will you.' He reached out for her hand. 'I woke up a few times and saw you sleeping in that nasty chair. Were you here all night?'

'Ever since you got admitted. Hospitals suck, and when you wake up, you should have a friendly face waiting for you.'

He squeezed her hand. 'Thank you.'

'I hope you didn't mind that my friendly face was asleep.'

'Best thing I've ever seen, asleep or awake. But you'd better get up and get your blood flowing again, take it from me. I don't know who picks out hospital furniture, but I'm guessing it's some kind of sadistic dungeon master.'

'I was just thinking the very same thing.' Lydia stood up and shook the pins and needles out of her arms and legs, wondering who Deputy Harmon – Terry – had watched over from an ergonomically bereft hospital chair. Maybe she would ask him one day.

There was a soft rap on the door, and then Sheriff Gannet announcing himself through the closed door. He walked in and gave them both reserved smiles, which was probably about as ebullient as he ever got, at least when he was on the job. During this whole ordeal, Lydia had observed a compassionate, competent man; one who took his role as leader very seriously. He wasn't the guy who was going to slap you on the shoulder, take you out to the golf course and lie to you, tell you everything was going to be okay.

'Deputy, Ms. Ascher,' he said, nodding. 'Everything's quiet, has been all night. Except for the media – they came in like a plague of locusts. Never thought I'd say this about the media, but I'm glad they're here. Bad guys don't always run from the cops, but they'll always run from a bunch of reporters with cameras.'

Deputy Harmon pushed himself up, wincing. 'Good morning, Sheriff. Did you find the SOB who did this to us?'

'Yes we did. He's in the morgue now.'

Lydia felt a tickling glimmer of hope. Two people had tried to kill her, and they were both dead now. There couldn't possibly be a third, could there? 'Do you know who he is, Sheriff?'

'Not yet. Ms. Ascher, I talked to the Minneapolis detectives a while ago. They have a safe house in mind for you in the city and they'd like to talk to you about it. They should be here soon. As a matter of fact, I'd better get downstairs to clear them through the lobby.'

A *safe house*, Lydia thought. Twenty-four hours ago, her house in the country had been safe, but not anymore.

# Forty-Seven

Lydia didn't know what to expect from Monkeewrench – the scant news stories about them she'd read in the past described them as reclusive, eccentric computer geniuses who regularly donated their time and software to law enforcement all over the country. Harboring a fugitive target of assassins seemed a little above and beyond the call of philanthropic duty, but according to Detectives Magozzi and Rolseth, Harley Davidson's mansion was better equipped for the job than a lot of high-security installations.

Maybe in Monkeewrench's line of work they were used to threats, maybe even death threats, and extreme personal safety measures were just part and parcel of doing business. Or maybe they were wildly paranoid and as eccentric as the articles had portrayed them. Either way, she was grateful for their offer of shelter, regardless of their motivation. But the most important thing was that they had requested her presence – she was the only one who might have a chance of deciphering any hidden messages in her grandfather's book. That made her feel like she actually had some control over her own fate and something to contribute to a larger cause – finding justice for Chuck and Wally and Otis and all the other innocents who hadn't been as lucky as she had been.

Yep, Lydia Ascher, thrust into crime fighting by her family's past, would become a superhero and staunch guardian of justice with the help of her little pocket rocket and a pulp fiction novel written by her grandfather. The only problem with that scenario was the novel wasn't yielding any hidden messages or clues, and she'd been poring over it for the past hour.

She set the book down on her lap in frustration and took in her surroundings for the twentieth time – it was a beautiful room in a grand home, filled with books, curiosities, and furniture that wouldn't have looked out of place in one of King Ludwig II's castles.

The king of this castle was tattooed and wore leather and had been named after a motorcycle. He looked pretty terrifying, the type of man you'd cross the street to avoid, but once you met him, he was anything but. Grace MacBride was a different story – she was a beautiful woman, not scary-looking at all, but when you met her, you got an instant sense of danger which didn't have anything to do with the big gun she wore.

She heard crisp footsteps in the hallway – Grace's riding boots, not Harley's heavy jackboots. There was a gentle rap on the door as Grace walked into the second-level library carrying a laptop computer. She'd been considerate enough to announce her arrival with a knock, perhaps in deference to Lydia's situation, but this woman wasn't going to wait for an invitation from anybody. And why would she? This was her turf, and even though Harley owned the mansion, Grace was the unequivocal leader here, which Lydia found impressive and admirable.

'Lydia? Have you found anything?'

Grace had arresting blue eyes that Lydia couldn't even begin to read, which was unsettling for a woman who made a living reading eyes and faces. 'Not really, I'm sorry to say. The problem is, none of this is my past, it's my mother's. There could be something plain as day in the text and I wouldn't notice it.'

'Your mother never mentioned anything unusual about it, aside from the fact that some of the places in the book were real, like the five-and-dime store?'

Something suddenly clicked in Lydia's mind. 'Now that you mention it, there is one odd thing.

My mother told me that going to the soda fountain at the five-and-dime with her father was one of her fondest childhood memories. She told me all about it, down to every little detail, including the address painted in gold letters on the front door. Five-six-five Main Street. Except in the book, the address of the five-and-dime is fourteen Oak Street. Why would my grandfather change the address?'

Grace's brows furrowed. 'Does fourteen Oak Street mean anything to you?'

'No.'

She settled into a chair next to Lydia and flipped open the lid of her laptop. 'Maybe it meant something to your grandfather. Let's find out.'

It didn't take Grace long to locate 14 Oak Street in Olean, New York, because the property was still operational, and had been for over a hundred and fifty years. Lydia felt her heart speed up. 'It's a cemetery. Oak Hill Cemetery. I didn't recognize the address, but that's where our family mausoleum is. Where my grandfather is.'

'He's buried there?'

'Well, not actually buried. After the plane crash, there were no remains, but they had a memorial service in the mausoleum and dedicated his drawer and placed a plaque.'

'Good catch, Lydia.'

It had been a simple statement of fact, really, but Lydia suddenly felt like a little kid who'd just won a game of Clue, figuring out that Mr. Mustard had done it in the ballroom with a candlestick. 'But why on earth would he change the address of my mother's favorite place to the cemetery where he would ultimately be interred? That's morbid. Cruel, even.'

Grace was struck by the eerie sense that dark tentacles of the past were slithering into the room. 'My only guess is he was leading her there because he left something for her. Something important enough to hide in the one place nobody would look: a tomb.'

Lydia looked down at the cover of the book. *'In Case of Emergency.'*

'And you're having an emergency. And look at the author's name. Thea S. Dixid. Scramble the letters, use a few of them twice, and it spells the Sixth Idea.'

Grace watched most of the color leach out of Lydia's face. 'I have to go to the cemetery. I have to go as soon as possible.'

'No. People are trying to kill you and if you move, they'll find you. And if I'm right about this and you lead them to the cemetery, they'll find what your grandfather went to great lengths to conceal from anyone except the one person he trusted most. Your mother.'

'But there might be answers there. There might be *the* answer there.'

'How far is Olean from Rochester?'

'About a hundred miles or so. Why?'

'My partners are in Rochester right now. They could go to the cemetery in your place.'

# Forty-Eight

It was early afternoon when Annie and Roadrunner got back to their hotel in Rochester. The suites here most certainly didn't compare to their luxury accommodations in New York City, and there was no Bergdorf Goodman around the corner, but they were flying back to Minneapolis in the morning. As long as there were clean sheets and twenty-four-hour room service, she could survive the night.

She got comfortable in a chair in the common room and stretched out her legs to cushion them on a tuffet because four-inch heels were beautiful murder and she'd been wearing one pair or another for the better part of their two weeks on the road.

Roadrunner collapsed in a recliner across from her and crooked his spindly arms behind his head. His long limbs made him look like a spider, and Annie always wondered what it would be like to be six-foot-eight and skinny as a straw.

'I think the meeting went well,' he said.

'You have an awfully charming way of understating your brilliance. You had that account sold in the first five minutes, and you know it. I was just window dressing. Which I don't mind one tiny little bit.'

'Come on, Annie, don't sell yourself short.'

She gave him a coy smile. 'Now, when have you ever known me to sell myself short? Why don't you call Grace and Harley and tell them the good news while I order us some room service and a nice bottle of wine.'

While Roadrunner worked his phone, Annie perused the menu and wine list. 'What do you think about trying some of the Buffalo wings? I mean, we're sort of by Buffalo, which is where they invented them, right?'

Roadrunner nodded, then lifted a finger. 'Grace!'

Annie watched as he listened for a moment, watched as his anticipatory smile faltered, faded, and died, killing her appetite along with it.

He apologized into the phone, ended his call, and looked up at her with troubled eyes. 'Wrong number.'

Oh dear. That was a very bad sign. 'Wrong number' was an emergency message Monkeewrench had established a long time ago if a secure connection was required, and Annie knew exactly how to respond according to protocol. She abandoned the room service menu to retrieve her computer and a special phone they all carried when they were on the road. In case of an emergency.

# Forty-Nine

Magozzi was staring at the smoke-stained log walls of Grundy's Bar, a great blue-collar hole-in-the-wall in St. Paul. Gino wasn't happy with Dahl's choice of a meeting place because it was the single bar in the greater metro area that didn't serve food, but Dahl was the one taking all the risks, so the choice was his.

The bar had been in its current location since opening as a speakeasy in the early thirties, and the place still had a secretive, dangerous feel. There were a few patrons at the rail, engrossed in a hockey game playing on the big TV behind the bar. Nobody was talking – it was the kind of place people came to to wind down after a shift or nurse their private sorrows in silence. The bartender looked like a mobster, and maybe he was.

Nobody seemed to notice that three men in suits were sitting at a corner table, even though the place probably hadn't seen a suit since Al Capone used to visit.

Special Agent Dahl was silently swirling a glass of Coke on a wet coaster, wearing a perfect poker face; Magozzi and Gino had opted for something stronger. They had laid down almost all their cards, including a recap of Malcherson's meeting with Shafer. Eventually Dahl raised his eyes, apparently having lost interest in his soda. No wonder – conversations like the one they were having required alcohol.

Dahl still looked like he belonged on the set of a surfing movie, but he'd lost his tan since the last time they'd seen him. 'I have no idea why you think I can help you with your homicides, Detectives,' he finally said.

Gino finished his beer and put his empty glass down on the table – it resonated a few decibels above what was socially appropriate in polite company. 'We just spent the past half hour telling you why. We're dangling on the end of a limb here. And by the way, we appreciate your time, so how about we don't waste it.'

Dahl's mouth ticked up a little. 'Excellent effort at diplomacy, Rolseth. Okay. Essentially, you just told me a group of innocent people are getting murdered because their predecessors worked on the hydrogen bomb almost sixty years ago, and they dreamed up some kind of secret program nobody seems to know about. And you suspect our government is behind it, killing its own civilians. Do you know how outrageous that sounds?'

'Touché, and an excellent effort on your part. Great technique, putting words in our mouths. But we never said anything about our government, or anybody else's government, which means you inferred that from what we just told you.' Gino let out a puff of air. 'We have a little experience interrogating people, too. Give us some credit.'

'After last fall, I'm not likely to ever underestimate you two.'

Gino rolled his head back and sighed. 'What we're telling you is a bunch of innocent people are getting killed after they signed on to Charles Spencer's website and started talking about the Sixth Idea, whatever the hell that is. Somebody with a .22 is killing the killers. And somebody sent a sniper – a frigging *sniper* – after Lydia Ascher when the first guy couldn't get the job done. And not a single one of our crime scenes has choked up any evidence we can use. No ballistics matches, no IDs. We're dealing with shadows, which makes it pretty damn hard to do our job.'

Magozzi ran his thumbnail around a heart-shaped groove that had been scratched into the old wooden tabletop. The tables had also been around since Prohibition, and bore the marks and scars of generations. There were a lot of tiny pieces of lives and their stories on this table that nobody would ever know. 'The only thing we have are chinchilla lady's prints.'

Dahl said, 'That's the woman you think was sent to kill Alvin Keller?'

'Right. NCIC popped a prints match, but there's a big black access constraint stamp on it.' He raised his eyes to meet Dahl's. 'What's that about?'

Dahl's eyes flickered, then stilled.

Gino had seen that no-compromise look on his partner's face a few times, the most recent when he was racing to save Grace MacBride's life. He knew better than to interrupt whatever eye duel he was fighting with Dahl.

'What the hell does that mean?' Magozzi gave him exactly two seconds to answer before leaning across the table. 'Not a good time to play coy, Dahl. The FBI runs NCIC and you're high enough on the ladder to know this shit, goddamnit. The body count is climbing.'

'I'm going outside for a smoke,' Dahl said, standing up, laying his cell on the table, holding out his hands to Magozzi and Gino, clearly asking for theirs without saying a word.

'It's frigging freezing out there,' Gino complained, even as he surrendered his cell and pulled on his coat.

Dahl cocked his head. 'When was the last time you had a cigarette?'

'Nineteen ninety-seven.'

'Tempted?'

'Oh, yeah. It's only been a couple decades. Damn habit lasts forever.'

Five minutes later, the three of them were shivering on the cold seat of a bus stop bench. Dahl didn't make a move to light up.

'You don't smoke, do you?' Magozzi asked.

'No. Never have. But it's a great excuse to leave a building. Just because Monkeewrench cleaned your phones doesn't mean anything.'

'Well, shit,' Gino mumbled. 'So, give it to us, Dahl.'

'The Bureau got a red flag when you ran . . . chinchilla lady's prints.' He winced a little. 'Do you nickname all of your victims?'

'Only when there are too many to keep track of.'

He nodded, as if that made perfect sense. 'Anyhow, that's standard with access constraints. Whenever any law enforcement runs prints on somebody with a federal cover on them, we hear about it. And when your request for an ID came in, I went to Shafer to see if I could clear it for you.'

'And?'

'He said forget that I ever saw it, and never mention it again. I've never heard those words out of his mouth before. Whoever put the access constraint on her file wanted to know if this lady ended up dead or detained. But they don't want anyone else to know anything about her.'

'Which means what?' Magozzi watched Dahl's eyes dart around nervously. There was plenty of paranoia to go around.

'She was one of ours.'

'You *know* that?'

Dahl nodded once, just barely.

Magozzi let that settle for a moment. Dahl had just given them a hell of a lot more than he should have, and he wondered why. Now Magozzi was going to repay the favor, and give him a hell of a lot more than he should. 'Our sources tell us she was KGB and that Interpol registered a death certificate for her three years ago.'

'That's our work,' Dahl said. 'She was turned.'

'Jesus,' Gino whispered. 'You're in on this?'

'Absolutely not.'

'Is Shafer?'

'I honestly don't know. I doubt it. He has orders, just like everybody else up and down the food chain. Access constraint can mean a lot of things. I only know what I know because I have a couple contacts who help me out from time to time.'

'So she's FBI?'

'Highly unlikely – we're just the federal arm of domestic law enforcement. This kind of work is outside the Bureau.'

'Do you know who she was working for?'

Dahl shook his head. 'She could be undercover for a lot of agencies. I don't even know the names of half of them. We get directives mandating access constraint without being told why, or who ordered it. Or she could be undercover for a black budget outfit, in which case you are never going to get to the bottom of this.'

The three of them sat huddled on the bench, silent, staring at the snow gathering on the sidewalk at their feet. Magozzi finally spoke. 'Why are you telling us this, Dahl? This isn't just your job on the line, it's your ass. This little chat of ours could send you to federal prison.'

Dahl turned and looked them both in the eye. 'I work for the Department of Justice. I took an oath to uphold justice. And you just made a very compelling case that an agent of the U.S. government was sent to assassinate Alvin Keller, an elderly citizen who honorably gave years of his life in the service of that government. That's not justice, that's an abomination.'

'I couldn't agree with you more. So, can you help us solve our homicides?'

'I don't know yet. I haven't seen Shafer since he met with your chief, so I have to take his temperature on this before I can give you any kind of answer.' Dahl fastened the top button of his coat, then got up from the bench. 'I'll talk to him. Give me your burner numbers and I'll call you when I know something. Where can I find you if I need to meet you in person?'

Magozzi scrawled phone numbers on a card and passed it over. 'We'll be with Monkeewrench. At Harley's.'

After retrieving their phones from the bar, the three men headed for their respective vehicles. 'Huh,' Gino muttered. 'So this is already on the Fed radar and we didn't even know it. Gee. Funny we never got a courtesy call.'

'Must have been an oversight.' Magozzi got behind the wheel of their sedan and cranked the engine. Frigid air blew out of the vents. 'Dahl's spooked.'

'He's not the only one. So what's your take on him? You think he knows more than he's telling?'

Magozzi thought about that, then shook his head. 'It didn't play that way. Shafer's got blinders on him and I think he wants to know what we know, just like we want to know what he knows.'

Gino snorted and scraped frost off his side window with a thumbnail. 'Too bad none of us know shit.'

# Fifty

Magozzi was parked in front of Gino's house, listening to a horrific, pseudo-jazz version of 'Walking in a Winter Wonderland' while he waited for him to change the shoes and socks that had been soaked during the trek through snowy Curtis Park to view Alvin Keller's body.

Gino had been inside for a while, which meant he was either raiding the refrigerator for leftovers, having a quickie with Angela after forty-eight hours on the job, or both. Whatever, Magozzi was happy for him, and happy to be sitting alone in a crappy sedan with a crappy sound system playing crappy music, just breathing for a while with no distractions.

His eyes wandered the neighborhood, looking for lights and decorations like he had as a kid. There were nods to Christmas at almost every house on the block – some kitschy, others more subdued. There was a nice pine wreath on Gino and Angela's front door, frosted white from the recent snow. It was studded with real pinecones and fake holly and topped with a fat red velvet bow. Magozzi knew this because he had the exact same wreath on his front door, courtesy of Gino's youngest – the Accident – who had recently joined Cub Scouts and was successfully learning the ways of fund-raising. They were starting them early these days.

'What did Angela give you to eat?' Magozzi interrogated Gino when he finally got back to the car, smelling like garlic.

'She fed me a piece of her mind for ruining my shoes, that's what. Damn. She almost raised her voice.'

'Come on. Cough it up. I can smell it, and Angela never forgets me.'

'She thinks you'd starve to death if she didn't feed you.'

'She might be right.'

Gino withdrew a foil-wrapped package from his parka pocket, just as Magozzi had hoped he would. 'Meatball sub with provolone, still warm. Extra peppers and napkins for you.'

Magozzi ascended to cheesy meatball nirvana and for a few brief moments all was right and good in the world. After his third bite, he jockeyed into sparse traffic on the boulevard that bisected Gino's neighborhood. Snow was still falling steadily, gathering in growing clumps on the lilac bowers in the center median. Years ago, the median had been lined with grand old elms, but the few trees that had survived the second major Dutch elm disease outbreak in the nineties had been uprooted by straight-line winds eight years ago. It had been a civic tragedy, and although the lilacs were pretty in the spring, they had an impermanent quality, like most things in the twenty-first century.

When Magozzi's phone rang on the sedan's console, he fumbled for it with messy fingers and it slipped out of his grasp. 'Shit. Gino, can you grab that?'

Gino reached for it and answered. 'Hi, Grace. Leo has his mouth full of meatball and can't talk right now.' He listened for a few moments. 'Dahl? Yeah, he's on the up-and-up, don't shoot him.' He paused and listened again. 'Okay, we'll see you soon.' He hung up and wiped a smear of tomato sauce off the screen with his glove. 'Dahl's meeting us at Harley's for a face-to-face.'

'That was fast. Something must have happened in Fedland.'

'Yep. Grace said they might have caught a break with Lydia's book, too.'

Agent Dahl was already there when they arrived at Harley's, waiting for them at the door. Grace, Harley, and Lydia were notably absent.

'So you're the butler now, Dahl?' Gino asked, his nose upturning at the distant aroma of something baked and sweet. 'How did you pull this off? I mean, Harley and Grace know you, but what gives? It took them two years to let us in without handcuffs and blindfolds.'

'Charm,' Dahl deadpanned. 'Pure charm.'

'Sure.' Gino looked around. 'Where is everybody?'

'In the kitchen. I was told not to leave the foyer until you two arrived. I got past the front door, but that's where the welcome wagon ended.' He looked up at the big spruce Christmas tree. 'Do you know there's a fifty-caliber handgun hanging from the inner boughs?'

'Harley gets really creative this time of year,' Magozzi said, moving closer to Dahl. 'So what happened with Shafer? Is this an official visit?'

Dahl shrugged. 'No. I'm off the clock until further notice.'

'So, off the books.'

'Yes. Which I'm certain is the only reason your friends let me in.'

Magozzi raised a brow. 'But Shafer sent you here.'

Dahl didn't answer right away. He didn't have to. Shafer wanted him here without his hands tied. If Monkeewrench came up with some important, ill-gotten information, Dahl could present it as an anonymous tip and Shafer would have plausible deniability if the shit hit the fan. In that case, Dahl would probably be the fall guy; a rogue agent teetering on the same gray line that Magozzi and Gino often confronted when it came to Monkeewrench. 'I'm here to offer whatever support I can,' he finally said.

Magozzi really didn't care what the backstory was – Dahl was an extra gun and an extra pair of eyes, and it was a reasonable assumption that they all had the same end game in mind – find the bad guys and keep Lydia Ascher alive. He gestured toward the kitchen, and Dahl and Gino followed.

Grace was on the phone, pacing the floor, and Harley and Lydia were sitting motionless at the breakfast bar, listening to the one-sided conversation intently. They all gave distracted waves to Magozzi, Gino, and Dahl, but nobody said anything that would interrupt.

Since the phone call was clearly important and nobody was talking, Gino grabbed a Christmas cookie from a plate on the counter to give his mouth something to do while he waited.

The room seemed airless until Grace finally hung up and acknowledged the newcomers with sharp blue eyes. 'Annie and Roadrunner are on their way to the cemetery,' she pronounced with no explanation.

'What cemetery?' Magozzi, Gino, and Dahl asked in unison.

# Fifty-One

Magozzi, Gino, and Agent Dahl chose lookout posts on the main level of the mansion, where they had clear lines of sight to the front gate, the alley in back, and the side yards and carriage house. Their role as guards was painfully redundant, because Harley's place was so wired up that everybody inside had the ability to constantly monitor security screens from a hell of a lot more angles than three pairs of cops' eyes looking out windows.

And far more effective than any human could ever be were the computers that were also monitoring the security screens with far more efficiency. The computer knew when a bunny jumped out from behind a shrub thirty or a hundred feet away and let you know about it the second it happened; the armed men inside would only know if there was a full-on assault of the property, and that just wasn't going to happen with Harley's yard lit up brighter than the Vegas strip and a whole lot of cops, on duty and off, trolling the neighborhood and watching the perimeter. And yet computers missed things sometimes, just like humans. And relinquishing all control to machines just didn't seem right.

They were all still cavemen at heart, Magozzi realized, protecting their perimeter, protecting their women. A gun was just a modern version of a club. Evolution didn't have a prayer of ever catching up with technology.

Magozzi looked away from the front hall window when he heard the soft hum of the elevator descending from the third-floor office. Grace and Harley emerged, carrying laptops. They both seemed calm, but there was an underlying current of urgency to their presence. It wasn't a social visit.

'Is everything all right?'

Grace nodded. 'Better than all right. Where are Gino and Dahl?'

'They're manning other battle stations down here.'

One corner of Grace's mouth twitched so slightly, anybody else would have missed it. 'Well, you're all doing a good job. Not a single barbarian has stormed the ramparts yet.' She stepped closer. 'The Beast just found something important, but it's nothing you and Gino can use and we're at the end of a trail. Do you trust Dahl?'

'He wouldn't have gotten past the foyer if we didn't trust him. I also have the feeling that his job is on the line just by being here.'

'Good. Because we need him.' She turned and cocked her head at Harley.

He walked over to an intercom mounted on the wall and pressed a button. His voice boomed through speakers that echoed through the house. 'Calling all knights in shining armor to the front.'

It took Gino and Dahl roughly thirty seconds to appear. They all clustered around Harley while he toggled up a screen on his laptop. It was dominated by a blinking map, a satellite photo, and a table of encoded computer commands. 'Ta-dah,' he said victoriously, waving a big arm toward the screen.

'What are we looking at?' Magozzi asked.

'A point of origin for the cyberattacks that took down Charles Spencer's website and hacked the Chatham Hotel server. The trail ends here. Whoever these bastards are, they bounced us around the globe a few times trying to hide their tracks, but there's no question in my mind or Grace's – these are your bad guys. Or at least some of them. We just don't know *who* they are. Not exactly, anyhow.' He narrowed his eyes at Dahl. 'Of course, we did absolutely nothing illegal to obtain this information, it all came from an anonymous tip.'

Dahl's nose was practically pressed against the screen. 'Of course. Where is this?'

'A house in upstate New York.'

'Who owns it?' Magozzi asked.

Harley rubbed his hands together. 'This is where it gets good and juicy. The owner is listed as a private foundation that just happens to be a nonprofit arm of Silver Dune Technology.'

'The same company that's making computer chips at AIF up in Cheeton.'

'You got it. For a charity, they've never been real big on publicity, but their 504C reporting checks out as far back as I could go.'

'What do they do?' Dahl asked, his eyes still riveted on Harley's computer screen.

'Their mission statement is "providing technology and infrastructure to developing nations." Basically, they set up wireless communication hubs in third world countries and give away shitloads of computers to facilitate commerce in poor, remote areas, so you don't have to walk a hundred miles carrying a load of yak wool or whatever to find out if there's actually a market for your stuff in a city center by the time you get there.'

Magozzi frowned. 'Not exactly nefarious. So this charity is some kind of a front?'

'Ninety-nine percent of it seems legit. It's the other one percent lurking in the shadows we have to worry about. I might add that they have had generous government subsidies over the years.'

Gino's imagination was taking the fast lane to the dark side. 'Great. So Silver Dune is some kind of a government front that suddenly decided it would be a good idea to kill U.S. citizens between philanthropic missions.'

Harley gave Gino a sympathetic look. 'You can spin this thing seven ways to Sunday. I'm just telling you what we know right now.'

'What about the Russian angle? Assuming this is all tangled up with the H-bomb and the Cold War never really ended.'

'It didn't,' Grace interjected. 'And if this is about the hydrogen bomb, you can be sure the Russians are involved. They were there from the beginning. But the hydrogen bomb went out of style with bouffants, dead in the water as a weapon after the testing ban in 1968. And it's not like you could hide secret detonations if you were still doing research. Harley and I think the Sixth Idea is about something else.' She looked around the room and preempted the question that was on everyone's lips. 'We don't know what.'

Magozzi tapped Dahl on the shoulder. 'The New York house is a little out of our jurisdiction and we don't have legal proof that connects it or the people in it with our homicides. The FBI is the only one who can work this. Think you can convince Shafer to run with it?'

Dahl was already slipping on his overcoat as he headed toward the front door. 'I don't think he'll need any convincing.'

After Dahl had left, Gino clapped Harley on the back. 'Stellar work.'

'Aw, shucks. Grace did most of it. I'm just a pretty face around here.'

'I'm guessing none of this information came from an anonymous tip like you told Dahl, so how the hell did you really get it?'

'The short answer? It's all about mistakes. Almost everybody makes them, overlooks something, forgets to close a door, or maybe they didn't even know the door was open in the first place. That's what we laser in on. All it takes is a missing patch on a neglected part of a server that permits an unauthorized command prompt, or a misconfigured firewall rule base, or –'

'Okay, gotcha. You guys are geniuses, end of story.'

Harley grinned. 'If you say so.'

Magozzi felt a little uneasy. He knew Monkee-wrench took risks all the time in their work; often very dangerous ones and always for the sole benefit of law enforcement and justice in general. Their cat-footed hacking was stealthy and elegant and their bold trespasses over the years had never been detected.

But no matter how brilliant, careful, or vigilant you were, there were times when you opened a door and a little something either snuck in or escaped, just slipped by without notice, like Harley had just told Gino. And the thought scared him.

He looked at Grace. 'This Silver Dune, we're obviously talking about some kind of institution. A well-funded one at that, and you broke down their door and connected them to some very nasty business. Are you sure you covered your tracks?'

Grace gave him a patient smile, the kind reserved for toddlers and naughty puppies. 'We did better than that – we left them a little parting gift.'

Magozzi cocked a brow at her.

'Let's just say we gave their system the flu.'

'Like a virus?'

Harley snorted. 'Hell, we gave their system Ebola. They're not going to be operational for a while.'

# Fifty-Two

'I don't have a good feeling about this, Annie.' Roadrunner was fidgeting and squirming in the passenger seat of the SUV they'd rented in Rochester.

Annie kept her eyes on the turnpike as she brushed Roadrunner's comment aside with a dismissive wave. 'Do you honestly think Grace and Harley would ask us to do something that would put us in danger?'

'I know they wouldn't. That's not what I'm talking about.'

Roadrunner's anxiety had been palpable the entire hour they'd been on the road, but as they got closer to Oak Hill Cemetery, it was reaching fever pitch, and starting to fray Annie's nerves. 'Oh, now don't you tell me you're all het up about visiting a little ol' cemetery.'

'Well, it's not like we're going to visit a dearly departed relative to pay our respects, we're basically going to rob a total stranger's grave.'

'We are *not* robbing a grave, we're following *instructions* from the grave. That book Grace told us about was a map, and we're going to execute the last wishes of the gentleman who wrote it because his granddaughter can't.'

'It's creepy. And what if we find something?'

'That's kind of the point, sugar. Come on, now, just relax. What we're trying to do now is hopefully save some living people, which doesn't leave us time to worry about the ghost of a man sixty years dead.'

'You believe in ghosts?'

'Of course not. I was just trying to make the point that we're on a mission here.'

Roadrunner sighed, then turned his focus to his phone, swiping through screens. He finally said, 'Annie, would you please take the next exit?'

'But our exit's not for another ten miles.'

'Yeah, but there's a gas station at the next exit.'

'We don't need gas.'

'I know, but I need to get something.'

Annie obeyed without question, because Roadrunner obviously needed a little cooling down, and if a gas station did it for him, then so be it. As she pulled into the parking lot of a mega-stop, a light, snowy mist started to coat the windshield.

While Roadrunner trotted inside, she stuck her head out the window and saw thick, dark snow clouds beginning to fill in the sky. Great. This was the part of the B horror flick when angry spirits opened up the heavens and stranded the protagonists in a very bad place where they would ultimately get sucked up into a demonic vortex.

Grave robbing, she snickered to herself. Such nonsense. She'd known Roadrunner for years, but she'd never even entertained the idea that such an analytical genius might actually believe in ghosts and spirits. As far as she was concerned, there was no point wasting precious time worrying about the possibility of paranormal horrors when there were already more than enough real-life horrors in the world to drive you mad a million times over.

*Don't ever whistle past a graveyard.*

*Why not?*

*Because you don't know who you'll wake up.*

Annie shivered a little and closed the window. It was getting colder outside.

A few minutes later Roadrunner trotted back out to the car with a cellophane-wrapped bouquet of sad-looking flowers. They had them at the checkouts of most every gas station or convenience store so the guilty or the rushed could pick up a last-minute peace offering for the aggrieved party in their life while they filled up their gas tanks. She'd gotten a few of those herself, a long time ago, from a man she'd ultimately had to stab to death. Not because of the last-minute, substandard flowers, of course.

But the odd thing was, she had always felt sorry for the flowers above all, that they had been singled out as inadequate for a floral shop and had been packaged and sent to languish in places where nobody appreciated them.

'What on earth, Roadrunner?' she asked, quickly terminating her strange, very dark train of thought.

'I am not going to visit a grave without an offering.'

Annie closed her eyes, summoning every last bit of forbearance and patience in her soul. 'That's a very nice gesture.'

The cemetery gates were open when they arrived – it was one of those grand old East Coast cemeteries that probably had graves dating back two hundred years and trees much older than that. The scrollwork iron fence was ornate and decidedly from a bygone era, but it had been well cared for over the years, as were the grounds. As Annie drove slowly down the plowed road into the cemetery, she saw a truck parked in front of what looked like a maintenance shed, where an older gentleman was sweeping the fresh snow off the front steps.

From what she could see, the three of them were the only living souls here.

She came to a fork in the road and stopped. 'Which way?'

Roadrunner was examining a map of the cemetery he'd printed out at the hotel. 'Take a right. That leads to an older part of the cemetery where the mausoleums are.'

'Are you doing all right, sugar?'

'I'm fine, Annie. Thanks.'

And he did seem fine. Calm, almost. 'I'm glad to hear that. No offense, but you were a little skittish on the way down here.'

He looked out the window and gestured. 'Yeah, I know. But look at all these tombstones. They're permanent memories of people, so many people. Generations of them, and they all meant something to somebody. It's almost . . . peaceful. Pretty. I wasn't expecting that.'

Well, Annie did have to admit that the place was pretty and so were the snow-dusted tombstones and monuments and the evergreen wreaths and swags that decorated many of them. And the people below the monuments were definitely in peace, but she'd never found solace walking among them. Or even driving around them. 'You were really expecting ghouls?'

Roadrunner looked over at her and gave her an apologetic half-smile. 'I always expect the worst. It's nice to be wrong.'

Annie had half a mind to tell Roadrunner that if you always anticipated the worst and it didn't happen, you were torturing yourself for no reason; and if you anticipated the worst and it did happen, you were just living through it twice. But now was not the time for sharing psychological chestnuts. 'Are we almost there?'

'It should be up on the left. Lydia said it was a big white one with a Grecian-style portico where the family name is. Buchanan. There it is.' He pointed ahead.

Annie stopped the car in front of an ornate stone structure that might have once been white, but was now discolored from decades in the elements. How many decades? she wondered. More than six, for sure.

She shivered a little as the weak late afternoon light, the softly falling snow, the shadows of surrounding trees played tricks on her eyes. She suddenly realized she had seen one too many horror movies in her life to feel good about prancing into an old mausoleum filled with the bones of a bunch of strangers. Maybe there *was* such a thing as ghosts, and maybe those ghosts wouldn't be very pleased by their intrusion into their sacred place of eternal rest.

*Don't ever whistle past a graveyard . . .*

'Annie?'

'What?'

'Are you ready?' Roadrunner was clutching the bouquet of flowers.

'Uh . . . do you think it's going to be dark in there?'

He looked a little alarmed. 'I never thought about that. We don't have a real flashlight, just the flashlight apps on our phones, and they suck.'

They should have thought of that at the car rental counter. *Do you have a flashlight we could borrow for our trip? Because we're going to be creeping around a cemetery at dusk and opening up a crypt and the flashlight apps suck.* 'We're going to have to prop open the door and let in as much natural light as possible,' she said with false confidence.

'There is no natural light. The sun's setting.'

Annie noticed sweat beading on Roadrunner's upper lip. 'Then let's do this before it gets darker than it already is. Do you have the combinations Grace gave us?'

'Yeah.'

They crunched through the snow toward the mausoleum, making the only sounds in this disconcertingly silent place. No birds sang; no wind whistled through the bare branches of trees; there wasn't another soul to be seen, at least not a living one. Annie decided cemeteries should have outdoor speakers playing Muzak at all times.

They paused at the door; there was a keypad, just as Lydia had said there would be – a modern, aftermarket touch that made it accessible to visiting family at any time, even without an appointment. Spur of the moment, midnight picnic with dear Uncle Bob? Sure, why not?

Roadrunner's hand was shaking a little as he pulled a piece of paper out of his jacket pocket and started punching in the combination. A few moments later, they both jumped a little when they heard the thunk of a lock disengaging.

They looked at each other. Annie saw fear in Roadrunner's eyes, and it was a pretty sure bet he was seeing the same thing in hers. Which was just silly. Silly, silly, silly, she'd let Roadrunner's superstitions and all those horror movies warp her common sense. She took a deep breath, lifted her chin bravely, and pushed open the door.

'Agh!' she took a halting step back.

'What? What!?'

Annie swept her hand in front of her face, nose crinkled in distaste. 'Cobwebs. God, they're everywhere. I guess those little bastards don't need a combination to get in.'

Roadrunner sighed in relief, actually smiled, then warily stepped inside, his head rotating back and forth. The place smelled musty and it was frigidly cold and really gloomy, but other than the cobwebs, it seemed nice enough and well looked after. And the best part was there were no boogeymen hanging out in the shadows, waiting to ambush them. In fact, there wasn't a sign that anybody or anything besides spiders had been in here to pay respects in a very long time.

There were stone vases mounted by each crypt drawer, all of them empty. Roadrunner found Lydia Ascher's grandfather's drawer in the gloom – Donald Buchanan, a brass plaque informed – and placed the gas station bouquet in the vase. It probably wasn't the most beautiful tribute he'd ever received, but it was something, at least, and he was glad he'd made Annie stop. 'Here it is, Annie.'

Annie was looking around, letting her eyes adjust to the darkness. The light from the open door was meager, but it was a godsend all the same. 'So . . . I guess we open it.'

Roadrunner gulped audibly. 'Yeah. But there's nothing inside, remember? It's just a memorial.'

'Well, if there's nothing inside, then why are we opening it?'

'I meant there's no dead guy inside. But there might be something else in there.'

*And if there is, what the hell are we going to do with it? Does it come with instructions?* Annie's breath was coming quicker now, and it sounded loud in her head in the absence of any other sounds. Neither of them moved for a moment, they just stood there and stared at the name plaque by the drawer, gathering their courage to either violate Donald Buchanan's final resting place, or fulfill a plan he'd conceived sixty years ago.

'Roadrunner, just open it.' Annie started stomping her feet back and forth, trying to warm them up. 'It's freezing in here, it's getting darker by the minute, and I would dearly like to get out of this place as soon as possible.'

Roadrunner took a deep breath and let it out in a frosty cloud. 'Okay.' His fingers were cold-stiff and shaky as he punched in the second code. Another lock disengaged with a click that echoed eerily in the closed space. 'I'm going to open it now, Annie,' he whispered, grasping the handle and slowly pulling out the drawer.

Annie pinched her eyes shut. Would bats fly out? Would there be bones, ashes, rats, mice, giant spiders, maybe some ungodly demon that would rise up and begin Armageddon? Or maybe a deadly fungus or mold spores that would kill them on the spot. The archaeologists who'd opened up Tut's tomb didn't fare so well.

'It looks empty,' he whispered.

Annie opened her eyes and very bravely stepped next to him, holding up her phone. The flashlight app was weak, but it was a little extra light all the same, just enough to illuminate something at the very back of the drawer. 'Looks like some kind of a portfolio. Grab that thing, honey, and let's hightail it out of here.'

# Fifty-Three

Annie had a death grip on the steering wheel of the rental as she squinted through the driving snow that was turning the expressway back to Rochester into a luge course. Her stomach flip-flopped every time she saw the traction control light flash on the dashboard, but at least Roadrunner wasn't freaking out, which he usually did during difficult driving conditions – he seemed totally preoccupied with the documents from Donald Buchanan's portfolio. Occasionally he would make little sounds and carefully shuffle the fragile old pages around, holding them closer to the faint library light above his visor.

'Don't hold out on me, Roadrunner. Did you figure out what the Sixth Idea is?'

He sighed and gently lowered the pages to his lap. 'It's a theory. These are notes, schematics, formulas – I'm no nuclear physicist, so half of this stuff might as well be Sanskrit.'

'What about the half that isn't in Sanskrit?'

'It's all about the electromagnetic pulse the bombs generated. He was trying to find a way

320

to harness the destructive energy and direct it specifically to selected targets. Wipe out the electrical and communications grid of a city, a country, a continent, without the mass destruction and toxic fallout of a multimegaton bomb. It would have been pretty bad news back in the fifties – nothing electrical would work. That's probably why Lydia's grandfather focused on building a generator in his book. But can you imagine an EMP strike today? The entire world runs on electronics and computers, and they'd be fried in an instant. Planes would literally be falling out of the sky, and that's just for starters. It would be catastrophic.'

Annie caught her breath. 'Oh my God. Everything would be gone in a heartbeat. No air travel, no transportation of any sort, no phones, no food, no water, no medicine, no money.'

'Yep. The supply chain would be toast. We'd be thrown back two hundred years. You take away electricity, computers, electronics, it would be the end of the world as we know it.'

Annie grunted. 'You've got that right, and people have been paranoid about it for years. And hackers have been threatening to do it for years.'

'Yeah, but if hackers took down a big power grid, they're just temporarily immobilizing the software that runs the system. Like the Stuxnet virus that shut down Iran's nuclear centrifuges. Iran eventually got them back up online. EMP destroys the hardware, the electronic components, from computers to transformers to cell phones. Everything would have to be rebuilt, and if you had a weapon like Donald Buchanan was theorizing . . .'

'You could strike again and again, as soon as there was something rebuilt.'

'Right.'

'But that's impossible. Nothing but a huge nuke can generate that kind of destructive EMP. Making a stealth, precision weapon out of it is science fiction.' Annie stole a glance at him. 'Isn't it?'

Roadrunner tipped his head. 'Well, the concept of a nuclear bomb was science fiction at one time, too. So was space travel. Science has a way of eventually catching up with fiction. And I could point out the obvious – people who had anything to do with the Sixth Idea or even any mention of it are suddenly getting killed. Why would you kill a bunch of innocent people over something that doesn't exist?'

Roadrunner had made a good point, but Annie didn't like the nihilistic tone their conversation was taking. Then again, she hadn't liked much about this entire day, especially the cemetery visit.

'Why do you think Donald Buchanan left all these cryptic notes for his daughter? What would she do with them? We don't even know what to do with them.'

'I don't know. Maybe he thought these papers would be some kind of leverage in the future. He was working for the government. Maybe he didn't trust the government any more than we trust it now.'

'Well, that's some solid thinking in any era.' Annie finally exited the freeway and headed toward their hotel. As she pulled into the parking garage and nosed into a slot, Roadrunner made a strange sound.

'What is it?'

Roadrunner flicked on the overhead dome light and handed Annie a sheet of paper with a hand-drawn schematic. 'What does that look like to you?'

Annie studied the paper for a long time. 'It looks like a crude version of the first logical map of ARPANET.'

Roadrunner bobbed his head. 'One of the progenitors of the Internet.'

Annie scowled. 'This doesn't make sense. These guys were building bombs, not computers.'

'What if they're one and the same? Computers produce electromagnetic pulses.'

'Yes, but we're talking millivolts, not megatons. The only thing a computer's EMP can hurt is its own motherboard if it's not arrayed properly.'

Roadrunner shrugged nonchalantly, but Annie could practically hear the wheels grinding in his head. 'Yeah. I suppose you're right. But what if you could tie millions of computers together all over the world and plant some kind of a doomsday switch, a chip or a virus or something, that would consolidate and amplify each computer's electromagnetic pulse? You could push a button, and boom – game over.'

'That is something I don't even want to think about. Come on, let's get up to the room and send this to Harley and Grace. I'll call and let them know.'

Annie dialed the Monkeewrench office as they walked through the lobby, her eyes lingering on the bartender, who was opening a bottle of champagne for a young couple, which seemed like a great idea at the moment. If anything warranted a glass or two of champagne, it was surviving a visit to a creepy mausoleum at dusk and retrieving a possible blueprint for a modern apocalypse. She shivered, still imagining the ghosts of cobwebs dancing around her face and neck. 'Gracie?'

'Annie. Are you back at the hotel?'

'Yes, and we had quite the excursion, thank you very much. We picked up a little present for you and we're sending the package. Are you up in the office to get it?'

'Yes, send it as soon as you can.'

'Give us ten minutes, we just got to the room. But don't get your hopes up too high. We have notes and sketches and that's about it. No answers.'

'That's fine, Annie. Thank you. Thank you both.'

Annie let out a dramatic sigh. 'Well, I'm not going to lie – you and Harley owe us.'

'It was that bad?'

Annie heard the smile in Grace's voice, which made her smile, too. 'We endured unimaginable horrors, and as it turns out, Roadrunner is extremely superstitious. He made me stop at a gas station to buy flowers for a dead man who wasn't even there. Is Lydia all right?'

'Safe and sound. She's resting in the bedroom next to the office.'

Roadrunner held his hand out. 'Let me talk to Grace for a minute.'

'Roadrunner wants a word, sugar. We'll see you in a couple days.'

'Grace, is Harley there with you?'

'I'm right here, buddy. We have you on speaker.'

'Good. Listen, I've spent the past two hours going over the paperwork we picked up in the tomb. It's not exactly light reading, so I wanted to give you a leg up on what I got out of it: it looks like Donald Buchanan was trying to weaponize EMP.'

'EMP was a result of big-ass nuke detonations,' Harley said. 'You can't get more weaponized than that.'

'No, I mean he was trying to figure out a way to generate EMP without the big-ass nukes and use it as a precision weapon to strike specific targets. You know, like destroy Moscow's power grid without the fallout and destruction of a nuclear strike. At least that was an example in Donald Buchanan's papers.'

Harley grunted. 'So basically, bomb whoever your enemy du jour is back to the Stone Age without the bomb. Damn. Donald Buchanan was a hacker at heart back when computers were just little infants.'

'Funny you said that. Because in all this theoretical physics stuff I found something we all know – a rudimentary schematic of ARPANET. Donald Buchanan was working on the basis for the Internet a full decade before it was even on anybody's radar.'

In the Monkeewrench office, Harley and Grace were silent for a long moment.

'Hello? Harley? Grace? Are you guys still there?'

'We're here,' Grace said quietly.

'Listen, I know it sounds a little wacky, but what if computers could be engineered to become a delivery system for EMP? Like through the Internet?'

When Grace finally hung up, she and Harley stared at each other as mental tumblers clicked into place. 'Silver Dune. They've been giving away computers all over the world for decades.'

'And manufacturing processing chips at American Iron Foundry up in Cheeton. The government took over American Iron Foundry during World War Two so they could build their bombs. What if the government is still running the place under the Silver Dune umbrella? Holy shit, Grace, ninety percent of the computers in the world use their chips. What if those chips are doctored up? Everybody in the world with a computer or a cell phone is potentially sitting on a mini version of an EMP bomb, and if you could link them all together through the Internet . . .' Harley took a deep breath. 'Man, is this the greatest, most insane conspiracy theory ever?'

'It's definitely insane. And totally improbable.'

They both flinched when the security alarm tripped.

Downstairs, a soft alarm sounded through Harley's mansion and Gino and Magozzi froze. 'What does that mean?' Gino asked.

Behind them, the elevator door opened and Harley clomped toward the computer station set up in the foyer. 'It means the security program picked up an anomaly on one of the cameras. Threat assessment is low, which means it's outside the immediate perimeter.'

'How do you know?'

'Because if the threat was imminent and inside the gates, you'd be hearing an alarm louder than a Metallica concert.' He poked at the monitor. 'Okay, here it is, live feed on screen sixteen.'

Magozzi and Gino crowded behind Harley. The security monitor showed a man walking down the empty sidewalk on the mansion side of the street. He slowed, then stopped as he approached the edge of Harley's property. As if posing for cameras he knew were there, he tipped his head upward in their direction. 'What the hell?' Gino finally whispered. 'This guy wants to be seen or what?'

Magozzi's borrowed shoulder unit squawked – one of the officers keeping an eye on Harley's and the neighborhood in general. 'Detective? I've got eyes on an individual approaching the gate.'

'We see that, Officer. Keep your position and keep watching.'

'Yes sir.'

Gino, Harley, and Magozzi continued to stare at the screen. Bizarrely, the man on the sidewalk suddenly looked up directly into one of the cameras positioned on the gate, then raised his hands palm-out to indicate he had no ill intentions. Presumably.

Gino's brows crept up his forehead. 'Holy shit. That's Arthur Friedman, our BOLO. Just a wild guess, but this guy didn't just stumble on us and Monkeewrench in an Alzheimer's stupor.'

'Jesus Pete,' Harley muttered. 'The last of the original eight. And he's a dead man walking out there on the street. We've gotta get him in here. Just make sure he's not carrying a nuke or a death ray gun in his pocket.'

'Gino and I will take care of it. Where are Grace and Lydia?'

'Upstairs. They're going to stay put until we figure out what this is all about. Listen, guys, I don't have time for details, but we just got off the phone with Annie and Roadrunner. They're back from raiding Donald Buchanan's crypt. Gino, I think we've got you beat in the crazy-train, outlandish-theory division.'

Gino puffed up indignantly. 'My outlandish theories are almost always right. Partially.'

'Let's hope ours isn't, but Arthur Friedman is probably the only guy on the face of the earth that can fill in some blanks.'

# Fifty-Four

Max was sitting in the back of a utility service vehicle. There were appropriate tools in the van, but none he would use, other than a safe filled with ample stacks of cash and passports from all over the globe and the usual array of electronics. Unfortunately, the electronics were useless here – he knew all about Monkeewrench, their skills and talents, and it would be impossible to breach any communications. It would also be impossible to access and kidnap Lydia Ascher, which was his most recent directive. His job here was going to be old-school: Wait. Watch. Terminate his mission if things got too hot, or wait for somebody to terminate the mission for him.

It had initially surprised him that Monkeewrench was harboring Lydia Ascher, but the more he thought about it, the more sense it made. They worked with the cops all the time, Detectives Magozzi and Rolseth in particular, who had drawn the unfortunate card of several homicides that apparently had roots too deep for any one person to possibly divine. And there was really no place safer than the corporate headquarters of a group of paranoid computer geniuses. He knew a lot of people just like them – some were white hats, some were black, but all of them were nuts. In fact, he knew of one in central Africa who had a crocodile-filled moat around his compound.

Max was pleased with his quickly accumulating bankroll, but also increasingly disheartened. His jobs had always been simple, well-paid tasks, but this particular job was quickly outgrowing his level of skill and compensation. Protect or kill, those were orders he could understand. But then they'd switched the game on him and he was now being ordered to kidnap and interrogate his charges about something called the Sixth Idea.

He thought about Alvin Keller, a helpless, sick old man who'd most likely died from sheer terror right in front of his eyes. And then there was Lydia Ascher, an innocent young woman. If he managed to get her into his custody, what would happen to her if she was turned over to someone like Ivan for further interrogation?

With this new shift in the focus of the mission and the increasingly distasteful tenor of events, he found himself thinking more and more about Montana, about retirement, about finally disappearing from the face of the earth. Whatever this Sixth Idea was, he didn't want anything to do with it.

The problem was, without a very compelling reason to terminate this mission, he was stuck here, because the people who hired him demanded results. And if results weren't delivered, he would be the one getting terminated permanently.

He checked his watch, then started up the van. He knew he would be under very sophisticated scrutiny from inside the house, and an idle service vehicle sitting around on a curb for too long without workers performing a task wouldn't escape that scrutiny.

But as he was about to pull away from the curb, he saw a lone figure walking slowly up the sidewalk, approaching the mansion's locked front gate. He was a tall, thin man in an oversized coat and his gait was unsteady and weary. The man stopped at the security box at Harley Davidson's gate and pushed a button.

Max took his binoculars from the case and focused on the man, whose face was lit up by the lights that flooded the yard and the sidewalk beyond. There was no question – this man knew exactly where he was going and what he was doing.

And Max knew exactly who he was. He dropped the binoculars on his lap and shook his head in disbelief. This was probably no laughing matter, but he couldn't stop smiling. Son of a bitch. *Son of a bitch!* he thought to himself. Arthur Friedman had fooled them all.

# Fifty-Five

Magozzi was standing in the shelter of Harley's front porch, watching the old man walk up to the mansion through falling snow. He had momentarily toyed with the ridiculous notion that Friedman was really an assassin with a perfect cover, sent here to kill Lydia. But that healthy-cop paranoia fizzled when he locked eyes with him. Arthur Friedman was a terrified and desperate ninety-two-year-old man, and he didn't look so good. His face was pale and gaunt and dark crescents rimmed his eyes. His overcoat was far too large for his frame, and his gait was cautious and shuffling.

*Jesus Christ, are you going to let this guy fall and break a hip on the sidewalk, Magozzi?*

He jumped down off the front steps and offered his hand. 'Please, sir, allow me.'

'Thank you very much, Detective Magozzi. My name is Arthur Friedman and I need your help. The same people who committed the homicides you are investigating will kill me if they find me.'

A million questions were racing through Magozzi's mind, but this was definitely not the place to ask them. 'We know, Dr. Friedman. You're number one on the list of people who might know anything about the Sixth Idea. We need to get you inside immediately.'

Dr. Friedman had wild, white eyebrows that lifted slightly. 'You know about the Sixth Idea?'

'We know it's getting people killed. Come in, Doctor.' Magozzi gently took Friedman by the elbow and led him inside. His arm was frail and bony beneath the sleeve of his jacket, and he was shivering. 'Obviously you don't have Alzheimer's.'

'Thank you for noticing. In truth, I was hiding at Meadowbrook, but no place is safe forever.' He stopped abruptly once inside the big double doors. The grandiosity of the mansion had stopped many visitors in their tracks, but there were also three people standing shoulder to shoulder, waiting for them, and they were all armed.

'Dr. Friedman, this is my partner, Gino Rolseth, and Grace MacBride and Harley Davidson.'

'Ah. Monkeewrench. I need your help most of all, which is why I'm here. I'm afraid something horrible is going to happen and you might be the only people who can stop it.' He paused and wrung his hands. 'But I'm not sure where to begin, because everything I have to say will convince you I'm a demented, delusional old man, and I don't think we have time for a psychiatric evaluation to prove otherwise.'

Grace's eyes sparked and fixed intently on Friedman's. 'Are you referencing the Sixth Idea, Doctor?'

Friedman nodded. 'How much do you know?'

'We know that Donald Buchanan had a visionary theory, foreseeing a future where computers were commonplace, producing small amounts of electromagnetic pulse that might somehow be harnessed into a weapon if all the computers could be tied together.'

Friedman staggered a little against Magozzi's arm. 'My God, how could you possibly know that?'

'We have copies of some of his documents,' Harley explained. 'In them is a crude schematic of ARPANET.'

He shook his head in disbelief. 'The Sixth Idea was indeed a theory back then. But I believe it exists now, and I'm afraid an attack might be imminent . . . Is there someplace I might sit down?'

Grace looked at Magozzi. 'Take Dr. Friedman to the den while Harley and I get Donald Buchanan's papers.'

Lydia was fully alert and sitting up in a chair when Grace entered the bedroom next to the office. Charlie was at her feet, pretending to be a guard dog. She looked composed, but her little gun was in her lap.

'False alarm?' she asked hopefully.

'In a way. One of your grandfather's colleagues is downstairs. A man named Arthur Friedman.'

Lydia's eyes widened. 'Why is he here?'

'He said he's here for help, but we haven't had a chance to talk to him yet, so stay upstairs until Harley or I come for you.'

'Does he know something?'

'I think he knows a lot, otherwise he wouldn't have found us, but I don't think he knows you're here, so let's keep it that way for the time being.'

'I'd like to speak with him. Unless he's here to kill me.'

Grace cocked a brow at her. 'He doesn't seem like the homicidal type. But let us make sure, then you can talk to him all you want. You have every right to hear what he has to say.'

'Once you establish that he's not here to kill me.'

'Exactly.'

# Fifty-Six

Magozzi was relieved to see Arthur Friedman slowly regaining color and strength as he huddled by the fire in the den, sipping from a hot mug of cocoa. Grace was sitting next to him, wisps of her dark hair backlit by the flames, creating a strange amber halo around her head. Her posture was tense and she was looking at Friedman like an entomologist might regard a newly discovered species of insect, but she was showing admirable restraint as she kept her questions mute.

'Thank you for this, Ms. MacBride. Now, where were we?'

'You said you thought an attack was imminent. What makes you think so?'

'Oh, yes, of course. First of all, I think there have been small-scale test runs of the Sixth Idea.'

'The blackouts?'

Friedman nodded. 'Yes. And because after years of inactivity, they're suddenly murdering anybody who might know anything about it. Trust me, if the Sixth Idea is a reality now, it's worth killing over to protect it and conceal it from the enemy. Or enemies, which seem to be proliferating at an alarming rate.'

Gino's frown was deep. 'With all due respect, Doctor, who the hell is *they*?'

'My former employers. Our government, or at least an esoteric, dark little branch of it.'

'But all the blackouts were in the U.S. Why would the government black out its own cities?'

'I would assume that at first they wanted to observe the testing closely, to make certain it worked as planned before launching it on an enemy. That's likely why the domestic blackouts were so short-lived and did little harm.

'But there were other attacks that our own media didn't find worthy of coverage. All but one province of Turkey lost power for ten hours last week. Minsk in Russia lost power for two days the week before, but none of this raises alarm bells. Power outages occur all the time, all over the world, for varying reasons. But what if these were all intentional? What if they never ended? And a larger attack – well, that would completely destroy anything electronic and the power grid could be crippled for months, if not longer. You could take down any regime in that time. Electronics rule the world now, and those who still have them could rule the world as well.'

Gino grunted. 'So our government is blacking out our cities and murdering innocent people so it can rule the world. Great.'

'Not so that it can rule the world, necessarily, but prevent others from attempting to.' Friedman let out a weary sigh. 'There are only two of us left – myself and a young woman, Donald Buchanan's granddaughter. I haven't been able to reach her, though.'

'Lydia Ascher,' Magozzi said. 'She's safe, Dr. Friedman. She was the one who led us to her grandfather's paperwork.'

Gino's face screwed up in distaste. 'Our government, huh? I pegged the Russians for this.'

'That was a valid assumption, Detective Rolseth, except the Russians don't have the Sixth Idea, although they want it badly.' Friedman gave him a dark smile. 'Ironic, isn't it? Our government is killing its own citizens and the Russians, of all people, are trying to save us. Detectives, I must ask about Alvin Keller. Has he been found?'

'I'm sorry, Dr. Friedman. He was found this morning. We believe his passing was from natural causes.'

Friedman closed his eyes and shook his head. 'The Russians kidnapped him for information about the Sixth Idea, and also to save him from the American assassins. His dreadful disease may have saved him from something worse.'

'How do you know all this?' Gino asked incredulously.

'Two Russians have been watching over me at Meadowbrook. A nurse named Vera and her friend Max. They speak Russian to each other, trusting that no Alzheimer's patient would understand, but I happen to be fluent.'

Harley entered the room quietly and laid a sheaf of papers on the hearth. 'These are the notes we have, Doctor.'

Friedman's hands started to shake. 'My God,' he whispered. 'This is a copy of Donald's original notes, in his handwriting. I thought these had all been destroyed or stolen years ago. Where did you find them?'

Magozzi shrugged uncomfortably, wondering if there was a good way to present this, or if he even should. But everything was pretty much on the table now, and there was no point in holding back. 'Donald left a message for his daughter that Lydia discovered. The papers were in his crypt.'

Friedman's eyes suddenly clouded, with tears or memories, or both, but then he smiled, showing a flash of age-yellowed teeth. 'Donald was a colleague, but he was also my best friend. And he told me time and time again that he would take the Sixth Idea to his grave. I had no idea he was being so literal.'

Grace refilled his mug from a carafe that was warming on the hearth. 'Dr. Friedman, tell us about the Sixth Idea. Tell us what we can do to help.'

# Fifty-Seven

'The Sixth Idea was Donald's baby, and something we all worked on for a short time before the project was ultimately scrapped. Or so we thought. As you have already surmised, his theory was to devise a globally interconnected network of millions of miniature EMP devices that could be selectively and remotely detonated. You could launch a surgical strike on a single building, a city, a country, a continent without the expense and massive devastation of a multimegaton nuclear bomb.

'The idea was that it would spare the people and cripple the technology that allowed corrupt tyrants and governments to rule and subjugate them. If we could disable the missiles and tanks, the transportation and communication of only the governments, the people would rise up to fill the vacuum with freedom and democracy.

'Like all brokers of chaos, we were deluded into thinking world peace was actually an achievable outcome, if only we had the proper weapon.

Of course, at the time, such a weapon was wildly theoretical. How could you plant millions of devices in hostile territories?'

'Enter the computer age.'

'Exactly, Ms. MacBride. Computers got smaller, the home computer was developed, and soon after that, everyone had to have one. The U.S. government, in a fit of false philanthropy, decided to give computers away to people who couldn't afford them – *all over the world.*'

Grace glanced at Harley. 'And if you implanted a doomsday chip in all of those computers, what you were really giving away were the components of a weapon that one day could be launched through the Internet.'

Gino folded his arms across his chest and leveled a harsh gaze at Harley. 'So this is your crazy-train theory you were trying to tell us about?'

'Pretty much.'

'Well, I'm impressed.' Gino looked around the room. 'Listen, I'm no expert on international policy, but if you could depose bad guys without massive human casualties, why would you want to stop it?'

Harley said, 'Because, Gino, once the Sixth Idea is out of the bag, it won't be long before everybody learns how to duplicate it. So you want to knock out Iran's nuclear program? Fantastic, I'm all for it, except then China or Russia or North Korea or somebody is going to get seriously pissed off and take out our whole power grid and everything that runs on it. And if you bring the U.S. to its knees, the rest of the world follows.'

'Don't forget the Islamist radicals,' Magozzi added. 'They've been trying to destroy Western civilization forever. If those crazy bastards got their hands on the Sixth Idea, they wouldn't have any moral qualms about using it to send the world back to the Stone Age and level the playing field.'

Friedman brightened and looked at Magozzi as if he were a promising young pupil. 'You just made the most important point, Detective Magozzi. Donald's theory was conceived during a different time, when mutually assured destruction protected the world from annihilation. If you are a civilized nation, you obviously don't want to destroy the world. The Cold War was bellicose and frightening, but in truth neither the U.S. nor the Soviet Union was ever going to start nuclear Armageddon – it was a stalemate from the very beginning. But those days are over. The terrorists changed everything – they don't care if they destroy themselves or the rest of the world, and the Sixth Idea is a perfect way to do it. Which is why we have to stop this.' He sighed and looked down into his mug of cocoa.

'As it turns out, medieval barbarism is perhaps the greatest weapon of mass destruction.'

Gino was fidgeting now, rubbing his thumbs together like he wanted to start a fire. 'Okay, that all makes sense, so can somebody tell me why our government would be stupid enough to take that risk and open Pandora's box?'

Friedman shook his head ruefully. 'We've done it before. Surely you've been alive long enough, Detective Rolseth, to realize that with great power comes great arrogance and a complete and utter lack of foresight. We unleashed two nuclear bombs to stop a war, and now that technology is not only available to anyone with the means to develop it, but already possessed by many nations – many unsavory nations who would like to destroy us. Donald understood that and it's what got him killed.'

Everyone's mouths formed silent O's; Grace was the first to find her voice. 'We thought he died in a plane crash.'

'He did, but that plane crash was no accident, and a couple dozen innocent souls died along with him. Donald was a fervent believer in mutually assured destruction in our time, when it was an effective deterrent, and he didn't think any one power should be in sole possession of something like the Sixth Idea if it were to become a reality. He threatened our handlers that he would go public if the project wasn't either exposed or scrapped. His plane exploded fifty feet off the tarmac two days later. Regrettably, the rest of us spent our lives looking over our shoulders, keeping our mouths shut.'

Friedman settled his gaze on Grace and Harley. 'I really have no idea how this can be stopped, or if it can be stopped – but since computers are an integral part of this, you seemed like the best hope, perhaps the only hope.'

Harley stood up from his seat and cracked his knuckles nervously. 'We traced cyberattacks related to one of the homicides to a house in upstate New York. The FBI is on the way and Grace and I already planted a bad bug in their servers. But I think we can make it worse.'

In the elevator on the way up to the office, Grace folded her arms across her chest and stared up at the polished wood ceiling. 'What's your idea, Harley?'

'Full-on assault. We're already into the bad guys' computers, so if we amp things up and kill the software, the chips are useless.'

'And if the software exists somewhere else?'

'This will buy us and the Feds some time. I've got this covered for now. Go get Lydia so she can meet Friedman.'

# Fifty-Eight

In the New York mansion, Zero looked at his four colleagues sitting around the table, thinking about how times had changed since the group's inception almost sixty years ago. The five of them still orchestrated the grand plan as their predecessors had, but over the years it had been necessary to call upon the talents of younger generations who had been born into a digital world. There were a dozen of them in the adjacent ballroom, where grand computers hummed and keyboards clicked.

Zero's mouth pinched in distaste at the muffled sound of exuberant voices coming from the other side of the common door. Some of them were barely into their twenties and acted like frat boys. So unprofessional. So undignified. And yet all of them were the best of the best, at the top of their field. Today they were celebrating the launch of their creation that would change the world, for the benefit of good men and women everywhere.

The intercom at Zero's right hand buzzed and a young voice he recognized but couldn't put a face to filled the room. 'Minus sixty, sirs. We're copacetic. In sixty minutes, Iran's nuclear program is going to be so fried it'll be like it never existed.'

'Thank you. We'll be in shortly.' Zero switched off the intercom and addressed the group. 'We're almost a year ahead of schedule and about to witness a whole new era of possibilities. Congratulations, gentlemen.'

There was excitement in the room, broad smiles and handshakes, but Three, always the spoiler, spoke up in his fussy, whiny voice while he stroked his wispy mustache, perhaps trying to coax it from the emaciated caterpillar it was into something more robust. 'But we still have some loose ends.'

'Alvin Keller is dead,' Zero snapped. 'Arthur Friedman is most likely dead as well, and even if he's not, his mind is – our people have confirmed that during their visits.'

'But Lydia Ascher . . .'

'Lydia Ascher is irrelevant at the moment. What is relevant is that in less than an hour, we are going to witness the birth of a miracle – a safer world. We'll deal with the last remaining detail afterwards if we deem it necessary.'

Some heated debate ensued at the table, most of which favored Zero's perception of things – with the Sixth Idea finally coming to life, a granddaughter of a dead scientist wasn't so important, at least for the time being.

Fifteen minutes later, as they were still debating, the intercom came to life again. Another young voice, this one panicked.

'Sirs, we can't execute.'

Zero felt a chill ride up his spine. 'Why?'

'We've been compromised.'

He heard loud voices in the background. 'Excuse me?'

'We've been hacked, sir. We were goddamned hacked.'

'Who was it? China? Russia?'

'We don't know. Whoever it was somehow got past our defenses and planted a virus that disabled our software and traced our location.'

*Traced our location?* Zero's mouth opened, and then closed. He heard his heart beating in his ears, felt it banging inside his chest. He didn't look at his colleagues around the table, afraid he would see his own terror on their faces.

They all knew what had to happen next. The rules were clear, immutable. Zero pulled out his keyboard tray and entered a numerical code. There wasn't much time to consider the consequences of those eleven keystrokes. Truth be told, he'd never imagined that this day would ever come. It had always seemed so perfect. They had the most magnificent weapon ever devised and they had guarded it jealously. Only five men in the entire world knew of its potential, and for the first time in history, a secret had been kept. Everything that had anything to do with the Sixth Idea was contained within the impenetrable walls of this house. And soon, sixty years of painstaking work and progress would be gone. So many lives and a weapon of sublime capabilities would be lost forever. But it had to be that way – whoever had breached this fortress could never be allowed to take possession of the Sixth Idea, and the only way to ensure that was to kill it; to wipe it entirely from existence as if it had never happened, as if it had never been conceived.

Immediately to his left, his second in command collected a sterling silver tray from a credenza behind him. It held five Waterford lowballs that shot colored arrows of light across the room. A decanter in the middle of the tray shimmered gold against its facets as he brought the tray to the table. His hands trembled as he made five generous pours into the lowball glasses.

Zero raised his glass, looked at each man, then said, 'Thank you, gentlemen. It has been an honor to serve with you.'

Then he looked down at his keyboard, pressed enter, and bizarrely, crossed himself. They all flinched involuntarily as they heard loud thunks throughout the mansion as heavy locks engaged on every door. And then the quieter but more sinister sound of hissing gas.

The five men at the table all heard the abrupt, urgent pounding on the door to the adjacent room, and the panicked voices.

'Sirs? Sirs! All our doors are locked from the outside and there's some kind of gas coming out of the vents that doesn't smell right! SIRS! WE CAN'T GET OUT!'

Zero's right eye began to twitch. He looked down so no one would notice. The voice on the other side of the door belonged to a young genius who had been so nervous, so excited about the possibility of working here that he had inadvertently blurted out his name when Zero had interviewed him. 'Please call me Tommy, sir.'

On the other side of the door, Tommy leaned his forehead against the wood. They had all heard the sounds of the locks clicking into place on the two doors that closed off their workroom.

At first, Tommy hadn't been alarmed, just startled. But then Frank collapsed at his desk, his face smashing down on his keyboard so hard it broke his nose and sent a gusher of blood over the letters.

Tommy moved first. Frank's desk was next to his, and they had become good friends over the years. He lifted Frank's face off the keyboard, saw his dead, open eyes, and felt quickly for a carotid pulse.

'Jesus.' He looked up at the others and didn't have to speak to convey the obvious. Frank was dead.

And then in the absolute horrified silence, they all heard the telltale hissing from the ceiling ventilator directly over Frank's desk, and the room deteriorated into chaos.

Men pounded on windows, threw chairs and their precious computers at glass that would never break. They threw themselves at doors that barely trembled in their casings, and the screaming and pleading was terrible to hear.

From the other side of the door, Zero heard another sound – the fingernails of men clawing at the wood of the door that separated them, and the pounding of fists that gradually weakened, and the screams that diminished and then died. And because he was suddenly very sleepy, he put his head on his hands and heard once again the voice of his Great-Uncle Elijah, who had lived through Auschwitz all those years ago.

I was one of those who survived, God forgive me. By cleaning the gas chambers after the horror. The first time I went into the stench and the darkness I saw a mountain of corpses piled on top of one another against the door, bloody gouges carved into the wood with broken fingernails stuck there like memories and accusations. It felt like my soul died that day, but I kept going back, day after black day, carrying out those bodies so I could live. Surely God will never forgive me for that.

Zero heard these words in his head as he fell into a pleasant, final slumber, hearing the dreadful scratches on the other side of that door. He was weeping as his breath finally stopped. *What have I done?*

# Fifty-Nine

Early morning sun was laying a faint bar of gold on the table in Harley's breakfast room, and even that feeble light hurt Magozzi's eyes. Dahl and Gino were sitting across from him and they both looked like they'd just come off a five-day bender in Vegas. Magozzi knew he looked as bad, and he felt even worse.

'You know why I'm here, Detectives.'

'Yeah,' Gino muttered. 'The Feds are taking over the case, which is exactly where it belongs, and I'm clicking my heels together to throw this pile of donkey dung into somebody else's lap. But what gives, Dahl? We've still got Lydia Ascher stashed upstairs and we'd like to be able to tell her she's going to see the light of day again.'

Dahl looked off to the side. 'You can tell her it's over.'

Magozzi scowled. 'Are you kidding? People have been chasing down this woman, trying to kill her for days, and you think she's going to take your word for it? That all of a sudden it's safe to show herself? You're going to have to do a hell of a lot better than that.'

Dahl leaned forward and said, 'Some of what I'm going to tell you will eventually become public once the investigation is closed. Some of it won't. For right now, none of it leaves this house. Agreed?'

Gino and Magozzi nodded.

'By the time our agents got to the house in New York, it was leveled to the ground. Gone. There was nothing left, and I mean nothing, except some partially incinerated bones and electronic components – a substantial amount of both – and those probably only survived because they were far enough away from the blast site.'

'Where was the blast site?'

'In the basement. There's a twenty-five-foot crater in the ground where the foundation was. It was rigged to self-destruct. Something scared the hell out of whoever was in that house – I'm guessing it was your friends hacking into their computers and finding their location. But whatever was in there is gone now, and it was obviously worth dying for.'

'But is it gone for good? Just because one house blew doesn't mean there aren't other houses just like it, other players continuing whatever twisted mission they had.'

'We've followed every associated lead so far. Silver Dune is gone. Any trace they ever existed is obliterated, including tax records. And American Iron Foundry in Cheeton filed bankruptcy yesterday. The plant was already gutted when our agents got there. The Cyber Crime Division came up empty because there was nothing left to mine.

'By all appearances, this was an autonomous entity that had a perfect doomsday switch for their operation. When you go to outrageous lengths to destroy something, you're not going to leave bread crumbs for somebody to follow in another place.'

'That's pretty damned sophisticated,' Gino grumbled. 'Way too sophisticated for the government to pull off.'

Dahl blinked at him, not sure if Gino had been joking. 'Or so sophisticated that *only* a government could pull it off. Our investigation will answer your questions eventually.'

'You just told us a lot without telling us anything.'

'Remember that, Detective Rolseth – I didn't tell you anything.' He looked at them both curiously. 'The Sixth Idea, Detectives. Did you ever find out what it is?'

Magozzi shifted uncomfortably in his chair. This was where things got dicey. Arthur Friedman had made a pretty compelling argument that the

Sixth Idea should stay buried, and Dahl had no clue Friedman had ever come here. They trusted Dahl, but in the end, he was government, which had apparently started this whole thing in the first place. 'Annie and Roadrunner found some old papers in Donald Buchanan's crypt. Early theoretical stuff on EMP, speculations about how it could become a weapon in the future. Nothing more than that.'

And that was absolutely true, Magozzi realized. The cemetery hadn't yielded anything more than what he'd just told Dahl – Monkeewrench had projected and envisioned how it might be a viable weapon in the modern era, but there was no proof it existed. Especially now.

'I see.' He stood up and gathered his coat and briefcase. 'I need to get back to the office, but I also need to take Ms. Ascher with me for a debriefing.'

Magozzi bristled. 'No way. You want to debrief her, you do it here. And only if you give us your word that the FBI is going to throw every single resource at her to keep her as safe as she needs to be, because I'm not so convinced this is over.'

'Really? You want to play this game?'

'It's not a game, it's a life, and I don't really give a shit who has jurisdiction.'

Dahl let out a weary sigh. 'Neither do I. Of course we're going to offer her anything she wants – a new identity, witness protection, a temporary safe house – it's her call, anything short of a beach house in Malibu.'

'Thank you.'

# Sixty

Upstairs in a sitting room, Grace was watching Lydia and Arthur Friedman. With Magozzi's and Gino's blessing, she and Harley had told them everything they knew – if there were two people in the world who deserved to know exactly what was going on, it was that pair.

Ever since she'd introduced them, the two had been clustered together on a sofa, talking nonstop. Well, actually, the doctor had been doing most of the talking, filling in some family blanks for Lydia. She had shed some tears, and from Grace's vista across the room, she thought she'd caught a glimpse of a few tears rolling down Friedman's cheeks, too; especially when Lydia had shown him the book, *In Case of Emergency*, and had told him the story behind it.

It was actually quite an extraordinary thing to watch – the two had seemed to bond before her eyes, tethered together by a tiny thread of the past, and yet that tiny thread had sewn an instant family where none had existed before. Grace understood this, and suddenly realized she was watching a version of her own past play out. She had been totally alone, without family, just like Lydia and Friedman, until she met Harley, Annie, and Roadrunner. And later, Magozzi and Gino had come into the fold. Now all of them were woven together by threads of the past and they would always be a part of one another's future.

An hour after Dahl had arrived, Magozzi and Gino finally rejoined them. They looked exhausted, but something in their faces had lifted.

Harley crossed his arms across his chest. 'You two look like a couple marathoners staring down the twenty-sixth mile. Did the house in New York answer some questions?'

'Yes and no. It went up in a fireball, and that fireball took everything with it, including the computers and the people inside. Agent Dahl thinks it was rigged to self-destruct.'

'Were they the same people who scrubbed the footage of Chuck's killers at the hotel and took down his website?' Lydia asked quietly. 'The same people who killed Wally and Otis and a lot of others and tried to kill me twice?'

'Yes, we believe so. But it's too early in the investigation to know anything for sure. As a precautionary measure, Agent Dahl said the FBI will offer you a protected safe house until things are resolved.'

Friedman's eyes lifted and connected with everyone's in the room before finally settling on Lydia's. 'They *did* have the Sixth Idea. They nurtured it from your grandfather's concept, protected it, and ultimately destroyed it when it was in danger of being discovered. They were the guardians. Albeit amoral guardians, but guardians nonetheless.' He took her hands in his. 'If your grandfather was alive today, this is the outcome he would have wanted. Without the senseless killing of all the innocent descendants, of course.'

'So it's over?' Lydia asked guardedly, hopefully.

Friedman shrugged. 'At least for now. But the concept of using EMP as a strategic weapon is as old as the first atom bomb. Somebody else will eventually re-create the Sixth Idea, it's just a matter of who will do it, how they will do it, and when.'

'What about the Russians who were watching you?' Grace asked. 'They were obviously onto something, and you are the last man left on earth who they think might be of use to them.'

'A very good point, Ms. MacBride. But since an Alzheimer's patient has been missing for so long in inclement weather, I will be assumed dead. That opens up a whole array of options for my future, as long or as short as that may be.'

'What will you do now, Arthur?' Lydia asked.

His mouth curved into a smile, sending rays of wrinkles across his face. 'Play golf every day until I die.'

Harley chuckled. 'Well, you're not golfing in Minnesota in December, which means you're planning on becoming a traveling man. Grace and I will work up a new identity for you. Like Detective Magozzi said, things aren't exactly ironed out yet, and until they are, you should fly under the radar.'

'I appreciate the generous offer very much, Mr. Davidson, but I have been looking over my shoulder my entire life and made all the necessary arrangements long ago.' He tipped his head at Lydia. 'And you, my dear girl – what will you do now?'

'Live my life. Try to make a difference. Get a bigger gun.'

'Good for you. Above all, be safe, but when things finally settle – and they will – don't run, don't hide. I spent two years hiding, living as a coward in a silent hell when I should have done something that might have prevented all the death the Sixth Idea left in its wake. I've done many regrettable things in my life, but that is the one that will haunt me most.'

Magozzi was watching Grace, mainly because he always watched her when they were in the same room together, but also because he knew what Friedman had just said resonated with her. Her face was as still and indecipherable as it always was, but there was a low-level frisson to her demeanor that hadn't been there moments before.

Gino cleared his throat. 'Leo, we've got a meeting with the chief in half an hour, we should make tracks back to City Hall.'

'Right. Is there anything we can do before we leave?'

'We're good, Magozzi,' Grace said. 'I'll let you out.'

The short elevator ride down to the main floor was quick, and Grace didn't say anything until he and Gino were almost to the door. 'What kind of safe house are the Feds offering to Lydia?'

Magozzi shrugged. 'We don't know yet, and Dahl probably doesn't either. He'll lay out some options when he debriefs her later today.'

'We'll keep her here until the Feds present something suitable.'

'That's really generous, Grace, but way above and beyond the call. You and Harley have done enough already.'

'We're not going to shove her off alone to a questionable safe house with a couple agents she doesn't know.'

'Hopefully, she won't need a safe house for long and she'll be able to go home soon.'

'She's selling it.'

'The lake house?'

Grace nodded. 'Yes.'

Magozzi's eyebrows lifted. 'Seriously?'

# Sixty-One

Later that night, Magozzi knew his future at last, and realized that it would simply be a continuation of the past. When Grace was asleep, as she was now, he could live out his fantasies, touching her as he would never dare when she was awake. He couldn't explain it, but there was something about her skin that shocked his fingers awake and some-times pushed him so close to losing control that he shuddered with the effort of holding everything inside.

Oh my God. That was nearly Neanderthal. And that meant he had gone over the edge.

But for this brief moment, he felt the curve of her back against his stomach, felt the soft press of Grace's back against his lower stomach, and thought maybe he could live with this for the rest of his life. Maybe it was enough. The trick was, you had to live for the moment, love the moment, in case there was never another.

Grace was blissfully asleep now, limp in his arms, and this was a rare thing. Life had taught her to be always alert, on guard, even in sleep, and he hated to think what had instigated that intense fearfulness.

But something had changed.

His eyes opened in the dark and his breath stilled. His hand went quiet, cupping her belly, feeling that tiny swell that had never been there before, as if something beneath his hand was talking to him.

Obviously no one knew yet. She was slender as always, you couldn't see it, you had to feel it – that soft rise of a normally nonexistent belly. He realized in that moment it wasn't just that something had changed. Everything had changed.

He was smiling as he fell asleep.

# Sixty-Two

Max was sitting on the front porch of his Montana ranch with a strong cup of tea and a plate of warm black bread with trout from his very own pond. Vera had done an excellent job pickling it. As it turned out, she was a superb cook.

His two golden retrievers were sound asleep at his feet. The vista in front of him was stunning, especially at sunrise – hues of purple and orange and pink painted geometric figures on the face of the distant mountain range in such a way he'd never seen in Russia. In the foreground was his herd of horses, grazing peacefully in abundant, flower-studded pastureland. Occasionally they would look up, as if they were enjoying the sunrise as much as he was. There had been times in his life when he'd had to eat both horses and dogs, but he so much preferred having them as companions.

Max didn't own a cell phone anymore, and he didn't have a landline. He didn't need any of that. He did keep a radio on hand for any emergencies with the animals or with his property; and he also kept a satellite phone, just in case he had an emergency of another sort. There was only one person in the world who knew how to contact him through the sat phone, and that person was calling now. He could answer or not. Nothing would come of it either way. But he did have a certain curiosity about how things had turned out for Ivan.

'*Dobroe utro, Ivan.*'

'Maksim! You just said "good morning," and narrowed down my search for you.'

'There are many places in the world where it is morning right now.'

Ivan uttered one of his rattling chuckles. 'I'm not searching for you, *tovarish*. Just inquiring about your welfare. You sound well.'

'I am. And you?'

'I am enjoying my retirement. Our last mission was an interesting one, was it not?'

'Not really. Business as usual.'

'I found it unsatisfying.'

'And why is that?'

'The Sixth Idea. I want to know what it is. So do our employers.'

'We don't have employers anymore, Ivan. Besides, the Sixth Idea never existed. It was a simple American decoy, and look how well it worked. Idiots are still chasing a myth sixty years later.'

'I'm not so certain it is a myth, Maksim. And there are others who share my sentiment. Arthur Friedman is still missing, and he is the only person in the world who would know.'

'Arthur Friedman is missing because he's dead, they just haven't found his body yet. And even if he were still alive, his brain has been dead and gone for a long time. Vera and I were there with him at the clinic, Ivan. We know this.'

'Yes, I suppose. But perhaps we should meet again to discuss this further.'

'I don't think so. And what does it matter to you? You should take your retirement more seriously. Chasing dragons is a young man's folly.'

'Yes, I suppose it is. So we part company at last. Enjoy the American Dream, *tovarish*.'

As Max ended the call, the dogs started whining in excitement and brushing their tails against the porch floor when they saw Vera walking up the stone path from the barns and gardens. She was carrying one basket of eggs and another basket of freshly harvested vegetables. This was indeed the American Dream. 'Ivan just called.'

Vera made a sour face. 'Trouble never dies.'

'Ivan would be difficult to kill. I believe those Troika cigarettes are what will ultimately get him in the end.'

They both looked up when the distant report of a fine Barrett sniper rifle cracked the still, silent morning air. Vera set her baskets down on the steps. 'Our ranch hand must have spotted a coyote.'

'He said they've been very aggressive lately,' Max agreed. 'I knew that rifle would come in handy here.'

# Epilogue

Magozzi was sitting on the bench at the end of the dock, beer in one hand, fishing pole in the other, just like he'd imagined on a cold December day five months ago. The lake reflected the deep blue of a perfect May sky and some purple flowers he couldn't identify perfumed the air from their terracotta pots on the shoreline terrace. It was a nice touch – something he never would have thought of, something he never would have done himself. Women were amazing creatures, creative in all sorts of ways most men would never be.

He smelled garlic and herbs wafting down from the open windows of his house. He heard the clink of glasses, the muted din of music, the rattle of the refrigerator's ice maker. And then the crackle of twigs and soft footsteps on the mossy path that led down to the lake.

'Catching anything?'

Magozzi turned and held up his beer. 'Bottle bass.'

Grace smiled and handed him a glass of iced tea flourished with a lemon wedge and a sprig of mint. 'I'm here to save you from that swill.'

'Well, thank the Lord. Without your civilizing influence, I'd turn into a full-on barbarian out here, drinking cheap beer and trying to kill innocent fish.'

Grace was in a sundress and sandals, as slender as she'd always been except for the growing swell of her belly. She'd been spending most of her time here with him, which made him happy; and she seemed happy here, too. For the entirety of their relationship, Magozzi had clung to tiny glimmers of hope that made him believe their lives might finally come together in an unexpected way. And now they were.

'Where's Charlie?'

'I think he's turned into a barbarian, too. Last time I saw him he was terrorizing squirrels in the woods.'

'No better job for a dog.'

'Harley just called. They're almost here.'

'So are Gino and Angela and the kids.'

Grace smiled. 'Harley bought some toys for the lake.'

'Oh yeah? Some floating loungers with cup holders in the arms, I hope.'

Grace gave him a mysterious smile. 'Actually, I think it's a little more dramatic than that.'

They sat in comfortable silence, sipping iced tea while they watched the sunlight break into shards on the water. It was quiet here, but full of life – fish jumped, turtles popped their heads out of the water, a pair of bald eagles soared overhead. Somewhere in the distance a horse neighed. It was a perfect day. Every day here was perfect. He'd stopped thinking of this as Lydia's house months ago.

Charlie started barking abruptly from somewhere in the woods, and they heard the honk of a horn, then car doors slamming.

'That's Harley,' Grace said, taking his hand. 'Let's go see the toys.'

They walked up to the house hand in hand, which seemed like the most natural thing in the world to Magozzi. When they crested the hill, he saw Roadrunner, Annie, and Harley waiting for them at the edge of the lawn with big smiles and even bigger coolers, blocking the view to the driveway.

'We're going to tear up the seas today, Leo,' Harley called down, then stepped aside to reveal a trailer with four WaveRunners. 'Pontoon is getting delivered later this week, along with a boat lift and everything else you need. Sorry, bud, but when you bought a lake house, you and Grace kind of gave up your privacy for the summer.'

Magozzi couldn't stop smiling, because Harley had used inclusive language. He hadn't said you gave up your privacy, he'd said you and Grace had.

*You and Grace. And in a few months, someone else.*

# Afterword

To Donald Hepler, a wonderful father and grandfather, who carried a heavy burden for many years; and to 'Chuck Spencer.' Although this is a work of fiction, portions of this story are based on actual events, both past and present, and are a part of our family history.

The flight from Los Angeles to Minneapolis as depicted in the second chapter, where Chuck Spencer meets Lydia Ascher, is written almost exactly as it happened to Traci a few years ago. In the book it seems like a freak encounter between two people who share an unusual family background, but in real life it was even more astounding than that – the real 'Chuck' was never supposed to be on my flight. It was only a last-minute cancellation and rebooking on a different airline departing from an entirely different airport that brought him to the last remaining spot on my flight – sitting next to me.

Also, very special thanks to Phillip Lambrecht and Michael Ebsen. Both made valuable contributions to the story.

Read on for a
sneak peek at
P. J. Tracy's new novel,

# NOTHING
# STAYS
# BURIED

Coming 2017

# Prologue

Something horrible was going to happen to Marla. Somewhere down the road there had to be payback for her perfect childhood, her perfect career at the veterinary clinic, her perfect apartment in Minneapolis, her consistently perfect life. Friends who adored her envied her in equal measure, and secretly waited for the tragedy to come, because they believed in the law of averages and the irrefutable balance of good and bad in every life. And also because in the darkest moments of their own less than perfect lives, they just had to believe that someday Marla would get hers.

'Good things come to good people,' her father was fond of telling her on those rare occasions when the shower of her good fortune made her feel just a little bit guilty. But if that were really true, why did the rest of the world believe the opposite? The notion that goodness was punished was so pervasive that even the language was permeated with warnings. Only the good die young. Nice guys finish last. No good deed goes unpunished. Phrases like that had often given Marla pause; made her think she should try harder to do something bad occasionally, like forget to return a library book, just to even out the scales.

And then she'd run over the bunny.

'Stop crying, Marla. And stop calling it a bunny. It was just a goddamn rabbit,' her father had tried to comfort her with semantics. 'Probably the same one that ate every lick of my spinach plants last week. Every last lick.'

But he hadn't known the worst of it, because she could never bring herself to say it aloud. The bunny hadn't died right away. She'd seen it in her rear view mirror, trying to drag itself off the road with its front legs, because the hind legs wouldn't work. She'd had to go back and run over it again.

It had been the right thing to do; but oh my God, that image in her rear view mirror would be with her to the end of her life, and although her father had felt great sympathy for her distress, he hadn't felt a bit for the rabbit. How could that be? How could you feel sorry for someone for being sad and not feel sorry for something being dead?

She spent the next week imagining that the bunny had been a nursing mother, and that somewhere baby bunnies were cold and mewling in a hidey-hole, slowly dying of starvation. She never admitted that to anyone, because people tended to think you were a bit unbalanced when you empathized with animals to the point of torment. But empathy was the disease Marla had inherited from her mother, and there were no boundaries to it. She couldn't help connecting to everyone and every thing she encountered; she couldn't stop speculating about their lives, their families, their pain – even that of silly rabbits that ate her father's entire spinach crop and then ran out in front of a speeding car.

Normally Marla didn't mind the night drive out to the farm, especially on a Thursday, when the freeway was empty. Tomorrow night the frenetic weekend race to lake cabins would fill the two lanes heading out of Minneapolis with a jam of lights, white and red, crawling bumper-to-bumper for sixty miles before it started to thin out. But tonight, and every other summer week night, the road shot straight and true into deeper and deeper blackness where the exits were few and far between. Her exit, just three miles up, was what worried her. That particular two-lane road was one bunny shy this week, thanks to her, and she greatly feared a repeat of last week's carnage.

She took the ramp more slowly than usual, stopped at the top and spent a long time looking both ways before easing right on to the two-lane road. There was no moon tonight, and the darkness seemed to swallow the beams of her headlights, as if she were shining them down the throat of a monster. She slowed even further as she approached the 'S' curve through the woods where the bunny had once lived, and that was the only reason she didn't run right over the large black shape in the middle of the road.

As soon as her headlights hit the thing, she recognized it as one of those large plastic bags the volunteer crews used to pick up the occasional litter on road clean-up days. Still, it had startled her, and she could hear her heart pounding in her ears as she pulled over on to the shoulder and stopped. She sat there for a minute trying to catch her breath, her fingers still curled tight around the wheel, eyes wide and fixed on the bag.

Relax, Marla. Blink, for God's sake. It's not an animal, not a person; it's just a bag of trash. Normally these bags were carefully placed on the shoulder for the township truck to collect, but this one was smack-dab in the middle of the two-lane road, and a genuine hazard to any vehicle coming around the blind 'S' curve at a normal rate of speed. It never occurred to her to simply drive around it and go on.

Her mind was already busy imagining a speeding car zipping around the first bend in the curve, slamming on the brakes, veering off the road and plowing head-on into a tree.

It was only after she got out of the car that she also imagined that same speeding car running into her while she was trying to drag the bag off the road, which made her move a lot faster.

It was surprisingly heavy, and it made a terrible scraping sound on the pebbly asphalt as she tugged and pulled it by inches toward the shoulder, and that was when she began to suspect what was really in the bag. She released it with a little squeal and a shiver, and backed away.

Motorists killed more deer on this particular curve than all the hunters in the county managed to bring down during hunting season. You didn't think much about what happened after the accidents unless you happened to see the road-kill crews making their rounds, loading grisly remains into the open-backed truck that hauled them away. Sometimes the job got messy, and then they had to use a shovel and a bag. Apparently this particular bag had fallen unnoticed off the back of the truck when it accelerated on the curve.

Marla looked down at the bag with a mixture of sadness and distaste, understanding the heaviness now, seeing the telltale swells and lumps that clearly marked a large object and not a collection of discarded cans and paper. At least she hadn't killed this one; hadn't witnessed its violent end, which made the job ahead a little easier. She wondered absently why it didn't smell, murmured a brief prayer that the bag didn't rip when she tried moving it again, then bent to her work.

This time she put her back to the side of the road and tried pulling the bag toward her. The large animal inside shifted and rolled with the first tug. Marla winced, but kept at it, right up until the moment the bag snagged on a sharp piece of broken asphalt, tore open, and a bloody human arm fell out.

Marla snapped upright and stifled a choked gasp. For a minute her mind didn't work at all, and then when it started up again it manufactured terrible pictures. Not that there was a dead person in that bag, because that was a reality she just couldn't accept at the moment. What occurred to her instead was that in the movies, just when the heroine thought she was safe, the supposedly dead person's hand jerked out and grabbed her ankle.

'Oh God, oh God, oh God,' she began to back very, very carefully away, toward her car, keeping her eyes focused on the inky blackness of the road ahead, because she didn't dare look down at the bag again.

And then suddenly, twin white lights pierced the darkness and began rolling toward her, faster and faster. Too small for headlights. They're back-up lights. Dear Jesus, there was a truck up there, so close, and she'd never even seen it. And now it was coming for her.

Marla was totally paralyzed for a few moments, trying to regain her composure, rationalizing for the sake of her sanity, because none of this made sense in her perfect world.

The truck is not coming *for* you, it's coming to *help* you. This is the country – people stop to offer assistance when they see a car on the side of the road, because in Buttonwillow, Minnesota, everybody was your neighbor, even if you lived twenty miles apart. It's probably somebody you know, maybe even somebody you went to grade school with. And there's a perfectly reasonable explanation for that body in the trash bag . . .

Marla snapped back to reality. No, no, no, there wasn't. There was no perfectly reasonable explanation on God's Green Earth for a dead body in a trash bag in the middle of a deserted country road. No perfectly reasonable explanation for this truck, suddenly appearing out of nowhere. And now, because she'd been thinking too much again, it was too late to duck into the safety of her car and screech away. Too late to call 911 or Jacob, because the truck had rolled to a stop a few feet in front of her car and now the driver's door was slowly creaking open. At that point, she abandoned all thought, succumbed to panic and instinct, and bolted into the woods.

Every inch of her felt like it was on fire as she leapt through the brush and bramble, dodging trees in the darkness, clambering over fallen logs, tripping over exposed roots and scrambling back to her feet. She knew these woods – Cutter Creek was to her right, and a few hundred yards up ahead there was a clearing and then Hank Schifsky's cornfield. Another quarter of a mile up was his long dirt driveway and his old farmhouse. She could make it.

And then she felt herself falling, felt her ankle give way as she tumbled down a steep, washed-out gully that hadn't existed when she'd run wild in these woods as a kid.

She choked back whimpers of fear and pain and dragged herself to the base of a large oak tree, trying to make herself as small as possible. And as stupid as it was, she hadn't lost hope; she was still waiting to hear the call of a friendly voice behind her. 'Ma'am? Ma'am! Don't run, I'm here to help you!'

But all she heard was relentless, crashing footsteps in the woods behind her. The raspy pant of her pursuer.

Something switched off inside of her. She divorced herself from her immediate reality, from her physical being, and retreated deep into the core of her soul. There it was peaceful, a place where she could think of her past and her future. She should have married Jacob. And if he'd still have her, she'd do just that. They'd have babies and live in Buttonwillow until the end of their days. They should have done it a long time ago, back when they were both eighteen and Jacob had given her the promise ring she still wore on her right ring finger, even though she was a grown woman.

The footsteps were getting closer now, crunching through the dead branches and old, dried leaves that littered the forest floor. Things couldn't end here. She had to leave something so Jacob and her father had known she'd been here, had made it this far, and could maybe piece together what had happened if she didn't make it out of these woods alive.

She pulled the ring off her finger and placed it by the base of the tree where she was hiding, and as she heard the labored breathing getting louder, she got up and started running on her swollen, ruined ankle, screaming at the top of her lungs.

The lights were what Walt would always remember. They didn't belong in this dark night in the countryside. They lit up the thick woods on the north side of the narrow road, throwing spooky shadows through the tightly packed tree trunks and brush.

They shed unwelcome light on the north side, where there was a turnaround with space enough for one car to park, for the daring anglers who skidded down the treacherous slope to drop their lines in the creek below. You fished at night during the few weeks when the suckers were running, but for the rest of the summer, only kids parked there at night to kiss and hold hands, and sometimes more than that before the clocked ticked to curfew.

The turnaround had been there as long as Walt had been alive. He'd parked there with Mary, his high school sweetheart, before sneaking back home, and he'd proposed to her there, too. Right there, where the path down to the creek carved a hole in a stand of cottonwoods far older than he was now.

All these things belonged here, had always been here, but not the lights, and yet tonight they were everywhere, startling the early spring frogs into silence, as if the whole place had been swept clean of night creatures.

Marla's car, the white Ford Explorer he'd bought for her when she graduated from college, was sitting in the turnaround, visiting the very spot where she might have been conceived all those years ago.

It was spotting from the gentle April rain that had just started to fall, and Walt's eyes brushed over it as if it wasn't there, because it shouldn't be.

He had been standing here so long while the Highway Patrol set up the lights and county deputies paced the grounds. He was glad the Highway Patrol was here. The more departments, the better. It gave the scene, the tragedy, a level of import that promised careful attention.

The crime scene techs, who looked like astronauts in their white suits and booties, hurried to cover that dreadful, bloody place in the middle of the road that was surrounded by blinking red lights and peppered with iridescent yellow crime scene markers. One of the techs, who had known Walt since he'd worked for him baling hay as a high schooler, looked over his shoulder at the old man.

'Probably isn't human blood at all,' he said with a fake, forced shrug. 'Raccoon, squirrel, deer more than likely.'

Walt didn't move. He kept looking at the plastic now covering the blood, protecting it from the rain. 'Marla hit a rabbit last week on this very road,' he said.

'Could have been a rabbit,' the tech said, but it was too damn much blood for anything that small and he knew it.

Marla had been missing for only a few hours, but out here, there were no time limits on reporting a missing person. This was Marla. They all knew her, like they knew every person in their district, and they knew she would have called her dad if she was going to be late for dinner.

A deputy approached Walt and tipped his brown, plastic covered hat. 'Mr Gustafson, is that Marla's vehicle?'

Walt hesitated because no one ever called him Mr Gustafson. 'It is.'

The deputy sighed and looked down. 'We'll find her, sir. Don't you worry.'

'Appreciate it.'

Jacob was here, too, coming out of the woods now, his face a frozen, unreadable mask. He'd been the first to arrive, getting here so soon after Walt had phoned him that he worried about how fast the boy had been driving, and how carelessly. He'd been sweet on Marla damn near for ever, and was the one person in this world who was as panicked as Walt, trying hard not to show it. He was Sheriff now, like his daddy before him, but he was more than that.

'How are you doing, Walt?'

'Not so good. Just like you.'

Jacob scuffed his boot through the agate stones scattered in the turnaround near Marla's car. Harry

Michaelson's Blue Tick hounds started baying in the far distance, the first dogs on site long before the patrol brought in their own hounds.

Jacob looked in the general direction of the sound as if he could see through the black of the woods beyond the lights, and looked back at Walt's face. It was partly in shadow, and he looked younger than his seventy-odd years, with his teeth clenched and his jaw muscles bulging as he looked toward the baying sound too. His pupils were dilated so wide, they ate nearly all of the blue of his eyes, and Jacob knew the man had to be dying inside at this moment. What had the dogs found? The seconds ticked by with interminable slowness before his shoulder unit squelched.

'Coons,' a voice came from the other end. 'A whole mess of 'em.'

Walt took his first breath in a while and released a shaky exhale.

He's in hell, Jacob thought, just like he'd been ever since he had gotten the call.

'Sorry, Walt. Damn Blue Ticks. The Highway Patrol dogs should be here any minute, and they don't sound at a Goddamned coon.'

Walt nodded, took another breath. He bobbed his head toward the Explorer without looking at it. 'Maybe she broke down.'

Jacob shook his head. 'Keys are still in it. It started right up. Tires are all okay.'

'Still, maybe it broke down earlier and just fixed itself sitting there. Maybe Marla . . . I don't know, started walking, got tired, fell asleep somewhere; she works so hard, you know . . .' His voice faded as he pressed a hand hard over his gut, because the agony was eating at him from the inside out.

Jacob looked away, pretended he didn't hear the absolute desperation in Walt's speculation, pretended he didn't see anything but a lot of people, a lot of lights, and an empty car.

*Nightmare. Jesus God, I'll do anything, just let her be safe . . .*

'What's on your mind, Jacob?'

'Walt, the hounds picked up a clear trail in the woods. It ended in a wash-out gully near the creek.'

'What does that mean?'

Jacob reached into his pocket and pulled out an evidence bag. 'I found this at the base of a tree in the gully.'

Walt took a sharp breath. 'That's Marla's ring. The ring you gave her in high school.'

'I think she left it for us, Walt.'

# THE BESTSELLING
# MONKEEWRENCH SERIES

# He just wanted a decent book to read ...

Not too much to ask, is it? It was in 1935 when Allen Lane, Managing Director of Bodley Head Publishers, stood on a platform at Exeter railway station looking for something good to read on his journey back to London. His choice was limited to popular magazines and poor-quality paperbacks – the same choice faced every day by the vast majority of readers, few of whom could afford hardbacks. Lane's disappointment and subsequent anger at the range of books generally available led him to found a company – and change the world.

*'We believed in the existence in this country of a vast reading public for intelligent books at a low price, and staked everything on it'*
**Sir Allen Lane, 1902–1970, founder of Penguin Books**

The quality paperback had arrived – and not just in bookshops. Lane was adamant that his Penguins should appear in chain stores and tobacconists, and should cost no more than a packet of cigarettes.

Reading habits (and cigarette prices) have changed since 1935, but Penguin still believes in publishing the best books for everybody to enjoy. We still believe that good design costs no more than bad design, and we still believe that quality books published passionately and responsibly make the world a better place.

So wherever you see the little bird – whether it's on a piece of prize-winning literary fiction or a celebrity autobiography, political tour de force or historical masterpiece, a serial-killer thriller, reference book, world classic or a piece of pure escapism – you can bet that it represents the very best that the genre has to offer.

**Whatever you like to read – trust Penguin.**